R0084653542

12/2016

Palgrave Studies in Literary Anthropology

Series Editors
Deborah Reed-Danahay
Department of Anthropology
The State University of New York at Buffalo
Buffalo, New York, USA

Helena Wulff
Department of Social Anthropology
Stockholm University
Stockholm, Sweden

This book series aims to publish explorations of new ethnographic objects and emerging genres of writing at the intersection of literary and anthropological studies. Books in this series will be grounded in ethnographic perspectives and the broader cross-cultural lens that anthropology brings to the study of reading and writing. The series will explore the ethnography of fiction, ethnographic fiction, narrative ethnography, creative nonfiction, memoir, autoethnography, and the connections between travel literature and ethnographic writing.

More information about this series at
http://www.springer.com/series/15120

Paul Stoller

The Sorcerer's Burden

The Ethnographic Saga of a Global Family

Palgrave Studies in Literary Anthropology
ISBN 978-3-319-31804-2   ISBN 978-3-319-31805-9   (eBook)
DOI 10.1007/978-3-319-31805-9

Library of Congress Control Number: 2016950035

Cover image © Corbis Super RF / Alamy Stock Photo

Printed on acid-free paper

This Palgrave Macmillan imprint is published by Springer Nature
The registered company is Springer International Publishing AG Switzerland

ALSO BY PAUL STOLLER

In Sorcery's Shadow (with Cheryl Olkes)
Fusion of the Worlds
The Taste of Ethnographic Things
The Cinematic Griot: The Ethnography of Jean Rouch
Embodying Colonial Memories
Sensuous Scholarship
Jaguar: A Story of Africans in America
Money Has No Smell
Stranger in the Village of the Sick
Gallery Bundu
The Power of the Between
Yaya's Story
Climbing the Mountain (with Mitchell Stoller)

Paul Stoller is Professor of Anthropology at West Chester University

CONTENTS

SERIES EDITORS' PREFACE

The Sorcerer's Burden is the first novel to be published in our series Palgrave Studies in Literary Anthropology. Our aim in the series is to publish works at the intersection of anthropology and literature that are grounded in ethnographic perspectives. We are delighted to present such a well-crafted story that conveys the experiences of an African scholar navigating between the world in which he grew up, in rural Niger, and the intellectual world of Paris to which he migrated and where he established a family with his French wife. Omar Dia, the protagonist of *The Sorcerer's Burden*, must find ways to reconcile his obligations to these two "homes" when he is faced with his own legacy as son of a great sorcerer. This story resonates with contemporary human experiences of global mobility, especially among those with cosmopolitan aspirations. Paul Stoller explores globalization through the prism of sorcery in Niger, a world seemingly far from that of Parisian academic life, and readers are taken into this world as Omar is drawn back into it.

Paul Stoller is one of the most lauded anthropologist-writers of our time. He has been praised for his ability to draw upon his ethnographic fieldwork to tell emotionally moving stories that deal with broad themes such as family ties, immigration, religious practice, the sensory aspects of living, well being, and death. In addition to two earlier novels 1999, 2005, Stoller is author or editor of 12 other books.[1] Stoller's ethnographic books and his memoirs are as compelling as his novels because he uses narrative ethnographic techniques to incorporate his own

---

[1] See Paul Stoller (1999, 2005).

experiences into those texts. Here, with Omar's story, he enters into the subjective experience of another person, which is more possible in the novel genre than in ethnographic writing.

As Kirin Narayan has pointed out, anthropologists have published novels since the early twentieth century. She characterizes the difference between fiction and ethnography as one of two approaches to representations of reality. In fiction, the author is "free to invent" whereas in ethnographic writing the author is accountable to the discipline of anthropology and its evidentiary standards.[2] Fiction frees anthropologists to invent characters and events, and to be creative in telling stories that may or may not be based on experiences or people they encountered during fieldwork. Both narrative ethnography and fiction, however, aim to tell stories that have emotional resonance.

The Sorcerer's Burden is informed by Paul Stoller's fieldwork experiences in Niger, a very poor country in Western Africa that lies in the southern region of the Sahara. A number of ethnographies and memoirs by Stoller have addressed his increasing knowledge as both participant and observer of sorcery among the Songhay, an ethnic group inhabiting Mali and Benin, as well as Niger, whose traditional livelihood is based on millet farming. Niger is a former French colony, which gained its independence in 1960. French remains its official language, although Hausa, Songhay, and Arabic are also spoken.[3] Although Islam is the major religion of Niger, as the novel shows us, indigenous religious practices involving magic and sorcery persist among the Songhay.

In one of his early ethnographic books based on fieldwork among the Songhay, Stoller describes his first experience, in 1970, at a spirit possession ceremony. He adds that "Although I understood none of its elements, the power of the ceremony overwhelmed me."[4] Later he would learn that "spirit possession is a set of embodied practices that constitutes power-in-the-world.[5] Diplomacy on the dune informs diplomacy in the Presidential Palace." Stoller paints the following sensuous picture of spirit possession:

---

[2] See Kirin Narayan (1999, 135).
[3] See Paul (2014, 2008, 1995, 1987).
[4] See Paul Stoller (1989a, xi).
[5] See Paul Stoller (1994, 636).

It is a white-hot day in June of 1987, and the mix of sounds and smells brings the spirits to Adamu Jenitongo's egg-shaped dunetop compound. Four mud-brick houses shimmer in the languorous heat. From under a thatched canopy at the compound entrance, the orchestra plays spirit music. The spirits like this place. Drawn by pungent smells, pulsing sounds, and dazzling dance, they visit it day and night.[6]

It was Paul Stoller who first formulated an anthropology of the senses in the late 1980s, with the now classic *The Taste of Ethnographic Things.*[7] Back in 1969 when he encountered the Republic of Niger, which was going to be his field site for decades to come, his initial reaction was: "At first Africa assailed my senses. I smelled and tasted ethnographic things and was both repelled by and attracted to a new spectrum of odors, flavors, sights, and sounds."[8] In the long run, though, it was his many returns to the Songhay that, he explains, "compelled me to tune my senses to the frequencies of Songhay sensibilities." He had to learn the language properly and make friends before understanding "that Songhay use senses other than sight to categorize their socio-cultural experience." Eventually, he realized that taste and smell are crucial for social relations, and that sound drives possession ceremonies and words in Songhay sorcery. Stoller even writes about "the sound of words."[9] And in *The Sorcerer's Burden* we also get to know Paris through certain sights, smells, and sounds.

This is a compelling novel that inspires reflection upon humanity and our current dilemmas regarding global power, spiritual power, and the power of family ties.

Deborah Reed-Danahay and Helena Wulff
Co-Editors, Palgrave Studies in Literary Anthropology

---

[6] Ibid., 1994, 634.
[7] See Paul Stoller (1989b); see also Paul Stoller (1997).
[8] Ibid., 4.
[9] Paul Stoller (1989a, 119–121).

Prologue

In West Africa they say that you can't walk where there is no ground. When Omar Dia was young he thought he could fly, but after having flown over a path that twisted and turned him to distant destinations, he returned to home in Niger, one of the most remote places in the world. Close to Omar's home in Tillaberi, there is an outcropping with a majestic view of the Niger River. It's called *The Place Where Stories Are Told*. For centuries Omar Dia's ancestors gathered there to listen to the old stories that connected the past to the present. Having finally returned to Tillaberi, Omar wanted to make sure that his story was told.

By the turn of the twenty-first century, Omar Dia's family had lived in Niger for more than 1000 years. Not many people have ever heard of Niger. Even though it is distant and unimaginably poor, Niger is a special place. In this little known corner of the world, people like Omar call their ancestors the "people of the distant past." Like those distant ancestors, Omar's people have been millet farmers or have been married to millet farmers. In June, the men plant the fields, and if the rains come when they are supposed to, they harvest the millet crop in October. When there are millet seeds in the granaries, the women pound them, transforming the grains into food—porridge, which people drink at noon, and a thick doughy paste, which, when covered with savory sauces, people eat at sunset. Such has been the way of life for Omar's people—year in and year out.

Omar could have easily lived this tranquil rural life, but he took a different path. Like every young boy in his village, he helped his father and brothers in the fields. He also shepherded the family flocks of sheep and goats. But he also loved to go to school. Once he learned how to read, Omar devoured every book he could find. His older sister, Salamatou, who was 10 years his senior, encouraged him.

People in Omar's family disapproved of Salamatou's independent spirit. They saw her as wild and bullheaded. Unlike anyone else in the family, she had gone to the Lycée and had even studied in France. When she returned to Niger with a degree, she became an important oral historian. Omar's family tried to arrange for her to be married, but she refused, saying that marriage didn't interest her.

Bolstered by Salamatou's unflagging support, Omar did very well in school, becoming one of the best students in Niger. At least that's what his professors told him. His teachers sent him to Niamey, Niger's capital city, where, like his older sister, he went to the Lycée, where he graduated at the top of his class. Eventually, his academic record took him to Paris, where he studied literature at the Sorbonne. He took to his studies with great passion, and again, the professors said he was one among the best students in France. They urged him to pursue graduate study. After several years of course work, he became passionate about French philosophy. Wouldn't it be exciting, he thought, to extend the insights of French philosophy to the study of African literature and film?

And that's what he did. He used the framework of French philosophy to write a thesis on the controversial West African novel *Bound to Violence*. The thesis soon became *Violence in the African Imagination*, his first book, the success of which surprised Omar. Soon thereafter he began to teach comparative literature in French universities. In time, he published two other books: *Above and Beyond Negritude*, an exploration of black identity, and *The New Griots*, a text on emerging African filmmakers. Critics showered these works with high praise. Radio and television journalists interviewed him. Newspapers invited him to write op-ed columns. His colleagues invited him to present a series of highly publicized lectures. In time, Omar was nominated and elected to a professorship at the Sorbonne.

Meanwhile Omar fell in love and married a French woman, Chantal Martin, an emergency care doctor. Chantal and Omar soon bought a lovely apartment and had two children: a son, Adam, and a daughter, Lilly. What a beautiful life, you might say. What a wonderful story, you might suggest. Alas, things, as Omar's father liked to say, are never the way they seem.

PART I

Paris, 2000

CHAPTER 1

Omar's carefully manicured life in Paris seemed perfect—a prestigious University Chair, a successful and beautiful wife, two lovely children, and a terrific apartment in a trendy Parisian neighborhood. What could be better? Then one day in November of 2000, he began to doubt himself. As he strolled into a hushed lecture hall to teach his class, he had the sudden and unexpected inclination to pinch his forearm. For some reason, he wanted to make sure this lecture event was more than a dream. His left eye began to twitch. A deeply repressed thought surfaced. How could Omar Dia, the oldest son of a millet farmer from Niger, have become an esteemed professor of comparative literature at the Sorbonne? Standing there before hundreds of people, another repressed realization swept into his consciousness: like most people in the world, he used external appearances to camouflage internal doubts. In public, he covered his body, which is as tall and thin as the desert trees that grow in his parched homeland, with the latest Parisian fashions. He liked suits of muted black and dark gray fabrics. Protected by these elegant clothes, he carried himself with grace, moving with calculated deliberation and speaking with quiet eloquence.

People said Omar was a handsome man. His face had smooth black skin, high cheekbones, and a strong square chin—all offset by black eyes. His wife liked to say that Omar's eyes suggested openness as well as vulnerability. People said he was cool and cosmopolitan. He used to believe what people said of him. How things can change—even in one day! Why would people want to sit and listen to him talk about literature and contemporary culture? His left eye continued to flutter, a tick that had plagued him during his childhood in Niger. How many years had he experienced the embarrassment of his eye flutter? Why was it twitching now?

Thinking these uncharacteristically uncomfortable thoughts, he steadied himself behind the lectern and took out his notes. As he looked up at the full house audience, his eye stopped fluttering. Omar took a deep breath.

That year the university had given him an enviably light schedule: one lecture a week from October to the end of June. His theme in 2000–2001 was "The African Intellectual," which was then a very hot topic in Paris.

The students liked Omar. After his lectures, they hovered around, asking many questions. Some days he'd invite one or two of the lingerers for coffee. His female students knew he was married. Even so, they sometimes flirted with him. If a female student crossed the boundary of respectability, Omar would always try to gently re-establish it.

Despite the light schedule, his academic duties took up too much of his time. He wanted to be a better father to Lilly and Adam. When he could, he took time from his schedule to watch Lilly dance, both at her classes and at her performances. She had the potential to become a graceful ballerina, but complained about having to practice too much. Adam loved to swim and joined a team at the neighborhood pool near the Bastille. During swim meets, Omar would shout encouragement to him and his teammates. Like any father, Omar tried to help his kids with their homework. Even so, Omar felt only a partial connection to his children. Would they ever learn about the African side of Omar Dia?

Omar could have bought an apartment in another part of Paris, but preferred to live near the Bastille. Many West Africans lived near his home. Mosques and Muslim butchers could be found on his street, the rue de Charonne. These elements gave Omar an indirect and mostly anonymous connection to his African roots. That's the way he wanted to live in Paris—comfortably close to his roots, but not entangled by them.

During his student days, Omar would return to Niger during summer breaks. As time passed, he found it increasingly difficult to visit home. The difficult conditions in Niger didn't bother him that much. Omar loved the Nigerien countryside—especially the glitter of the Niger River in late afternoon sunlight and especially *The Place Where Stories are Told*. None of these bucolic pleasures reduced the bitter animosity that his presence triggered in the family compound. His younger brothers, the sons of his father's second wife, called him a white man with black skin. They accused him of abandoning time-honored family traditions. Weary of this venomous rancor, he soon decided to spend his time in Paris. When he got married and had children, his visits to Niger stopped altogether. Even when his beloved mother died, he remained in France. In his mind he had become a French intellectual, an authority on the French philosophers no less, who was comfortable in his skin.

Or was he?

On the day he began to doubt himself, Omar realized that his indirect and anonymous connections to things African were insufficient. Somehow, someway Omar needed something to fill the gaps, to be more fully connected to his wife and kids, to complete himself as a human being. Little did he know how that autumn day would forever change his life!

"Good afternoon," he said in a voice, which, since adolescence had been deep and resonant. He always taught late in the afternoon, spending most mornings at his apartment or at his café, which was on the corner of the rue de Charonne and the Boulevard Voltaire. Sometimes Omar would meet his colleagues there.

"My topic today," he announced, "is *La Sape*, which, as you may know, stands for *Society of Revelers and Elegant People*. Looking at the way I'm dressed, you could say that I myself am a potential *sapeur*." He paused for effect. "Given my very conscious presentation of self, some people might take me for a sapeur, a young African immigrant living in Paris, who spends most of his money on the latest fashions."

"Today I'd like to talk about the cultural aspects of 'la sape.' Imagine yourself as a young African man or women in a Bacongo neighborhood of Brazzaville, Congo. It is the early 1960s, the era of independence. Life has limitless possibility. You've come to the city, you've learned French. You go to the cinema. Your young life is full of dreams. And yet, your lot is hard. You are poor. You come from a country of limited opportunity. What can you expect?"

Omar walked to the left of the lectern and continued. "You expect to join your comrades in the cafes. You go with them to the cinema. You dress like Jean-Paul Sartre, Albert Camus or Simone de Beauvoir. In more recent times you might take on the persona of Roland Barthes or, better yet, Michel Foucault. You become one of the 'intellectuals,' and you try to make your club the place where people wear the most elegant clothes. Dressed as intellectuals, you debate *Being and Nothingness*, or *The Stranger, or The Order of Things*, and you enter a space that knows no boundaries. In your club, you are 'condemned to be free,' to borrow from Sartre, but you don't care, because you breathe deeply the air of expectation and promise." Omar paused for dramatic effect and scanned the audience to measure the effectiveness of the lecture.

"But like life, fashion is fleeting," he continued. "Just as existentialism or structuralism as an intellectual fashion faded in France, so the existentialist clubs disappeared in Brazzaville. Independence swept the whole region into the tide of political intrigue and social violence. The young "existentialists" threatened the State. And so to protect themselves, they drifted into the surrounding bush. The State did not put out the fire of their youth, however. Several years later, Bacongo youths, single, unemployed, and alienated by state politics, triggered a new round of prestige dressing. Like the existentialists, they formed new clubs in which they displayed their sartorial flair. By dressing in the latest French designer clothes, these young people competed to become "The Great Man." In this way, La sape was born."

Enjoying his connection to the audience, Omar went on to describe how la sape was no longer confined to Brazzaville, but had taken on global dimensions. He discussed how it had become a rite of passage for young Congolese men who would leave Brazzaville with little or no money and travel to Paris. They would arrive at Roissy Airport and take trains to the Place de la République. There they would meet other Congolese young people and find lodging and work. Therein would begin a yearlong adventure in which they would work and save money to buy the latest fashions, which they would show off at African dance clubs. At the end of their year, they would return to Brazzaville, the latest fashions stuffed into their suitcases, and would proudly attend a ball at which judges would select the best-dressed young man who would become the "King of the Sapeurs."

A student raised her hand. "Mr. Professor," she said, "is the sapeur phenomenon an exercise in masculine vitality?"

Omar appreciated this question. "Indeed it is," he responded. "These young men are alienated from their ethnic traditions, which are disappearing with the deaths of elders. They are also alienated from mainstream European culture. They are, after all, young, black, and relatively poor. This modern rite of passage enables them to feel strong here in Paris and re-integrates them into their own emerging societies. By dressing in the latest fashions, they are saying: Look at me. I'm cosmopolitan."

Omar, of course, could say the same thing about himself. Feeling the alienation of the sapeurs, he too dressed to say: "Look at me. I'm cosmopolitan." In a flash, he wondered: Who am I? What am I doing with my life?

That day, there were many more questions: some good, some confused. They provided the impetus for a vigorous give-and-take of ideas. Omar attempted to discuss the questions that provoked them to think and perhaps to ask additional questions. In such circumstances, time usually moves on in a flash. And so, the class session came to an end.

Students hovered around the lectern and asked more questions. Usually he welcomed further discussion, but on that day, fully experiencing the sour taste of discomfort, he didn't want to linger and didn't want to have coffee. For a moment, he no longer wanted to be "The Professor." He simply wanted to gather his things, rush to the Metro, and go home.

CHAPTER 2

Freed from the public responsibilities of being "The Professor," Omar hastily made his way to the rue des Écoles. The street glistened with the remains of a passing shower. Thick gray clouds gave the sky an ominous sheen. A cold northwest wind ripped down the street. Chilled to the bone, Omar reached the Boulevard St. Michel–wide, busy and full of vehicular and pedestrian traffic. Turning right he made his way toward the Seine and descended into the Paris Metro's warm embrace. He entered a packed car and stood among a motley assortment of passengers: tall, short, fat, thin, clean, dirty, white, brown, yellow, and black. Some of the passengers wore business clothes-suits, which, like Omar's outfit, had been crafted from muted black and gray fabrics; others sported jeans and tee shirts, which, from their sheen and odor, hadn't been laundered in a very long time. Omar noticed a young African man, who, like him, stood tall in the car. Like Omar, he had put on a charcoal gray sport coat. When their gazes locked, Omar nodded, silently signifying a bond between them—two sapeurs acknowledging their camaraderie.

In the Metro car no one knew Omar, which gave him a feeling of reassurance. Although most people in the crowded Metro car were, "dazed and confused," to borrow from a popular American film title, Omar wondered about the total strangers cohabiting his space. Who were these people? What were their life stories? Were they happy, sad, upbeat, or suicidal? And if, by chance, they looked at him, what judgments would they make? A few of them might make racist judgments. They might see him as another black man, trying to "dress up" like a sophisticated European. Was he a thief or a potential terrorist or simply a mysterious exotic figure who had fabulous stories to tell? What judgments would his African comrade make? He knew one thing: no one in the Metro car would think that Omar held the Chair in Comparative Literature at the Sorbonne.

After one change of Metro lines, the train came to Omar's exit, the Bastille, liberating him from the discomforts of strangers. The cold wind made him shiver. He walked past the shops on the rue de Rivoli, making his way toward the rue de Charonne. Turning left onto his street, he followed the curve of the road as it snaked upward toward his building. He walked briskly, looking downward to avoid any kind of eye contact with what seemed at that moment a cold, damp, and alien world. Suddenly, an African woman tugged his arm and spoke to Omar in Songhay, the language of his ancestors. "Help me, Sir. Help me."

Tall and stout, the woman wore an open raincoat over her print cloth outfit—a top and wrap-around skirt made from what appeared to be thin cotton dyed light blue. A soft white headscarf framed a square face. Years of exposure to sun and dust had clouded the whites of her eyes. "What can I do for you?" Omar asked in Songhay.

"You can help me. I know you can."

"How could I help you?" Omar had no idea who this woman might be.

"My husband is dead. A sorcerer has cursed us," she said breathlessly. "My daughter is wasting away. She eats, but can't keep her food down. I have nightmares. I can't sleep." In desperation, she grabbed Omar's sleeve and pulled it.

Omar looked at the woman's hand on his sleeve and tried to remain calm. "We're in Paris," he said. "These things don't happen here."

"They do!" she insisted, loudly. "They're happening to my family."

"But what can I do about it, Madame?"

"You're Omar Dia."

Surprise stiffened his body. "How do you know my name?"

"You're the son of Issaka Dia."

For years, Omar had avoided the burden of being Issaka Dia's oldest son and potential successor. Omar's father was a great sorcerer who had learned his science from his father who had learned it from his father and so on. Members of Omar's family had been practicing sorcery since the end of the fifteenth century. Omar felt much love for his father, a big, tall man who gathered attention wherever he appeared. From an early age, however, he wanted no part in the family practice. If you lived close to Issaka Dia, how could you avoid the specter of sorcery? People continuously came to the Dia's dunetop compound in search of health and well being. Barren women sought fertility. Men without wives sought a powder that would make them irresistible to a particular woman. When spirits made people sick with possession, the possessed sought relief. Yes, the desperation of this poor woman on the rue de Charonne had a familiar ring. It viscerally reminded Omar of why he had studied so diligently, why he had felt so relieved to attend the lycée in Niger's capital city, why he had breathed deeply the air of liberation when he began his studies at the Sorbonne in Paris. Indeed, his years in Paris had shielded him from his father's legacy.

The flutter returned to his left eye. Would this woman disrupt his carefully contoured life in Paris? "I am the son of Issaka Dia," he said, finally. "But I know nothing about sorcery."

"It doesn't matter," she said, continuing to tug on his sleeve. "You have his power in your blood." she continued. "Blood is obligation. You must help us."

The phrase "blood is obligation" struck him as if he had been shot with an arrow. From the time he was a small child, members of Omar's family would often repeat the phrase "blood is obligation." How unlikely for him to confront this obligation on the streets of Paris! Omar wanted to disappear. If this woman knew about his family, other compatriots in the city, all believers in "blood is obligation," might want Issaka Dia's oldest son to cure them of sorcerous curses. He put his hand over his eye to calm it. His stomach tightened. Was his beautifully stitched life in Paris about to unravel?

Omar knew what to do. He'd follow his time-honored prescription for confronting conflict: escape to more a peaceful place. He jerked his arm back, which freed his sleeve from the troubled woman's grasp. "I can't help you."

He walked away from the sorrowful woman, hoping that she wouldn't follow him home. As he made his way up the rue de Charonne, he looked back. Immobilized, the woman stared straight ahead, her arms hanging limply at her sides. As Omar approached his building, he thought about the woman's logic. How could blood carry the power to heal? How could someone like Omar, who knew nothing of magical incantations or healing plants, cure a person of an illness generated by sorcery?

Omar finally reached the warm confines of his building. Unlike many of the venerable structures on the rue de Charonne, Omar's building, which had been constructed in the 1970s, had been upgraded to make it more attractive to potential buyers. From the sidewalk, the glass security doors opened on to a courtyard that featured a reflecting pool with a fountain. In the spring and summer, the pool, surrounded by flowering bushes and strategically placed benches and high-backed wooden chairs, created a bucolic space. Weather permitting, Omar would often take a book, sit on one of several wooden chairs, and read for hours.

In short order, Omar had taken the elevator to his floor. Taking a soothing breath, he crossed the threshold to his home, which smelled of simmering beef stew. Omar and Chantal lived in a spacious rectangular-shaped three-bedroom apartment in which all of the rooms overlooked the courtyard. The kitchen, which was long and narrow, occupied one end of the space. Omar didn't care much for the kitchen, but Chantal loved to cook and had insisted on an up-to-date culinary space. Accordingly, they bought fancy food mixers and choppers, and a large stainless steel refrigerator. The dishwasher and trash compactor had high-tech features, which reduced their energy bill and helped to preserve the environment.

The dining and living rooms were situated next to the kitchen. In contrast to their large living room with its black leather sofa and chair and glass coffee table, the dining room was rather small. Persian carpets, which Chantal adored, covered the parquet floors. Chantal, who also collected art, decorated the apartment walls with paintings and stocked the étagères with sculpture, mostly abstract stuff, fashioned from iron. A hallway lined with over-stuffed bookshelves led to the bedrooms. Omar and Chantal slept in the large bedroom. The kids shared the second bedroom and the hall bathroom. The study, the third and smallest bedroom, was Omar's refuge. As a confirmed modernist, he furnished it minimally—a sleek desk without drawers on which he placed his laptop computer, a small printer, a small photo of his father, and a snake-like desk lamp. One wall was lined with books. He decorated the other walls with enlargements of his book covers, properly framed, as well as diplomas and plaques that commemorated prizes won and honors bestowed. A particularly colorful Persian carpet, from Kerman, provided a degree of color and warmth to what could be considered a rather stark room.

"Chantal," Omar cried, when he entered the apartment. "You home?"

"In the kitchen, Omar." Short, thin, and olive-skinned, Chantal, who was what the French liked to call *une brune*, effused an almost palpable energy. She wore her black hair short and straight and had piercing black eyes. As on most days, she wore black slacks and a white blouse.

Even though she presented a very take-charge, no-nonsense image, perhaps a necessity for an emergency care doctor, she possessed incalculable warmth. Her smile could melt the iciest personality, and she always considered the welfare of others before thinking about her own desires. She had tried so very hard to give Omar a full and happy life, but his professional and existential pre-occupation was a continuous source of argument. Chantal put the family first. Omar wanted to put family first, but other issues—especially the pre-occupation with his work—took precedence. When Chantal got angry, she'd sometimes say that Omar cared more about French philosophers than his family.

"Are the kids home?" Omar asked, walking into the kitchen.

"They've gone to the Matracs for dinner and a sleep-over." She smiled devilishly. "We've got an evening to ourselves, dear. Maybe we'll have a little time… I've put up some beef bourguignon and bought some wine–a Burgundy from 1996. Won't it be nice to have a cozy evening?"

"Just what I need," he admitted, looking at the floor.

Chantal's smile set into a deep frown. "What's wrong?"

"Tough day, Chantal. I'm feeling down."

Trying to control her frustration, Chantal put her hands on her hips. "Go and sit down. I'll get us some wine."

She filled two wine glasses with the Burgundy and brought them to the living room. Omar took a sip and looked at his wife. "I had a very strange day, Chantal."

"How so?"

"I had a full house of students, but began to wonder why they would want to listen to someone like me."

"Oh come on, Omar! You're one of the best known scholars in Paris!" She always found Omar's existential ruminations frustrating, but tried to demonstrate support for her husband.

"So they say," Omar said, appreciating Chantal's efforts to make him feel better.

"You waste your time with such shitty thoughts," Chantal said. "You're a brilliant man and a wonderful teacher."

"I gave the lecture," he said, not hearing what Chantal had said. "They asked me questions, but I felt like an impostor. Sometimes I feel that Paris is an alien world where things are not what they appear to be."

"We have a good life in Paris, Omar," Chantal stated.

"Yes, we do, but today I wanted to escape the students. I didn't want to be The Professor. I wanted to be free of obligations." He shook his head. "I wanted to disappear not just for a day, but maybe for weeks or months."

Chantal frowned. "Do you have doubts about us?"

He shook his head. "No, Chantal. Try to understand. We live together, have kids together, but you don't understand everything about me."

Chantal sipped her wine. "I guess you can never completely understand another person, no?"

"Something weird happened today," Omar observed.

Worry creased Chantal's face, particularly between her eyes. "What happened?"

"This African woman from Niger stopped me on the sidewalk a few feet from our apartment building."

"That's not unusual."

"She said she needed my help."

"Did she want money?"

"No. She said she'd been the victim of a sorcerer's curse."

"But what could you do about it?"

"I told her I knew nothing about those things." He sipped his wine. "Know what she said? She said I could help her."

"Why would she think that?"

"She knew about my father. She knew that I was Issaka Dia's oldest son. She said that I had power in my blood."

"Power?"

"The power to heal illnesses caused by sorcery."

"But you live in France, not Niger," she said, her jaw clenching. "You're a literature professor at the Sorbonne. That world is far away, Omar."

"I'm not so sure, Chantal. During my lecture today, I suddenly started to think about my father. Then on my way home I just happened to be confronted by a woman, who wanted to be cured of a curse."

"It's coincidental, Omar. There's no way to explain what happened to you."

"That's one way of looking at it," he said nodding his head. "But there's another way. Maybe my father is sending me a message. He's trying to teach me something. I felt his presence today."

"That's impossible," Chantal said.

"You don't know my father," Omar stated.

"Can he transport his presence more than 4000 miles?"

"That's what they say in Tillaberi. They say that my father and his fathers could travel great distances. They say that my ancestors could fly high and far like vultures."

"That's a wonderful story, Omar," Chantal said calmly.

"When things get back to normal, you'll see that what happened today was a series of coincidences."

"Maybe so, Chantal. Maybe so."

Just then the phone rang. Omar thought it might be the Matracs calling about one of their kids. Maybe Lilly forgot to pack her toothbrush. Perhaps Adam had a stomachache.

Chantal picked up the phone. "It's for you," she said, "your brother in Niger."

Fear gripped Omar's gut. No one ever phoned from Niger unless they bore bad news. Five years before he had gotten a call from his brother, Abdoulaye, announcing the death of his mother. "Hello," he said in French.

A torrent of Songhay greetings rang in his ear. Omar's brother, Abdoulaye, asked after his health and the well being of his family. He paid homage to Omar's work. Omar responded in kind, asking after the well being of the kinsfolk in Tillaberi, the family village in Niger. Formulaically, they responded to these questions positively. All was well with the folks in Tillaberi. All was well with Omar's work and family in Paris. They both knew, of course, that all wasn't well, but it would have been unthinkable to say so at the beginning of a conversation. Omar didn't know how to begin the real conversation. Abdoulaye took charge. "Older brother," he stammered, "our...our father, Issaka Dia, is not well. He's weak with a bad sickness. He's told us the date of his death and...and it's near."

"May God be with him," Omar said to his brother.

"He says," Abdoulaye continued, "that he's got a lot to tell you. You know, the secrets of the family. You're the oldest son. It's your birthright."

This news made Omar's legs shake. "I don't want to know the family secrets. I read and write, younger brother. I search for the truth."

"That's right, older brother. Father says that you, like him, look for the truth. You must come to Tillaberi to sit, listen and become the owner of truth."

"Father wants me to become the owner of truth?"

"He does."

"But I just can't pack up and leave. I've got to work. My family's here."

"Blood is obligation," Abdoulaye said.

Omar cringed but said nothing.

"We ask you to come home now."

Suddenly, the events of the day made perfect sense. Omar's father's presence manifested itself during the lecture and the confrontation on the street with the Songhay woman. In the world of sorcery, Omar remembered, coincidence does not exist. There is a cause—and an explanation—for every event. The events of the day had been a prelude. His father had sent Omar feelings of doubt about his identity in France, doubts that the woman in the street had reinforced tenfold.

Not knowing what to expect, Omar knew what he had to do. Blood is obligation, he said to himself. "I'll come in the next few days," he told Abdoulaye.

"God is great," Abdoulaye said.

Omar hung up the phone and looked at Chantal, whose face betrayed worry. "What's wrong?" she asked.

"My father is dying," Omar said. "I've got to go to Niger to be with him during his last days."

"Then you must go at once, Omar." She paused a moment. "Do you want me to come with you? The Metracs can look after the kids for a week or two and I can take off from work at the hospital."

"I love you for asking, Chantal, but I need to go alone. I'll make the arrangements."

"Don't you want me there with you?"

"It's too dangerous. Something happened a long time ago and it would be dangerous for you to come."

"You've never mentioned this danger to me."

"I don't want to talk about it right now."

"What's wrong with your eye, Omar?"

"It's a long story. My eye hasn't fluttered since I was a kid. I thought I had left that behind. When my eye twitched the kids in my village made fun of me. I was miserable. I wanted to escape. They'd say, 'Look at Omar; he's a freak.' I can't believe that my eye's acting up again. Why is this happening to me?" He put his hand over his eye to calm it. "I may have to be in Tillaberi a long time."

"How long?"

"Several months at least."

"What! What about us? What about your teaching?"

"I have to go." How could Chantal understand what Omar had to do? She had never been to Niger or to Tillaberi. Omar had shielded her and the kids from the murderous conflicts in the family, and he did not want things to change. "My father's time has come. He knows exactly when he'll die."

"How can he know that?"

"He's a sohanci, a great sorcerer. The great ones know the dates of their deaths."

"How can that be possible?" Chantal wondered.

"It's not possible in our world," Omar said. "In my father's world, impossibilities become possibilities." He paused a moment. "In my father's world, Chantal, life gets very complicated."

"So you have to go," she said with resignation.

He nodded and slumped his shoulders. "I don't want to go, but I'm the oldest son, which means that Issaka Dia will reveal to me the family secrets. It's called the sorcerer's burden. I've avoided it my whole life, Chantal." Omar shook his head. "I don't know how I'll cope, but I have to return." Omar took his wife's hand. "Blood is obligation, Chantal."

Chantal's face set in a frown. "I don't like any of this, Omar. It's just too sudden and too difficult."

"Chantal, I love you and the kids. I love my life in Paris, but I need to be with my father. There's no choice."

PART II

Tillaberi, Niger 2000–2001

CHAPTER 3

The news of Omar's father's illness steered him into a bank of fog. He became listless, dreamy, and undirected. He wondered how this turn of events would change his marriage. When Omar didn't know where to turn, he would contact his older sister Salamatou in Niamey. Like Omar, Salamatou had kept her distance from the family. As a strong-willed and educated woman, she left university teaching to become a dynamic administrative official in Niger's Ministry of Higher Education. In Niger, however, her success made her an undesirable female. Even if she had let the family try to arrange a marriage, it would have been difficult to find a match. Rumor had it that Salamatou preferred women to men—a radical choice in a place like Niger.

When Omar talked to Salamatou about his dilemma, she urged him to come to Niger, but to stay only for a small amount of time.

"You are torn apart, Omar," she told him.

"I know, but I don't want to go. How can I go on like this?"

"You need to come to Niger to try to mend the tears, Omar, but God knows you don't want to stay too long in Tillaberi." she said. "It's too dangerous."

"I'm afraid what they might to do me," Omar said, "but I need to go there."

"I understand, Omar. Just be careful," she stressed. "Hold your tongue. Don't let them get to you."

Omar loved his sister. She was the only person in his family who understood the conflicts and doubts that he had long ago repressed. It was a pity that their life courses had steered them in different directions. After she completed her studies, Salamatou hadn't remained in France. She never told Omar why she had severed her ties with France. Even though she lived relatively close to the family compound in Tillaberi, she never visited—too dangerous, she would say. "Maybe we'll spend some time together when you come to visit? I hope so."

"I'll look forward to it, older sister."

"So, you'll go to Tillaberi and sit with Issaka Dia?" she asked.

"Yes."

"You know, if you spend too much time there, your life will change."

"I'll still be a scholar," Omar insisted.

"Maybe you will. Maybe you won't. But if you stay there too long, you'll get sucked into sorcery. You might even discover something new about yourself—something you might not like."

"I don't know about that."

"I do, Omar." She cleared her throat.

"Can you come up to Tillaberi?"

"You know I can't do that."

"Then, I'll come to see you."

Omar quickly made arrangements for his trip to Niger. He bought an open-ended round-trip airline ticket and arranged for a taxi to take him directly to his father's compound in Tillaberi.

In short order, Omar found himself on a smooth five-hour flight from Paris to Niamey. When he exited the plane and walked down the stairs to the tarmac, the Nigerien heat grabbed his body. He slowly made his way to the Reception Hall, square, empty, whitewashed, and stifling, which led to the police officer's station, where, if all went well, his documents would be inspected and stamped. By the time sweat had saturated his matching shirt and trousers, he retrieved his bag and received a customs officer's cursory inspection. Beyond the customs gate, he found his driver, who held a sign with his name.

"Monsieur Dia," he asked as Omar approached him.

"Yes."

"I admire your father. Three years ago, he healed my brother."

'He did?" Omar asked, his head still in the clouds.

"Yes," the man stated. The driver was very tall and thin and had jet-black skin that stretched tautly over his face. He wore brown dress slacks and a loose-fitting white dress shirt. "My brother went to see the French doctors. They could do nothing for him. Then he went to Tillaberi to see Issaka Dia. He came back to Niamey a healthy man."

"My father," Omar said, "is a powerful man."

"He's the descendant of Sonni Ali Ber—our great King and sorcerer."

"That he is," Omar said.

"And so are you, Monsieur Dia. It's my honor to take you to your father's house."

"Thank you."

They walked into bright midday sunlight. Like most days in Niger, this one was quite hot—perhaps 95 degrees—but a cool breeze from the west made the dry heat bearable—even refreshing.

After many years of absence, the prospect of returning to Tillaberi frightened Omar. Just saying the word "Tillaberi" made him think of his family's expectations—sacrificing your personal desire to the will of the group. Granted, in many Songhay families a person had to make daily sacrifices. Being a descendant of Si, also known as Sonni Ali Ber, the great sorcerer king of the Songhay Empire, brought on deep expectation. Sonni Ali Ber's reign of conquest, destruction, and territorial expansion began in 1464 and continued on until his death in 1491. But there's more, for Sonni Ali Ber practiced a powerful and much feared sorcery. It was said he could shape-shift into a vulture and survey his enemy's positions. It was said that he used sorcery to vanquish his most powerful foes. This knowledge was passed from father to son. Omar's grandfather passed it on to his father, the oldest among his brothers. And one day the time would come for Issaka Dia to pass on the family's secrets to Omar, his oldest son. From an early age, the weight of obligation pressed heavily on Omar's shoulders, so much so that he developed a nervous twitch in his eye, so much so he wanted to run away. And that's exactly what he did, first to Niamey, Niger's capital city, and then to Paris. By time he got to Paris, he had calmed down—no involuntary eye twitches.

The more time Omar spent away, the more he felt that he lived in a world quite alien to that of his father. In his younger days when sometimes he visited Tillaberi, he usually felt uncomfortable. When he got married, Chantal wanted to meet the family, but Omar refused to take her to Niger—too busy he would say. After the children were born, Chantal wanted them to meet their African relatives. She thought they should know their grandfather, aunts, uncles, and cousins. Omar steadfastly refused, which angered her.

"It's too risky for the kids," he would always say.

Chantal thought that Omar's stubbornness had robbed the children of a rich heritage. Omar, though, wanted no part of his African past. He wanted to protect his children from the irresolvable conflict in his family.

When Omar was young, the trip from Niamey to Tillaberi was fraught with perils. The torrential rains, which usually pounded Niger in August and September, reduced the road to a barely passable muddy track. Then for the next ten months, the brutal Nigerien sun baked the road into a rutted, bumpy pathway that destroyed shock absorbers and broke axels. Because drivers paid little heed to these potential dangers, the roadside was the grisly scene of horrible accidents—overloaded buses, the famous Mille Kilo vans stuffed with passengers and cargo, hitting a rut, losing control, and tumbling down an embankment, killings dozens of poor peasants. Then there was the "bridge of death," a narrow concrete structure, with no protective barriers, that spanned a 30-foot *wadi*. If two drivers approached the "bridge of death" from opposite directions, they'd sometimes play chicken, racing to see who could cross first. To the left and right of the bridge, the rusting hulks of vehicles whose drivers had lost the game littered the wadi. Nigeriens thanked God that these accidents did not occur every day. The same could not be said for other events that would slow the pace of travel: blowouts, caused by acacia thorns that nestled in sandy stretches of roadway; engine malfunctions, caused by the negligence of local mechanics; or the frustrating "*panne d'essence*," caused by drivers who miscalculated how much gas they needed to travel between Niamey and Tillaberi.

Did those past fates await Omar as he traveled from Niamey to Tillaberi? It was hard to know. The road had long since been paved. Potholes had replaced road ruts. Cars no longer crossed the "bridge of death." As for Omar, he was the sole passenger in a new, fully fueled vehicle. How times had changed Niger! How times had changed him!

In these new conditions and circumstances, the trip from Niamey to Tillaberi passed without incident—no flat tires, no engine breakdowns, no accidents, only a continuous stream of cool air on his face and the blur of the bush outside his window. As they passed the ferry crossing that led to the Niger's west bank, the driver wondered about Omar's father.

"He must be old now, your father."

"He's well over 90," Omar said.

"You've been living in France, Monsieur Dia?" the driver asked.

"Many years," he said. "I work there and have a family—a wife and two children."

"May God grant them a long and healthy life!"

"Thank you," Omar said, feeling embarrassed. He had been so preoccupied with his own dilemmas that he hadn't even asked the driver about his life. "What's your name?"

The driver smiled. "I'm Garba Hima." For a tall man, Garba had a surprisingly thin raspy voice. "I live in Niamey, near the vegetable market—two wives and seven children. The older ones go to school. The oldest boy is very smart—number one in his high school class."

"That's wonderful, Garba. Please call me Omar," he said. "Is your family in good health?"

"Yes, except for my four-year-old son. When he was two we took him to the clinic. They gave him a shot, but it severed a nerve in his leg. Since then he walks with a limp."

"May God lighten his burden," Omar said, using a formulaic Songhay idiom.

"Amen," Garba intoned. "The others, Inshallah, are in good health."

"My father," Omar said, "is old and sick. "It's his time. That's why I came all the way from France." He looked out the window onto a vast desiccated brown plain dotted with green bushes here and there. "It's been many years since I've been to Tillaberi." He took a deep breath. "I'm Issaka Dia's oldest son."

Garba looked at him for a moment and lapsed into silence. What more could be said?

CHAPTER 4

As they drove further north, the vegetation thinned out: fewer trees, bushes, and waterholes; more sand, brown clay, and rock. In time, Tillaberi Mountain, a large gray cone that dominated the village, came into view. As always, the sight of the mountain stiffened Omar's spine. For many generations, his family made yearly sacrifices on the mountain's summit, the place from which his ancestors derived much of their magical power.

They came upon a military checkpoint. Dressed in fatigues and seated on battered metal chairs, two soldiers lazily swatted at flies as they fought off sleep. Having no interest in a mere taxi, they waved them through. They drove through town, following the main road, which featured an assortment of mudbrick boutiques, dry goods shops, a primary school, a secondary school, a health clinic, as well as a line of sand-stained cement buildings. Constructed during the colonial period, these structures housed the regional government. The market, which would fill up with buyers and sellers on Sundays, was still situated on a plain that gradually sloped toward the Niger River. Tillaberi hadn't changed all that much.

Driving through town brought on a flood of memories, Omar thought of his days in the primary and secondary schools, remembering some of his classmates. What had happened to them? Some had probably become minor civil servants who worked for the forestry service, the police, or the post office; others had probably become peasant farmers who cultivated millet or rice. A few might have gone into business. Omar tried to remember their names, but could only recall one or two of them. Because he was the son of a great sorcerer, no one had wanted to be Omar's friend. His classmates feared that friendship with him might endanger them. They giggled when his eye twitched on the playground and in the classroom. The fearful townspeople kept their distance from all of Omar's brothers and sisters. That's why the family lived so far away from the center of town. Omar had a miserable childhood.

Omar's schoolmates could leave their homes and arrive at school in five minutes. It took him almost one hour to walk from their Tillaberi Mountain compound to the primary school. When he went to secondary school, the trip took 90 minutes. Those long walks reinforced his isolation and fueled his resentment. How he had wanted to escape Tillaberi!

When they reached the north end of town, Omar asked the driver to turn off onto a dirt track, a path that would eventually wind its way to the family compound. They descended a hill, crossed a small bridge that spanned a wadi, and drove up a steep embankment. This neighborhood, called Zongo, housed recent arrivals to Tillaberi—members of nearby ethnic groups—Fulan herders, Hausa leatherworkers and butchers, Tuareg blacksmiths. From rickety tables in front of their mudbrick houses, small-time merchants from Mali and Burkina Faso sold kola nuts, dried dates, sugar cubes, and cigarettes—not in packs but in clusters of two and three. At night, men—old and young—came to Zongo to visit the brothels.

They came upon the outskirts of town and followed tracks into the bush—a plateau dotted by a few acacias and thorn bushes. Omar's family homestead had been built in the midst of a land so barren that it looked like a moonscape. In such parched circumstances, water became a precious commodity. In town, most people fetched water from the Niger River. In the bush, people gathered water from seasonal ponds or from wells. Fortunately, for Omar's family, there was a deep well in the compound, which meant that his female relatives didn't have to walk very far to find water.

After several minutes of driving, the compound finally came into view. Surrounded by a four-foot fence fashioned from dried millet stalks, the compound, shaped like an oval, shimmered in the midday light. With the expansion of the family, the compound had grown. What once was a relatively small household had become something of a community in which lived Issaka Dia; Issaka Dia's second wife, Maymouna; Omar's brothers; his father's sisters; Omar's cousins; and their wives and children.

Omar invited Garba Hima for lunch.

"I'd like to, but I should get back to Niamey."

"But I insist, Garba."

"Okay, then." He popped the taxi's truck and gathered Omar's leather bags. They clapped three times outside the compound door, also fashioned from millet stalks, to announce their arrival. Someone moved the door to reveal an opening in the compound fence. A young boy, perhaps six years old, dressed only in tattered underwear emerged from the compound. Brown streaks of dried dirt stretched across his black skin. His shaved head glistened in the bright sunlight. Staring blankly at them, he said nothing. What a contrast they presented to him. He was barely dressed. Omar and his driver were dressed like Westerners, Garba in his aforementioned brown slacks and white shirt and Omar in his airplane attire, a shirt and matching pair of dress slacks in muted gray—the essence of La Sape.

After what seemed an interminable moment, the boy turned toward the compound. "Hey, hey, hey, people are here. People are here."

A tall bull-necked man walked toward the compound entrance. A billowing black robe, which is called a *boubou*, covered his thick body. He had wrapped a black turban around his head—the costume of Songhay sorcerers who wear black, the color that symbolizes the vulture, their ally and familiar. On seeing Omar, the man's square face creased into a wide smile. "God is great. God is great." They shook hands. "Older brother," said Abdoulaye, "we praise God that you are here."

"God," Omar said, "is the owner of strength," he responded, reciting one of his father's favorite sayings.

Abdoulaye beamed with delight. "Who is your friend?" he asked, looking at Garba Hima.

Omar made introductions.

"Be our guest." Abdoulaye said to Garba. He motioned for them to enter the compound. "Hey everyone! Hey!!! God be praised! Our oldest brother, Omar Dia, has returned. God has brought him here."

As they walked into the compound, the family surrounded them. Maymouna, the mother of Omar's younger brothers Moussa and Seydou, came forward. Her aged breasts lay flat against her chest. Strutting up to them in her homespun indigo blue wrap-around skirt, she began to sing the praise poetry of Omar's ancestors. Invoking the name of "Si," Omar's ancestor, the fifteenth century Songhay king, she repeatedly thrust her index finger skyward.

Si flies in the night.
Si flies when the rooster crows.
Si Baru (Sonni Ali's son).

Si Almine (Si Baru's son who first came to Wanzerbe, village of sorcerers).
Si, who can kill man between the head and the hair.
Si, who can kill a man between the shoe and the foot.
Si who can kill a man between the shirt and the neck.
Si, who is all powerful.
Si, who sees the past and predicts the future.
Si, who is our father and protector.
Praise to Omar Dia, grandson of Si, who has returned to the land of his ancestors.

Omar's younger brothers, Moussa and Seydou, who like Abdoulaye, wore black boubous, also came forward. While Abdoulaye spent much of his time farming and assisting Issaka Dia in his work as a healer, Moussa and Seydou were musicians. Seydou played the one-string violin, called the *godje* in Songhay; Moussa played the gourd drum, which is called the *gasi*. During spirit possession ceremonies among Omar's people, musicians play these instruments to bring spirits into the bodies of mediums. During the dry season, Moussa and Seydou traveled from village to village, offering their services. Omar considered Abdoulaye, who was close to his age, a serious and quiet man who possessed an even disposition. Moussa and Seydou took after their mother, Maymouna, a talkative hot-headed woman.

"Older brother," said Moussa, "nice of you to return after so many years."

"Older brother," said Seydou, eyeing Omar's fashionable clothing. "You dress like the white man." Seydou fingered Omar's sleeve. "Very nice. Very nice." He grinned. "How are our in-laws in Paris?"

"They are well," Omar answered.

"How long since your last visit?" Moussa asked.

"It's been a long time. You both were young boys when I went to France. Now you are strong men with wives and children," Omar said, trying to reduce the palpable tension.

"Yes," said Seydou, "we honor the family tradition. We live here and honor our father. And you....you left us..."

Omar had expected these resentments but not at the very moment of his arrival. Why had he come to Tillaberi? How he wanted to escape from a compound of spiteful relatives who wished him ill.

"That's enough," Abdoulaye interjected. "Omar has come home, which makes us happy, which makes our father happy."

Moussa cleared his throat. "What's with your eye, older brother?" he asked.

Seydou faced Omar. "Yes, there's much family business to discuss. As the oldest son you have to step forward." He snickered. "Good luck, older brother." He playfully slapped Moussa on the back and the two brothers walked away.

"Put your uncle's things in my house," Abdoulaye said to one of Omar's nephews. He turned to Omar. "Father wants you to sleep with him in the spirit house—a great honor."

Speechless, Omar nodded.

Meanwhile Garba Hima, who had been a silent witness to a small slice of the family drama, continuously shuffled his feet, scratched his head, and hunched his shoulders.

Omar turned toward Garba and grinned. "Abdoulaye," he said, turning back to his brother, "it was nice to invite Garba Hima to lunch, but his boss expects him back soon. He doesn't have the time to lunch with us. Isn't that right, Garba?"

"That's true," Garba said. "Thank you for offering the lunch, but I've got to get back."

"We understand," Abdoulaye said.

Garba smiled with relief. Who knew what might happen during an afternoon in a compound of sorcerers—all dressed in black? He left with dispatch.

CHAPTER 5

Omar looked at the spirit house, which, during his long absence, hadn't changed. It was still a thatched hut, shaped like a beehive, situated at one end of the family compound. Adjacent to the spirit house stood the spirit canopy, nine wood posts that supported a thatch roof, under which musicians played spirit music. Omar's brothers had built rectangular mudbrick houses for the rest of the family. These homes, each of which consisted of two rooms and a corrugated tin roof, hugged a millet-stalk fence, creating a common clearing in the compound's center, a space where goats and sheep were tethered. A small round mudbrick house, fashioned for cooking, had been constructed near the compound entrance. Close to the spirit hut, two acacias shaded the well, which Omar's grandfathers had dug in the distant past.

"For now, come to my house," Abdoulaye said. "Father's sleeping. After lunch, we'll see him." Abdoulaye lived next to the spirit house.

"I'm hungry," Omar confessed.

"They're making a meat stew and rice." Abdoulaye looked at Omar's clothes. "You're home. Wear a boubou. You'll be more comfortable."

Omar hadn't worn a boubou in a very long time. "That makes sense."

Abdoulaye pointed to a small thatched enclosure next to his house. "Go there to wash. You'll see a bucket and soap." He handed Omar a thin blue towel. "Wash. Then we'll get you dressed. Then lunch."

"Thank you, Abdoulaye."

"We're happy you're here, older brother."

During his long absence, Omar had forgotten just how unsatisfying it was to wash one's body with a cup, a cake of scentless lye soap, and a bucket of cold water. Even so, it felt good to wash away the grime of travel. As he rinsed the soap from his hair, the difficulty of his circumstances flooded his consciousness with dread. He hadn't lived in "compound conditions" for a very long time. How would he react to the food? Would the well water make him sick? And what about the obvious tensions in the family? In Songhay families, the sons of one father and different mothers, who are called *bab'izey*, usually competed for family resources and power. That had always been the case in Omar's family, which is one reason he ran away as soon as he could. As soapsuds seeped into his eyes, he winced. Shit, he said to himself, how would he be able to spend time in this god-forsaken place?

Moments later, Omar entered Abdoulaye's house. He found his brother seated on a pillow positioned on a palm frond mat. Abdoulaye pointed to a table in the house's back room on which there was a neatly folded pile of black clothing. "Put those on," Abdoulaye said, "and sit with me."

Putting on billowing drawstring trousers and a matching black tunic brought to Omar an unexpected sense of calm as if his ancestors had touched him. He fingered the large black boubou, which had been embroidered in gold thread around the neck, and wondered if it belonged to his father. He folded the boubou over his arm and entered the front room. He'd wear it when they went to visit Issaka Dia.

Abdoulaye patted a pillow. "Sit there. They'll bring us lunch soon."

He passed Omar a bowl of fresh milk. "How long has it been since you drank sweet milk from one of Niger's cows?"

Taking the bowl, Omar smiled at his brother. "In God's name, it's been a very long time."

Omar took a sip. It was thick, warm, and sweet. The deep aroma of milk fat flooded his mind with childhood memories of cold mornings during the cool dry season. Issaka Dia would wake him before dawn and place him next to a small fire he had started. Hunched over the fire, they'd share a bowl of warm, fresh milk. Issaka Dia would gaze eastward toward the red rim of the eastern horizon and talk to his oldest son about the past, present, and future.

"Omar," he said on those and many other occasions, "in heaven's name, you have the spirit of our ancestors. I'm proud of you."

In the glow of these early morning fires, Issaka Dia would sometimes throw his cowrie shells to look into Omar's future. Each time he'd throw the shells, he'd predict a path full of recognition and fine deeds, of success and distant travel. Each time he'd throw the shells, he'd also see a space of loneliness and isolation. Like any father, Issaka Dia worried about his son. And yet, he knew that one day Omar would return home. "In time," he liked to say, "your path will lead you back here to the land of your ancestors."

Omar smiled inwardly. The shells, he said to himself, never lie. "Brother," he said to Abdoulaye, "how goes it with you?"

"All is well with my wife and children—two boys and three girls."

"You are blessed," Omar said. When they were kids, Abdoulaye followed Omar everywhere. Before he entered primary school, he'd accompany Omar on errands. When Omar took the long detestable treks to school, Abdoulaye would walk with him.

"Too far to walk alone," he'd say.

Back then, they forged a bond. Some people might say that having the same father and mother in a polygamous household forged their bond. That might have been the case. Omar had always liked Abdoulaye. Even as a child, Abdoulaye put the concerns of others ahead of his own. If their mother needed onions for the evening meal, Abdoulaye would volunteer to walk to the nearest market, a considerable distance, to get them. Sitting next to Abdoulaye, Omar knew that his brother's kindness and warmth hadn't diminished with age.

"I'm grateful, Omar. How is your family?"

"They're in good health."

"I'm happy for you," he said. "Why haven't you brought them here to meet us?"

"It's a long story, Abdoulaye," Omar said, sighing. "They'll come one day, soon."

"I hope so."

Abdoulaye, of course, knew why Omar hadn't brought his family to Tillaberi, but was too polite to bring up what had transpired in the past. Omar didn't want to talk about it either. So, he passed the bowl of milk to Abdoulaye, who took a sip. "Brother," Omar said. "It feels good to be here. I'm happy that you've been looking after our father."

"I've learned from him. I've learned about the spirits and have followed the path of plants."

"You'll become our spirit possession priest, then?"

"That's my destiny."

"And you're learning to be an herbalist?"

"Yes. I mix medicines that heal people. Almost every day, people come to see me." Abdoulaye took another sip of his tea. "That's my path." He looked deeply into Omar's eyes. "Father is saving his greatest secrets for you."

This statement made Omar shudder. He had never wanted to embrace the physical and psychological burdens of sorcery. Why couldn't his brother Abdoulaye accept this burden? Abdoulaye seemed to willingly accept the difficulties of being a spiritual guardian in rural Niger. His even-tempered disposition suited the stressful rigors of a life in sorcery. Why hadn't Issaka Dia picked him as a worthy successor? Omar hunched his shoulders. "Abdoulaye, I think you should receive these secrets. I've been away for too many years. I can't accept the responsibility. How can I take up the sorcerer's burden? You should take it up."

Abdoulaye shook his head. "You are the oldest son. Issaka Dia has picked you. He knows what kind of person can follow the path of power. He's wiser than we are."

Omar touched Abdoulaye's forearm. "But don't you feel anger in your heart? You've been here all these years. You know about plants. You've looked after father. And me, I've been away."

"You've been away, Omar, but there's no anger in my heart," Abdoulaye stated. "Issaka Dia shows us the way and it will be good."

Abdoulaye's words forced Omar to confront the difficulties of his situation. Ever loyal to Issaka Dia, Abdoulaye would never step in to assume responsibilities, which, at least in their father's mind, had been reserved for Omar. Was there no escape? How could he get back to his comfortable life in Paris? Right then and there, Omar resigned himself to listen seriously to what his father had to say. If his father gave him an object, Omar would accept it and treat it with respect. Somehow, he'd find a way through this trying time and get back to his life.

CHAPTER 6

Just outside of Abdoulaye's door, someone clapped three times. "Food here," a thin, soft voice uttered.

"Bring it in," Abdoulaye requested.

She glided in like a gentle breeze, her sweet scent filling the space. For some reason, her scent, which seemed familiar, made Omar shake. She was a tall, strong-boned woman dressed in a wrap-around skirt and a tank top that revealed smooth shapely arms and a long neck. She averted Omar's gaze, but he noticed the crease of a smile around her full lips.

Saying nothing, she placed a large and a small enamel pot before them.

"What is it, today?" Abdoulaye asked the woman.

"Rice, meat and squash sauce," she said.

"God be praised. It's my favorite," Abdoulaye said.

Omar continued to stare at the woman. Why did she look so familiar?

"We expected older brother today," she said, to Abdoulaye. "That's why we made this sauce."

"Who are you?" Omar asked with a European boldness that did not fit the situation. In Niger, men are usually circumspect around adult women they didn't know.

By looking at Omar directly, the woman unexpectedly met his boldness with a measure of her own. Smooth black skin covered a face framed by high cheekbones and offset by large deeply set black eyes, a strong straight nose, and a large sensual full-lipped mouth—"a black goddess," Omar thought. "I'm Uncle Ali's widow," she said to Omar. "I'm also your cousin."

"What's your name?" Omar insisted.

"Fati," she said in her thin, high-pitched voice.

"I'm Omar," he said, reacting socially more like an African in France than one in Niger.

"I know," she said, again averting his gaze. "I have work to do," she said as she slipped outside into the sunshine and walked away.

Abdoulaye opened the casseroles and handed Omar one of the two wooden spoons that Fati had brought. He poured the steaming sauce on the rice, looked at the food and said: "Praise be to God." He began to eat. Omar followed suit. The first spoonful of the spicy food brought back memories of Omar's late mother. Tall and thin, his mother always spoke slowly, carefully, and quietly. She had an oval face with large cloudy eyes. She didn't smile very much—except when she saw Abdoulaye and Omar. At mealtimes, she always made sure that Omar and Abdoulaye got extra portions of food. Following the evening meal, Omar would go to her house to talk. She always wanted to know what he had learned in school. He often complained about his isolation.

"It's not easy to be a sorcerer's son," she'd always say.

Omar would nod in agreement and tell her of his plans to travel to Niamey and to France. "I don't want to bear the sorcerer's burden," he'd say to her.

"Follow your heart, my son," she'd say to him. "Follow your heart."

In her own quiet way, Omar's mother was a remarkably wise woman. Why had she become so distant to him? Their bond of love had been strong, but not strong enough to bring him back from France—back to his mother and a life in Tillaberi. She must have missed him. She must have harbored deep disappointment in her oldest son.

"Older brother, the food?"

"Delicious. It makes me think about the past, about our mother."

"I miss her every day," Abdoulaye said. "She was kind. She knew our traditions."

Omar picked up a bowl of water and took a swig. "Yes, she did." He paused a moment. "Abdoulaye," he said, wanting to bring the conversation to the present, "why has Fati not remarried? She's a beautiful woman."

"You know how it is, Omar. She's a widow of a sorcerer from a family of sorcerers. Who would want to marry her?"

"She'd make someone a fine wife," Omar said.

Abdoulaye grinned. "She'd make you a fine wife, older brother."

"Not me," Omar said avoiding Abdoulaye's gaze. "I've got a family in France."

"Why not a second family here? You're a Muslim. You have money—a perfect match."

"No, no," Omar responded, waving at his brother. "It's not possible."

"If you married Fati and had a family here, we'd see you all the time."

Omar shrugged his shoulders. "I'm not going to marry her—just wondering about her."

Abdoulaye stood up and patted Omar's shoulder. "Men like to wonder about beautiful women, no?"

"That, my brother, is the truth."

CHAPTER 7

After a sumptuous lunch, Abdoulaye suggested a siesta. Being exhausted from the physical and emotional displacements of the journey, Omar willingly obliged. As soon as he lay down on his brother's bed, he fell into a shallow sleep, tossing and turning in the still afternoon heat. He dreamed of his mother, remembering her face the day he left Tillaberi for Paris. Her unblinking eyes bore into his soul, filling him with a deep remorse. Maybe they both realized that Omar had decided to abandon his family's way of life. On that day, Omar's mother neither smiled nor waved goodbye. Her face seemed frozen. Years of living in the households of sorcerers, who are not supposed to betray emotion, had fashioned in her a deep stoicism. As he was about to turn his back on her, he noticed a single tear rolling down her cheek. What had he done to his dear mother? Why had he forsaken her? Omar bolted awake in a cold sweat.

His head spinning, Omar rolled off his brother's bed and staggered toward a wall. Where was he? What was he doing in this house?

Just then, Abdoulaye came in. "Are you okay, older brother?" he asked. "Bad dreams?"

"I dreamed of our mother."

Abdoulaye sighed. "I dream about her a lot."

Omar turned and walked toward his brother. He took his hand and looked into the latter's eyes. "Thank you, Abdoulaye. Without you, I wouldn't be able to do this. This is a difficult time."

"Baba always says that we must be mindful and patient."

"That's the truth, my brother."

For a few moments, they stood in silence, holding hands and savoring the comforting bond that had been quickly and effortlessly re-established. The muezzin's call for late afternoon prayer echoed in the dry air and brought to an end what had been a special moment for Omar.

"Older brother," Abdoulaye said, "time to visit father. Get yourself ready."

Omar went to a water jug and dipped a plastic cup in it, drawing out cool water that he used to refresh his face. He took the black boubou his brother had given him and put it on. As they left the relative cool of the house, the late afternoon heat took hold of him like an angry wrestler. Sweat beaded on his brow. Slowly, they walked the few paces to Issaka Dia's straw hut. Abdoulaye had long tried to convince the old man to live in a more comfortable mudbrick house, but Issaka Dia had refused, preferring his conical home with a floor of smooth wadi sand.

After clapping three times to announce their visit, Issaka Dia asked them in. "Praise be to God."

They then entered the hut where their father had always eaten, slept, and performed rituals. As children, they learned that no one entered the hut unbidden. The hut had always been a place of mystery and power, where supplicants and even family members treaded lightly and with the utmost respect. Inside, the ribbons of sunlight streamed through the thatch. Issaka Dia's *lolo*, the sacred iron staff of the sohanci sorcerer, stood in the sand right next to the hut's center pole. Scores of blood-caked rings had long ago been slipped onto thicker parts of the staff. Small pots and miniature sandals hung from the rafters. Issaka Dia used these objects to make offerings to the Atakurma, the elves of the bush. Hatchets, whose necks had been adorned with small bells, had been wedged between the hut's wooden skeleton and its grass covering. The deep, sweet smell of Bint El Sudan, an oil-based perfume, filled the air. As always, the spirit hut filled Omar with awe.

Issaka Dia, whose bed stood to one side of the hut, had propped himself on several pillows. Illness had withered his once large and powerful body into what looked like a bent tree branch. Dressed in black drawstring trousers and a loose-fitting black tunic, he raised his bony arm and beckoned them closer. The parched skin on his face stretched tightly over his high cheekbones. His head had been shaved, revealing a smooth scalp that glimmered in the filtered afternoon light. He smiled, revealing a mouth with only a few stump-like teeth. As always, his eyes, large and deeply set, burned like beacons. "Omar," he said weakly, "is that you, my son?"

"It is, Father. I've come to sit with you."

"God is strong," Issaka Dia said. "God has answered my prayers." He turned toward Abdoulaye. "When did your older brother arrive?"

"Around noon, Father. He had lunch and took a siesta."

"Pap, pap, pap. Wonderful Abdoulaye. Make sure that he's comfortable. He needs to be very strong."

"I'll look after him, Father."

"Abdoulaye will take good care of me, Father."

"I know he will." He beckoned Abdoulaye close to him and whispered in his ear. Abdoulaye looked up at Omar and smiled. "I'll see you later, Omar." He left Issaka Dia and Omar alone. Omar glanced at the hut's opening. "Why did you send him away?" he asked.

"Because, my son, we have important things to discuss. I will die three nights after the next new moon and I have much to teach you. When I'm finished, I'll do what I have to do and you will be the one."

That meant that Omar's father would die in roughly one lunar month, for the current new moon had just appeared. Although Omar had been taught that great sorcerers know the exact time of deaths, the certainty of his father's proclamation unnerved him. How much could he teach Omar in one month? Omar also knew that when his father died, Issaka Dia would vomit his sacred chain and expect his oldest son to swallow it. Omar didn't want to take on these heavy burdens. He didn't want to swallow his father's sacred chain. He feared that he would choke on it. Why had Issaka Dia picked him to bear the sorcerer's burden?

"Father, I'm not worthy. Give your power to Abdoulaye," Omar said.

Issaka Dia laughed softly and then coughed. "Why do you speak this way? Blood is obligation."

"Yes, I know. But I've been away, Father. I live in France. My wife is French. I have no head for the ways of our ancestors. Abdoulaye would be a more worthy successor, a better guardian of the family traditions." Omar cleared his throat. "I didn't choose to be your first-born son. Why does being the oldest son make me your successor?"

"It doesn't."

"Everyone says that it does," Omar said

Issaka Dia spat tobacco on the sand. "They're wrong, my son. A sohanci looks into a person's heart. That's how he knows if a person can take on the sorcerer's burden."

"I don't understand, Father."

The old man shifted his position. "Do you remember when you were in school, and your grandfather lay dying in this very hut?"

Omar remembered the slow death of his aged grandfather. He must have had a cancer that gradually consumed his bones. Toward the end, the poor man could hardly move. "Yes, I do."

"Do you remember the day he asked all of his grandsons to gather around his bed?"

"Of course."

"Tell me what happened."

Omar's grandfather gave each of his grandsons, including Abdoulaye and Omar, a tiny baby chick. He asked them to hold the chicks in their open palms. The helpless chick shook in the young Omar's open palm. Then Omar's dying grandfather ordered his grandsons to squeeze their chicks to death. "You saw what happened, Father."

"I know. Tell me anyway."

"Everyone killed their chick, except me."

"That's right. You couldn't kill a helpless creature. Right then, I knew that you would be the one to take up the sorcerer's burden. You have to value life to be trusted with the power of death."

"You never told me! You let me move along my path, thinking that as the first-born, I had certain obligations—obligations that I did not desire."

"It was good you didn't seek power, Omar. Those who seek never find what they're looking for. A person does not come to power, Omar. Power comes to a person. Ever since that day, my son, I had my eyes on you. Ever since that day, I knew about you."

"I didn't know, Father."

"Many people knew it, Omar. That's why some people in the family wanted to hurt you. When you were young, they tried to kill you."

Omar remembered discovering poisonous snakes in his house and death magic objects among his books and notebooks. Issaka Dia had protected him from those threats, but he had still feared for his life. When Omar went to Niamey to study at the lycée, Issaka Dia was relieved. "It's too dangerous here for you. You've got to leave. You'll be gone for many years," he said, "but you'll be back. At first, you'll come to visit, but your head and heart will not be with us. You'll spend much time away, but one day, when your path has opened, you'll come back and be fully with us. Back then," Issaka Dia said, "I wanted you to leave. Now I want you here with us."

"Is it still dangerous, Father?"

"It's always dangerous in our world, my son. People will challenge you. They will try to make you sick. They may try to kill you. But in my heart I know that you are ready to take on the sorcerer's burden."

Omar didn't share Issaka Dia's confidence. "Father, my life is elsewhere. I don't want these family obligations."

"Blood is obligation, my son." He waved his arm at Omar. "We've talked enough for now. We'll eat and sleep in this hut. We'll talk late at night when no one can overhear us. Come back later tonight." Issaka Dia groaned as he lay down on his bed. Minutes later he had fallen asleep.

CHAPTER 8

After leaving Issaka Dia's hut, Omar retreated to Abdoulaye's house. He sat on a low wooden stool and looked at the clay water jugs that lined one wall of his brother's mudbrick house. The conversation with Issaka Dia deepened his misgivings about the sorcerer's obligations. He still couldn't fathom why Issaka Dia had chosen his wayward son to take up the sorcerer's burden. There had to be more to the story than Omar's reaction to his dying grandfather's test of character. Issaka Dia must have had other reasons for choosing Omar. How Omar wished that his father had picked someone else. He wanted to leave Tillaberi and return to his life in France. His eye began to flutter.

"Older brother," Abdoulaye said. "How goes the late afternoon?"

"It goes well, Abdoulaye." Omar looked at his brother, who smiled at him. Dressed in his black boubou, Abdoulaye was a powerful figure of a man, a person who was, as they say, comfortable in his skin, someone who liked his life. When Omar thought of his life in France, he realized how much he liked the complexities, if not all the particularities of his life in Paris. He loved to spend leisurely days at home reading the latest thinking on literature and philosophy. He also liked to teach and enjoyed the admiration his students showered upon him. He loved his wife and children. What would become of that life? In Tillaberi, Paris seemed very far away.

Abdoulaye found a second stool and sat down and stared at his brother's fluttering eye. "When we were young, your eye used to flutter when you were troubled. Are you troubled, Omar?"

"I am, Abdoulaye. Issaka Dia has much to tell me—many secrets and many burdens." Omar told his brother that he did not want to take up the sorcerer's burden. Omar's hesitance seemed to comfort his brother.

"Power does not come to those who seek it," he stated.

"What am I to do?" Omar asked his brother.

"Like the good person you are, you'll meet your destiny. You'll meet with Issaka Dia and accept whatever he gives you. That's how our heritage passes from generation to generation."

"And when that heritage has been passed to me, then what?" Omar asked.

Abdoulaye looked at Omar and smiled. "Then you'll do what our father always says." He paused for effect. "You'll follow your heart."

Abdoulaye's words reminded Omar of stories that Issaka Dia liked to recount. Late in the afternoon, Issaka Dia liked to talk about the great sorcerers of the past and how they helped the kings and chiefs to wage war, how they sickened the evil chiefs and healed the good ones. Issaka Dia used many proverbs to tell his stories. The logic of these stories was frustratingly circular. Caught up in the telling, it took Issaka Dia a very long time to get to the point. As Omar became a young man, he no longer wanted to listen to the stories. He preferred to read books and dream of his escape to Europe. How ironic it was that after a long European hiatus, Omar was once again mired in a world of allegorical tales. Would Omar ever tell stories this way?

"Omar," Abdoulaye said, breaking the silence that had settled between them, "it might be good to take a ride in the bush. The bush is beautiful in the afternoon."

"What a terrific idea, younger brother!"

It was a hot and hazy afternoon. They mounted their horses and rode to the east.

"Omar," Abdoulaye said, "we should go to *The Place Where Stories Are Told*."

Perhaps Abdoulaye had inherited Issaka Dia's capacity to read another's thoughts. "What a good idea!"

Omar remembered childhood rides to the wondrous spot that overlooked the Niger River basin. The smooth canter of their stallions quickly led them away from the family compound. They followed sandy paths that tracked to the east toward a line of sandstone buttes that rose steeply and sharply from vast red clay plains. Riding eastward and upward, they crossed boulder-laden gullies that, when the rains come, became raging mud streams. To the right and left, Omar took in the acacias and tamarind trees that somehow managed to survive Niger's heat, dust, clay, and sand. Along the banks of the gullies, he noticed the blooms of plants, the roots of which are used to treat skin rashes. As they climbed higher and higher, the sparse vegetation thinned out even more. Even in the dry desolation that marked the higher ground, robust plants emerged from crevices in clay and rock. Seeing these plants always reminded Omar of the resilience of the Songhay people, who for centuries have lived—and lived well—in this unforgiving environment.

Omar followed Abdoulaye ever higher on the path. Behind them to the north, Omar saw the paved road that cut through the heart of Tillaberi, the town where his family had lived for many generations. That road followed the curve of the Niger River north until it came upon the Malian border. Glistening sunlight marked the movement of cars traveling both north and south. Through the late afternoon haze, Omar could just make out Tillaberi's radio tower. Government functionaries used it to gather data on weather conditions. Finally, Abdoulaye and Omar reached their destination: a long, flat, and smooth piece of rock that buttressed two towering sandstone buttes. Looking east from this vantage, Omar could see a plain dotted with scrub that pancaked to the next line of buttes barely visible in the hazy distance. A few green clusters, most likely acacia, tamarind, and jujube trees, marked water holes in the distance. Turning toward the west, Omar gazed down upon the valley of the great Niger River, a ribbon of sparkling water that cut through a narrow band of green—a maze of rice fields and gardens—which, after several hundred meters, gave way to the ever-present tawny brown of sand. They dismounted and sat on the smooth rock surface. Not worrying about their horses, which were used to this routine, they looked upon the world—the majestic Niger River valley bathed in the golden light of late afternoon. The whir of the afternoon wind surrounded them with "the sounds of silence," to borrow from a popular American song.

This perch had always been Omar's favorite place in the world. When he was a child Issaka Dia brought him there. As they gazed upon the vast basin of the Niger, Issaka Dia would tell Omar to open his ears so that he would understand the stories, tales that were always about their ancestors. Their ancestors, his father would say, came there to talk about the lives of their ancestors. "This is *The Place Where Stories Are Told*," Issaka Dia would tell Omar. "One day, you will bring your children to this place."

"How long has it been since you've been here, Omar?" Abdoulaye asked.

Having spent so much of his life in France, it had been a long time indeed. "It's been too long. I've forgotten how much I love this place."

"It's an important place for us. It's an important place for you, Omar." Omar nodded.

"Why have you been away for so long? We're your family. Your roots are in this land, Omar."

He shook his head. "I can't talk about this right now, Abdoulaye. It's complicated."

"We've got time. My mind is open to your words."

"You're a fine man, Abdoulaye. Maybe we can talk about this another time."

"As you wish, Omar," he said standing up and turning in the direction of their family compound. "Follow me. I've got some work to do in the bush and I'd like your help."

Descending the steep trail that had led them to *The Place Where Stories Are Told* they found a path that cut through scrub brush, rock and scattered acacias and tamarind trees. To their left, the afternoon light brought into the relief the craggy outcroppings of Tillaberi Mountain. Straight ahead, they saw a long, desiccated plain that sloped down toward a depression that formed a pond, the waters of which glimmered in the sunlight. In a silence broken only by the rustle of robes in the wind and the clop of hooves on sand, they headed toward the pond. A donkey brayed in the distance. Occasional gusts kicked up clouds of dust, the stale odor of which permeated the air. The vast emptiness of the bush gave Omar a rare feeling of peace and well-being. He remembered taking his dog for childhood walks in the bush. They would leave early in the morning or late in the afternoon and trek into the emptiness. His dog would sometimes chase down a hare and bring home a wonderful lunch or dinner. More often than not, they returned empty handed. How he had loved those forays into the unknown. What was it about the bush that made him feel so good? When they reached a rise just above the pond, Omar remembered something his father used to say: "We find harmony in the bush. Where we find harmony, we find power." That, Omar finally realized, was the power of the bush.

Just then, Abdoulaye pointed left toward a tall termite hill that swept up from the plain like a volcano. "We should inspect that termite hill, Omar."

Scores of termite holes dotted the bush near Tillaberi. They had always fascinated Omar. How could these simple winged creatures, which often swarmed after a rainstorm, create such majestic structures? He didn't understand why Abdoulaye wanted to inspect an innocuous termite hill.

They dismounted. When Abdoulaye reached his destination, he moved the palm of his hand over the termite hill's rough surface.

"Are you looking for something?" Omar asked.

Abdoulaye continued his search and then suddenly stopped. His body shuddered. "Omar," he said, "come and take a look."

Next to his brother's hand, which he had placed near the hill's base, Omar saw a round shape outlined on the surface. "What's that?" Omar asked.

"It's an antelope horn—bad magic. We need to break the spell."

As Abdoulaye spoke, Omar visualized his apartment on the rue de Charonne near the Bastille. In his mind's eye, he saw his wife and kids. How very far he had ventured from that reality! "Please explain, Abdoulaye."

"We need to find sticks to remove the antelope horn," he said. He then explained that the horn had probably been filled with sorcerous objects of some sort. If that was the case, it could prevent rain from reaching Tillaberi. "You see," Abdoulaye said, "that termite hill lies on the path of rain. If there's a bad charm on the path of rain, the rain will miss a village." In short order, they found sharp-ended sticks and began to dig around the horn. "Last year," Abdoulaye said, "we'd see the rain coming and it would often fall to the north and south of our fields. Last year people in neighboring villages had a much better harvest than did the people of Tillaberi. Maybe this charm explains what happened."

Due to the rock-like hardness of the clay, it took some time to dislodge the antelope horn. When they did, Abdoulaye held it upside down and shook it to free whatever had been placed inside. Several objects encased in leather fell to the ground.

"Bad magic?" Omar asked.

Abdoulaye nodded. "We've got to burn these things and bring harmony to the bush…"

"Sorry," Omar said, "I didn't bring any matches."

"I always bring matches when I walk in the bush," Abdoulaye stated. "I'm always looking for bad magic. Our ancestors led us to this one today."

They quickly gathered a pile of twigs, lit a fire, broke the antelope horn into bits and pieces, and threw everything into the flames. Standing over the flames, Abdoulaye recited a formula.

What is in my mind is in your mind.
What is in my heart is in your heart.
What is in my mouth is in your mouth.
My mind-heart-mouth thinks-feels-says
The spell is broken.
The flames have sapped its power.

Abdoulaye repeated the formula three times, three being the number associated with males. He then spit three times into the fire so that the words might enter the flame and do their work. Abdoulaye looked at Omar. "We have to bring back the harmony of the bush. Do you remember the *genji how?*" he asked.

The genji how, an incantation Omar had memorized as a child, is the principal incantation of Songhay sorcerers. It restores harmony to a world continuously torn apart by jealously, betrayal, cruelty, and war. "Yes, I do."

They stood over the flames and recited the sacred text three times:

In the name of the High God.
In the name of the High God.
I speak to the east.
I speak to the west.
I speak to the north.
I speak to the south.
I speak to the seven heavens.
I speak to the seven hells.
I am speaking to N'Debbi.
And my words must travel until, until, until they are known.
N'Debbi lived before human beings.
He gave to human beings the path.
He gave it to Soumana and it was good for him.
Soumana gave it to Niandou.
Niandou gave it to Belma.
Belma gave it to Wijindi.
Wijindi gave it to Issaka.
And Issaka gave it to me.
What was in their lips is in my lips.
What was in their minds is in my mind.
What was in their hearts is in my heart.
Today I am infused with N'debbi and it is good for me.
N'Debbi has seven hatchets and seven picks.
He gave the big rock, Wanzam, to Dongo.

He evades the capture of the blind.
He evades the capture of the ancestors.
The force—the force of the heavens—protects all.

They spat three times to the north, south, east, and west. In so doing, they restored harmony to the bush.

Abdoulaye stared at the flames that had subsided a bit. Having completed their task, he extinguished the fire with sand. "This is our work, Omar."

CHAPTER 9

On his first day back in Africa, Omar had flown from Paris, taken a taxi to Tillaberi, reunited with his dysfunctional family, begun the slow process of adjusting to a different climate and diet, met the beautiful Fati, his cousin and uncle's widow, and rode out into the bush where he and his brother Abdoulaye found and destroyed a destructive charm. The events produced in Omar an unexpected surge of energy.

After a satisfying dinner of millet, pounded into a thick paste and covered with a tasty peanut sauce, Omar wandered about the family compound. Flickering lantern light marked the site of soft conversations, the murmur of which echoed in the night air. Because the compound was so far from Tillaberi, the family did not receive many visitors, especially at night, which meant that most of the conversations took place between family members. Omar drifted to a group of his female relatives, including Fati, who earlier that evening had once again brought him food.

"How goes the evening?" he asked.

"It goes well," they answered.

"Sit down," Omar's father's sister said, "and bring us your words." She had wrapped herself in a coarse, indigo blue homespun cloth.

What a wonderfully poetic way, Omar thought, of asking someone to join the conversation. "I give thanks," he said to his father's sister, whose name was Hampsa. "I give thanks."

A porcelain teapot sat atop a small rise of charcoal that glowed in a brazier. A box of sugar cubes and seven glasses, one large one and six small ones, had been situated on the palm frond mat on which they sat.

The deep aroma of steeping tea saturated the air around them. Fati added seven cubes of sugar to the steeping pot and then, positioning the pot high above the large glass, poured a stream of tea into it. She then emptied the glass back into the pot. She repeated this pouring ritual three times. Then, she filled six small glasses with frothy tea and gave a glass to everyone.

They sipped the tea. It was strong and sweet.

"Tea is our pleasure," Hampsa said. "It's our medicine."

"It's also good for talk," said Maymouna, Omar's father's strong-willed second wife.

As a child, of course, Omar had been introduced to tea drinking. At the time, he hadn't much cared for it. It was sometimes too sweet and always too strong. If he drank the required three glasses, it made sleep difficult, if not impossible. "I remember the pleasures of tea," he said as he sipped some into his mouth.

"Omar Dia, we welcome you back to your home," Hampsa said. "You came all the way from France. You honor us. May your stay here be full of health and well-being."

"Thank you, my aunt. It's a great honor to be here."

"You're with your family now. Our thoughts are your thoughts."

They continued to sip tea.

"We heard tonight some news of the bush," Maymouna stated. "What did you and Abdoulaye find out there?"

"We found bad magic buried in a termite hill and destroyed it."

"Do you know how to do that?" Maymouna asked, sneering slightly.

"No. Abdoulaye did it."

"Aha. They don't teach those things in France, do they?"

"No they don't."

"My sons Moussa and Seydou know how to do these things. They also find bad magic. They're strong descendants of our ancestor, Si, and know how to bring harmony to the bush."

"They're strong men," Omar said, thinking about how much he disliked the arrogance of his two younger brothers. "I would have welcomed their company this afternoon."

"They'll soon be back. They'll teach you much about our ways," Maymouna said. "You'll see."

Fati looked at Omar. "We talk so much about our life here. What about your life in France?"

Maymouna spat tobacco onto the sand. "Why should we care about France? In the past they tried to kill us, but we were strong. We're still strong."

"All true, my mother," Fati said. "But I'd like to hear from my cousin about France."

Maymouna grunted.

"Well, cousin?" Fati said.

Omar tried to explain how he lived in Paris. He described his apartment and talked about his work at the university. "I speak," he told them, "and many people listen and write down what I say. For that, they pay me. I also write books which people read."

"How many people come to hear you speak?" Fati asked.

"Sometimes one hundred people will come," Omar answered. "Sometimes more than two hundred people come to listen." Changing the subject, he described the shops, markets, and parks of Paris.

"Is it true that in Paris," Fati asked, "people put fences around trees and that rivers have walls instead of banks?"

"It's true, Fati."

"Why would people do that? It's like putting the trees and rivers in prison."

Omar laughed and wondered about Fati's wonder. "I don't know, Fati." Just then he realized that he had avoided the subject of his wife and children—his family life in France. He knew why: Fati's beauty attracted him. Here he was alone in Niger, in Tillaberi, living in the same compound with a beautiful widow. She must be lonely. She must miss the company of men.

These lascivious thoughts shamed Omar. He had just left his wife and children in Paris and there he was thinking about another woman. He'd have to be careful with Fati. He would try to dampen his desire for her.

"Paris is a strange place," Fati observed, "but the pictures of it I've seen are very beautiful. I don't think I'd like it there—too dirty, too many people."

They finished their tea, slowly hoisted themselves from the ground, and wandered off to their houses. Omar's combination of tea and adrenaline fought off fatigue. Mentally and physically alert, he walked toward the spirit hut to meet with his father.

CHAPTER 10

Omar found his father propped up on several pillows. A lump of tobacco filled out his lower lip. Upon seeing his son, a smile transformed Issaka Dia's face into a patchwork of wrinkles. "Welcome my son. Welcome."

Omar greeted his father and asked after his day.

"All goes well," he responded. "I thank God you've come."

Considering the hour and his condition, Issaka Dia seemed remarkably well, but the sight of him did not diminish Omar's concern for his health. "Baba, shouldn't you be sleeping now? It's late."

"Bap, bap, bap, bap, Omar. I've been sleeping too much. Besides, what we talk about should only be discussed late at night." He paused for a moment. "Are you tired, my son? You've come all the way from France, have you not?"

"Yes, Baba, but I'm not tired."

"Good, then," he said. "You're ready to hear the history of our family." Issaka Dia shifted his position on his pillows and prepared to tell the tale. "Are you ready, my son, to hear the truth?"

"I am, Father."

"Then so be it. In the time of the distant past, the time of our ancestors, the time when our fathers ruled Songhay, the kings, our ancestors, lived in Gao."

"Is it the same Gao as the town in Mali?"

"It's same town, my son." Issaka Dia spit out some tobacco. "Our ancestors, the Dias and the Sonnis ruled Gao for many centuries. They were brave warriors and they also practiced powerful magic. They used magic to fight their battles."

"What kind of magic, Father?"

"They knew how to fly to locate the enemy. They could make themselves disappear. In battle, arrows and swords would not pierce their bodies. They knew how to make a person so crazy that he would not know his front side from his backside. Everyone feared and respected our fathers. People said that they were the offspring of fire."

"You mean that our ancestors could handle fire?"

"I mean that our ancestors were so full of power that they could not only handle fire, but also burn anyone who came too close to them." Issaka Dia shifted his position yet again. "With their power our fathers built a great empire in Gao. They built a special magic house where they kept their most powerful objects. Before a king died, he would pass on to his heir, the first born son, the *gind'ize gina*, the first sound, the most powerful sound in the world."

"Could someone ever defeat such powerful men, Father?"

"For a long time no one could touch them, especially the all-powerful Sonni Ali Ber, the last of our ancestors to rule Gao. Early in his reign, Sonni Ali Ber was told that his sister, Kassey, would give birth to a son who would one day take away his power. Soon thereafter Kassey did give birth to a son. Fearing for her son's life, she secretly gave her infant, who was called Mamar, to a friend, a woman of the Bariba tribe, who lived on an island in the Niger River."

"'Do not reveal my son's identity to anyone,'" Kassey told the Bariba woman. 'In time, he'll reveal his identity.' Mamar remained on the island and grew into a strong and brave soldier, who, in time, became one of Sonni Ali's generals. From his mother Kassey, he learned the great magic of the Sonnis. From his caretaker, Jitu, he learned the southern magic of the Bariba. When he had won the respect of thousands of loyal soldiers, Mamar converted to Islam and plotted the end of the reign of the Sonnis."

"And then what happened?" Omar asked.

"With the power of his magic, which surpassed even that of Sonni Ali Ber, Mamar came to royal feast in Gao. He presented himself to the king.

"'I, General Mamar,'" he said, "'pay my respects to the invincible Sonni Ber.'"

The king acknowledged his great general who had won many battles and who had expanded the territory and increased the wealth of the empire. "'Do you have good news for me?'" Sonni Ali Ber asked.

"Mamar stepped forward. "'I do,'" he said. "You know me as Mamar, general of the Songhay armies. I am also Mamar, son of Kassey, your sister, and I am here to end your rule and take my place as king. With that Mamar's magically anointed spear flew toward the King. Sonni Ali Ber died instantly as the spear pierced his heart. Mamar proclaimed himself King of the Songhay and took the name, Askia Mohammed."

"What happened to our ancestors," Omar asked, "the descendants of Sonni Ali Ber?"

"The descendants of Sonni Ali Ber threatened Askia Mohammed. Askia Mohammed sent out soldiers to kill our father's fathers. They found and killed all but one of Sonni Ali Ber's male descendants. When they found the last holdout, Si Baru, Sonni Ali Ber's oldest son, they cut off his head and threw his body into the great Niger River. But Si Baru, the first sohanci, possessed very powerful magic that defied death itself. Si Baru's severed head rose up in the sky. As the river carried the headless body to the south, the head followed it downstream. Head and body floated over the rapids and entered the mouth of the Garuol River. In the name of God, head and body moved upstream for seven days. At the end of seven days, the body washed up on a distant shore. Just then, the head rejoined its body and Si Baru regained consciousness. Local people surrounded our ancestor and sang his praises. They welcomed him to their country."

"'What do you call this place?' Si Baru asked."

"We call it Wanzerbé," the people said. "And what is your name?"

"I am Si Baru, son of Sonni Ali Ber," he said.

"The people bowed to their new king. 'We welcome you, Si Baru, May we all prosper here.'"

"Si Baru married local women who bore him children. Our ancestor taught his children how to fly like vultures, how to disappear, and how to make someone crazy. Si Baru's children passed the knowledge on to their children. That is how we became the offspring of fire. And now I will pass this knowledge on to you, my son. We are all of the same blood. Blood is obligation." Issaka Dia shifted his position once more and coughed. "I'm tired now, Omar. Sleep here with me and think about your obligations."

"I will, Father. I will."

Issaka Dia lay down on his bed. Soon the soft rumble of gentle snoring filled the hut. Omar blew out the lantern and sat down cross-legged on a straw mat a few feet from his father's bed. How could he, of all people, learn to fly like a vulture? Could he truly become an offspring of "fire"? As Omar lay down on the mat, doubt coursed through body. In Paris, he had become soft. He liked his spacious apartment and soft bed. Would he be able to sleep on the rock hard palm frond mat? If he had to worry about these minimal comforts, how could he ever become the successor to the great Issaka Dia? Did he want to? Slowly and quietly, Omar got up and slipped out into the night air, which was cool and refreshing. A vast moonless sky loomed above him. The Milky Way divided the sky into equal halves as if some invisible presence has stretched a loosely stitched strip of white cloth across the heavens. A shooting star streaked across the southern horizon. The wind carried the aroma of wood smoke, probably the last throes of a dying fire. Donkeys brayed in the darkness. Why had Omar come to Tillaberi? What feelings had propelled him to his father's bedside? He felt bewildered and troubled. Slowly, he dragged himself back to Issaka Dia's hut and laid down. Staring up at a ceiling fashioned from twigs, the mantra "blood is obligation" lulled him into a deep, dreamless sleep.

CHAPTER 11

Several days passed before Issaka Dia again spoke to Omar. In the interim, Omar tried to adapt to the daily routines of his family. He'd wake with the cock's crow at dawn and slowly roll his aching back off the palm frond mat. Then he'd take a large metal tea pot, dull as the gray of an elephant's hide, fill it with water, and slip out of the hut to wash his face and hands. Abdoulaye would then greet him and ask after his health. Together they'd join Issaka Dia in the spirit hut. By then, one of Omar's young nieces would have brought them some tea and the warmed-up leftovers of their dinner. Sometimes, she would bring them fried millet pancakes—a real treat. During these breakfasts, Issaka Dia spoke little, if at all. After breakfast, family friends would come to visit. Occasionally, someone would consult Abdoulaye about a physical or emotional problem. Omar would watch as Abdoulaye threw cowrie shells to divine the problem. Then Abdoulaye would prescribe a solution—a course of herbal medicines, a sacrifice, a snippet of domestic advice. Issaka Dia slept most mornings and most afternoons. They would wake him for lunch, usually rice and a stew with a few chunks of meat swimming in a pot full of green and viscous gumbo sauce. In time, Omar would look forward to lunch, which was always eaten in silence, and his siesta, which now refreshed him. In the late afternoon, Abdoulaye and Omar would walk in the bush and talk about the family. In the evenings, the beautiful Fati brought them a dinner of millet paste smothered with a meatless peanut sauce—delicious. After dinner, Omar would talk with Abdoulaye or chat with Fati and his female relatives.

After a week of this routine, Omar entered the spirit hut to sleep. He found his father propped up on his pillows. "It's time for talk," he announced.

Omar grabbed a long leather pillow and sat down on the ground next Issaka Dia's bed. "My head is open, Father."

"That's good, my son. One day, you will tell these stories." He coughed several times and smiled.

"Si Baru, son of Sonni Ali Ber, married local women in Wanzerbe. He had many children to whom he taught his great magic. He taught them about the Atakurma, the little people who are the guardians of the bush. He told them to go to the bush every Sunday and leave the Atakurma a bowl of milk and some honey. In this way, the Atakurma would protect the village from the dangers of the bush. He told them how to respect the trees and plants of the bush, how to ask for forgiveness when cutting bark off a tree or breaking the stem of a plant. He showed them how to mix potions that would heal the sick or sicken the unworthy. He fed them much *kusu*, the food of sorcerers. They ate kusu that made them invisible, kusu that protected them from spears, arrows, and bullets, kusu that enabled them to fly like a vulture." Issaka Dia smiled and paused. "Our fathers were invincible, Omar. In the name of God, they were strong and unspoiled. Time has weakened our magic, but we must try to keep it strong. Our people need us to be strong, Omar."

"I hear you, Father."

"Good," he said. "In time the Empire of Gao weakened. Askia Mohammed was strong—a good general and a good king. But as he aged, his many sons fought each other to become king. The princes became fat and lazy. The Fulan and Tuaregs fought the rule of Songhay and finally, the Arabs came from the north and the Empire broke apart. The descendants of Mamar…"

"The Maiga?"

"Yes, we call them Maiga. The Maiga fled to the south and settled among the farmers. They married local women and became chiefs."

"Did they settle in Wanzerbe?"

"No. Only our people lived in Wanzerbe. Outsiders were not welcome—especially the Maiga, whose fathers had killed so many of our ancestors. The Maiga feared the power of our fathers."

"As they should have," Omar interjected.

"And so, the Maiga, the princes of Songhay, traveled to Wanzerbe to talk with our fathers. They asked our fathers to perform magic to protect their lands from enemies. In this way, our fathers became the guardians of Songhay. They asked the spirits for rain, for good harvests, for strength against enemies. 'And if a person becomes a mean chief,' one of the princes once told our fathers, 'then you, the descendants of Si, must make things right, you must teach him a lesson.' The burdens were great, but our fathers took them on. They were respected and feared."

"In time they split into two clans," Issaka Dia continued, "the red sohanci who are descendants of Si through both the father and mother. The white sohanci are descendants of Si only through the father."

"And what are we, Father?"

"We are red sohanci. We've always married within the family, my son. Our pure blood makes us strong."

"Is it so?"

"It is so, my son," Issaka Dia retorted formulaically. "There came a time when wars ravaged our lands. One season the Maiga princes fought one another; another season they'd fight our neighbors the Fulan, the Tuareg, or the Zarma. There were many raids; the soldiers took many captives and filled their villages with slaves. During this time, the chief of Ouallam, to the east of Tillaberi, sent a man to Wanzerbe to ask our fathers for help. War had ruined his country. Seyni and Ousmane, sons of Soumana, the greatest sorcerer of his time, volunteered to help the chief of Ouallam. They transformed themselves into vultures and flew east from Wanzerbe to Ouallam. They performed great feats of magic and Sadyara, the snake god, appeared on the land and in the sky. In fear enemy soldiers fled Ouallam and the farmers returned to their fields. The chief asked the brothers what they wanted in return for their work. Ousmane, the older brother said: 'I want to become the chief of Ouallam.' The Ouallam chief welcomed his new leader whose power guaranteed peace and prosperity."

"And what happened to Seyni?"

"Your grandfather?" Issaka Dia asked rhetorically. "He married a woman who was both a descendant of Si and a witch. They moved to Jessey, a village in the Ouallam country. They had many children. When the French came, they moved us to Simiri, where my brothers still live. In Simiri, we protected the chiefs. We made them strong. Other chiefs brought us to their villages, and we made those villages strong. We prospered in Simiri. We ate meat and drank milk and received the gifts of people from far and wide."

"But how did we come to Tillaberi?"

"Bap, bap, bap, bap. Sorcery causes many problems in families, my son. There's much jealously in this compound."

"There's jealously among the brothers here," Omar observed.

"Jealousy is our greatest enemy, my son. In Simiri, all of my brothers wanted to become the next sorcerer. They wanted the great secrets. I was the first-born and my brothers were jealous of my birthright. They plotted against me. At the time of the French war, they tried to deceive me so they would get your grandfather's great power. My father understood this business. To guarantee my safety, he sent me to live with relatives in Tillaberi. Once I married and established a compound, he came to live and eventually die with us. When he died, I alone received his great secrets and great objects." Issaka Dia coughed and tried to catch his breath. "But the hatred and treachery are still with us, my son."

Issaka Dia lay down on his bed, closed his eyes, and fell asleep. Omar wondered how much of this sordid history would repeat itself. He bent down, slipped out of the spirit hut, and emerged into the night air. A brisk wind blew in cool air from the west. As always, stars filled an inky moonless sky. In this vast expanse, Omar felt terribly alone. His family was there, but they had little or no comprehension of his life. They didn't know or care about his accomplishments. They had never listened to his lectures and couldn't read any of his books. They would never see his apartment in Paris or meet his wife. They didn't know the names of his children. And yet, there he was in Tillaberi, eldest son of Issaka Dia, the most renowned sorcerer in western Niger.

In the silent darkness of the compound, Omar noticed a lantern light flickering in one of the grass huts—Fati's hut. In need of some comforting conversation, he walked over to the hut, fashioned from bush grasses, and softly clapped three times.

"Enter."

Fati sat on her bed but Omar was much too focused on her appeal to notice anything else about her space. She had wrapped a homespun indigo cloth around her body. "I couldn't sleep, and I saw the light," Omar said.

She smiled and patted the bed beside her. "Come and sit," she said softly. "You're welcome here any time." She patted the bed again. "Come and sit."

Omar sat down barely able to contain himself. His heart pounded against his chest. Despite his obvious desire for Fati, Omar steeled himself to maintain a respectful distance. He was, after all, a married man with children who had, out of principle, resisted the sexual advances of his students. "Yes," he said hesitantly, "I couldn't sleep. I've been talking with Issaka Dia. He's started to teach me, but I'm troubled, Fati. In France, I sleep well. Here, I'm lucky to get a few hours of rest. In France my eyes are at peace. Here they flutter."

Staring down at her knees, Fati nodded and then looked up at Omar, her large black eyes clear and unblinking. "They say that sorcerers never sleep well because they're protecting their villages from the bush spirits or from bad people." She paused a moment. "Maybe it's your fate to sleep the sleep of sorcerers."

"Maybe so," Omar admitted with no small measure of skepticism.

"Maybe it's your fate to do good in the world," she said. "Maybe you're destined to help people. That's why you here. That's why you've come all the way from France."

Fati's words somehow slowed the beat of Omar's heart and brought him some peace. How could Fati understand so much about Omar's situation? How could such a short exchange of words bring him such comfort? He had no idea. "Thank you, Fati," he said momentarily pushing back his desire for her, "you've made me feel better." Omar stood up and looked down at her. "Can I come back some other evening to talk?"

"Yes."

CHAPTER 12

The more Omar learned about the family, the more troubled he became. How could he negotiate his way through what seemed a minefield of family conflict? With the proximity of Issaka Dia's death, his time in Tillaberi would be short. Issaka Dia didn't waste time on trivial matters. He completed the family history, much of which Omar had heard before, and gave Omar the lowdown on the trustworthiness of his surviving brothers. Then they dove into the science of sorcery.

"Some of my brothers in Simiri will demand that you give them my power objects. Don't give them anything," Issaka Dia said. "They all have bad characters. My objects of power are for you and Abdoulaye and no one else." He paused. "Do you understand, my son?"

"I do, Father."

"They'll also want you to teach them what I'm teaching you," he said. "You must respectfully refuse."

Omar nodded.

"Tonight I give you divination," Issaka Dia announced. From under his pillow he produced a black cloth satchel. "These are my shells. My father gave them to me. His father gave them to him. These shells carry the voice of Wambata."

"The spirit of the cemetery?"

Issaka Dia laughed softly. "Yes, but also the spirit of divination. Wambata sees the past in a gourd of blood, the present in a pool of water and the future in a bowl of milk. She sees above and below." He coughed and continued. "There's a white satchel near the center post. Give it to me."

Omar found the cloth satchel and gave it to his father. Issaka Dia untied it and slowly took out a mirror. "This, too, is yours, Omar. If you balance a coin in the center, you'll be able to see deep into a person's past and far into the future. Try it," he said giving Omar the small mirror.

Omar placed the mirror on the sand, found a coin, balanced it on the mirror, and saw absolutely nothing. "I see nothing, Father."

Issaka Dia laughed. "Exactly as it should be, my son. When you're ready, your path will open. It took years for me to see the past and future in the mirror. Your time will come—with patience."

"I'll take good care of these, Father."

He smiled. "I know you will, my son."

"What about the shells?"

"Ah, the shells," Issaka Dia answered. "I almost forgot. If you want to hear the shells, I must start you on your path. Give me the small bowl with kola nuts in them."

Omar found a black bowl with two kola nuts floating in a small amount of water.

"Now take the kola nuts," Issaka Dia continued, "and place them over your closed eyes. Then, you must come close to me."

The kola nuts felt cool and soothing on Omar's eyelids.

"Keep them over your eyes," Issaka Dia commanded. Then he recited an incantation: "What is in my heart is in your heart. What is in my head is in your head. What is on my lips is on your lips. Hear me, Wambata. Give your power to my son, Omar. Give him the gifts of sight and sound. Allow him to follow my path." Issaka Dia pressed softly on the kola nuts and then blew air on Omar's face. "Keep your eyes closed, my son," he ordered as he lifted the kolas from Omar's eyes. He broke open the kolas and examined them. "Yes, my son, Wambata will give you the gifts of sight and sound. In time, she'll help you to see and hear the past, present and future. Praise to Wambata."

"Praise to Wambata," Omar repeated.

CHAPTER 13

Omar left Issaka Dia's hut that night blessed with the sight that, true to the ways of Songhay sorcerers, would develop over a long period of time—maybe decades. As he walked toward his brother's mud brick house, he wondered about his own blindness. How many years had he spent with his eyes closed to the central destiny of his life?

The tension in the family compound was palpable. Upon seeing Omar, the seething contempt of his youngest brothers plunged into him like dull knife. And what did Abdoulaye really think of his "European" brother? What did his other relatives—both blood kin and in-laws—think of their wayward kinsmen? Why had he come to this godforsaken place? Convinced that he should return to Paris as soon as possible, he again noticed the flickering light of a lantern in Fati's hut. Feeling out of sorts, Omar walked over and clapped three times to request entry.

"Who's there?" Fati asked in thin high pitched voiced.

"It's Omar," he said softly with no small amount of tingling in his stomach.

"Come in," she said. "Come in."

Omar bent down and pushed himself through the hut's opening, noticing for the first time how carefully Fati had arranged her home. She had covered the fine wadi sand floor with several straw mats. Colorful striped blankets had been stretched across the hut walls, giving the place the feel of a nomadic tent. On one side of the circular space, she had placed a blue armoire next to which was a matching sideboard, an open drawer of which revealed an array of cloth neatly folded and arranged into piles.

Wrapped in a light blue cloth, Fati sat on her bed, a four-poster crafted from local wood. Connected to the posts, netting had been folded up onto the mosquito net's cloth top. Fati smiled at him and his heart beat hard and fast against his chest. Go slow, he said to himself. She is a beautiful and sexy woman, but Omar was a married man with two children. He lived in another world. What could he possibly have in common with someone like Fati?

Fati patted her hand on the bed.

Omar remained standing, staring at her. He didn't know what to do.

"Come and sit," she said. "Come."

Slowly, Omar sat down next to her. "I was walking and saw your light," he said softly.

"I hoped you would," she said, her black eyes sparkling in the dim light. "Now you're here."

"I was talking with my father," he said, changing the conversation in an attempt to control his desire.

"He's teaching you powerful things?"

"Yes," Omar said.

"And you don't know if you want to learn such things."

How could she know about his psychological dilemmas? "That's the truth, Fati." He said. His chin sank toward his chest and looked at the straw mat on the floor. "I feel out of place."

"You're not out of place," Fati asserted. "I see what your father sees in you. You're the right one to take on the sorcerer's burden."

Omar shook his head. "My brother Abdoulaye should be the one. He's the one." Omar's left eye began to flutter.

Fati put her hand over Omar's eye. Her hand was warm and soft. His eye relaxed. "May I call you Omar?" she asked in her thin voice.

"Of course."

"Omar, you're the one to take up the sorcerer's burden. I sense it in you."

Her words filled Omar with desire—not reassurance. Not wanting to complicate his life, he tried to quash his need for her. But she simply sat there, wrapped seductively in her blue cloth, smiling sweetly in the flickering lantern light. At a very difficult moment, she believed in Omar. Sitting in the dim light Omar's life flashed before him. He saw a young boy ashamed of his family's heritage, a young boy running from pre-ordained destiny, a young boy who feared for his life. In the end, who was he? What were his responsibilities and obligations? What did people expect of him?

How would he go on? These questions shot through his mind like meteors streaking through the black sky, burning brightly, and then fizzling into nothing at all. In seconds, he had navigated himself back to Tillaberi, back to Fati, and back to the brutal present, a moment during which those existential questions lost their meaning. In that present, Omar found himself on Fati's bed in the silence of her hut. Slowly he turned toward Fati and stroked her arm. Her smile deepened. She lay back on the bed. Omar untied Fati's blue cloth. She spread the arms of her body, black and firm from the hard work, and opened her life to him. They effortlessly slipped into each other's being. A deep contentment soon washed over Omar, a happiness that he had never experienced. His world would never again be the same. Omar then knew that he would have to find a way to make space in his life for the sorcerer's burden—a way of healing the world.

CHAPTER 14

Omar easily slipped into the rhythm of compound life. The crows of roosters and the brays of donkeys would wake him every morning just before dawn when the cool air was free of dust. He'd slip out of his father's hut and walk over to Abdoulaye's two-room mudbrick house. There he'd join his brother next to a small fire the latter had built. As the fire crackled, they'd sit silently in the gray morning light, listening to the wind whirring and birds chirping. In time, Abdoulaye would put embers from the fire into a brazier, pour water into a metal pot, and heat it up for some morning coffee—Nestlé's instant, imported from Cote d'Ivoire and bought in a dry goods shop in Tillaberi. When the water was ready, Abdoulaye filled the two mugs, stirred in two teaspoons of coffee granules, and added one teaspoon of dry milk. He then dropped in one cube of sugar for Omar and added three cubes for himself. After several sips, he asked after Omar's sleep and the state of his health, the traditional Songhay greeting for early morning. Then, they'd plan their day.

Some days they'd walk all the way to Tillaberi to buy matches, sugar, dates, and tins of coffee and dry milk. On Sunday, market day in Tillaberi, they'd trek over the dunes to river's edge—Tillaberi's market space. There they'd buy onions, garlic, ginger, sorrel paste, and powdered baobab leaves. Sometimes they'd buy a bit of beef, mutton, or goat. Usually, they'd treat themselves to kebabs, or even an ice-cold Coca Cola. They'd also buy gifts for their female relatives—fragrant soaps, vials of oil-based perfumes, and bolts of colorful print cloth. They bought candy for the children. Omar had always loved the bonhomie of the market—a sea of smiling faces, the din of brotherly and sisterly recognition. And then upon their return, Omar loved to see the beaming faces of the family—so grateful for the modest gifts they had brought.

A steady stream of clients came to visit Abdoulaye during the mornings and afternoons. Omar's brother had won the reputation of being the most knowledgeable herbalist in all of western Niger. Like a good physician, Abdoulaye would examine his patients carefully and announce his diagnosis. He would then search through his apothecary of powdered plants to find a medicine that would successfully treat the ailment. He would then either mix an herbal paste for infected cuts, insect or animal bites or give the patient a combination of powders and explain carefully how to prepare them and how many times a day he or she should drink the concoction. Abdoulaye prescribed these latter kinds of medicines for people suffering from a wide variety of disorders—dysentery, intestinal parasites, malaria, and hepatitis. Abdoulaye introduced Omar to resins that, when burned on a brazier, produced aromatic smoke that stopped a life-threatening episode of asthma or calmed the frayed nerves of someone in the throes of a panic attack.

Abdoulaye taught Omar how to mix herbal concoctions. He taught him when to use the plant's root for one condition and its leaf for another. Omar admired Abdoulaye's deep knowledge of herbal medicine as well as his heartfelt concern for his patients.

"Abdoulaye," Omar told him on several occasions, "you are good to teach me this."

"Older brother," he replied, "it's my pleasure. Many years ago Issaka Dia said I should follow the path of plants. He taught so much about them. In truth, I'm still learning." He paused a moment. "Your destiny differs from mine, Omar. Like father, you will walk the path of power. To do that, you need to know about plants that heal the body and calm the soul. Issaka Dia will teach you about spirit plants, amulets, and magic. It's your path to use the special medicines. They've been passed down father to son from the time of our great ancestor, Si."

"Abdoulaye," Omar said, "you've walked your path with grace and humility."

Between spoonfuls of lunchtime *doonu*, a nutritious millet porridge that they mixed with milk and sugar, Abdoulaye and Omar would continue to discuss herbal medicine and magic rites. At least once a week, they'd eat rice and spicy sorrel sauce that had a few chucks of mutton or goat—hardly the delicious French cuisine Omar had grown used to in Paris! Lunch usually made Abdoulaye and Omar quite sleepy, which meant that they would routinely take siestas.

Omar enjoyed late afternoons best of all, for that was the time that they would take strolls in the bush. Sometimes, they'd mount two of the family horses—they had three Arabian stallions—and ride deep into the bush. They followed paths that Omar had taken as a child, especially the path that led them up to the flat surface between two buttes, *The Place Where Stories Are Told*. On occasion, they'd ride to isolated villages, where people lived completely off the land. One late afternoon, they visited Gusuberi, which consisted entirely of straw huts that surrounded a large pond. When they got to the village, a swarm of children, chirping with delight, surrounded them. A group of men and women clapped their hands and greeted them. They knew that Omar and Abdoulaye had come to help them. The brothers dismounted and two boys, dressed only in tattered and soiled shorts, led their horses to the pond.

"Welcome, Abdoulaye Dia," an old man said. He wore a frayed tunic that had once been white, but now looked more like the dull brown of the dusty countryside. "We welcome you to our village."

A naked young boy, his skin streaked with dried mud, ran up to them and presented a gourd.

"Fresh milk for the travelers," the old man said. He looked at Omar with curiosity. "Who is the man you ride with, Abdoulaye?"

"He's Omar Dia, my older brother and oldest son of Issaka Dia."

The old man extended his hand to Omar. "I'm Ibrahim Ali, chief of this village. Your visit honors us. I'm sorry we cannot offer you more than fresh milk. Times are hard here."

"I'm honored by your generosity," Omar said.

"Are you a healer like your brother?" Ibrahim asked.

"I know very little," Omar said, "but I'm learning."

"Your brother," Ibrahim said, "has been coming here for many years. He's brought us health and happiness. When our babies are sick, we summon him. When the spirits take one of our sons or daughters to a crazy place, we summon him. When worms wander through our intestines, we ask for him. Even when good fortune reduces our sickness and suffering, he comes to visit. He's our brother and protector."

"You honor me and my family," Abdoulaye said.

Ibrahim Ali led them to a small grass hut in which someone had spread two palm frond mats between which was a clay water jug. Two long red-dyed leather pillows with tasseled ends had been placed on the mats.

Abdoulaye took out a bag of cowry shells and several satchels that contained medicinal powders.

"We sit here," Abdoulaye said, "and people come to seek advice or treatment. This, Omar, is one of the sorcerer's burdens."

As soon as they sat down, a young woman holding a crying infant stooped to enter the hut. Thin as a millet stalk, she looked no more than 18 years old. She handed the screaming two-year-old to Abdoulaye. "He's burning up," the woman said. She wore an indigo wrap-around skirt made from homespun cloth, a top whose shape and color, a one-time blue, had suffered from hundreds of washings—immersion in the water hole, a good scrub with lye soap, a series of wet slaps on a boulder, the African version of agitation, and a good dry in the Sahelian sun.

Abdoulaye held a kicking and screaming child in front of him. "Look at him, Omar. What do you see?"

"It's his ear," Omar said. Just behind the ear, Omar saw a swelling from which ran a stream of yellow pus. "Looks like the cyst burst."

"It broke this morning," the woman said.

Abdoulaye took out a black cloth bag and fished out a gourd and a small pestle, which he gave to Omar. "We are going to mix a paste that will suck out the pus and dry the wound." He gave Omar a green powder, which he identified, and filled up one-half of the gourd. "Omar, add water and mix it into a paste."

Omar did as instructed, and soon a thick green paste formed in the gourd.

"Now, dab the paste over the wound."

After talking softly to the child, Omar pasted the medicine over the wound. It began to dry immediately. The child calmed down.

Abdoulaye took out a small piece of knotted cloth and opened it, revealing a reddish powder. He whispered its name to Omar and then asked the woman if she could get fresh milk.

"We get milk every morning from our cow."

"Good. Put three pinches of this powder in the child's warm milk, morning and night. This will give him strength."

The woman took back her child and, after praising their efforts, left the hut.

Soon thereafter, they heard three claps outside the hut, announcing another visit. A young man, built thickly like a wrestler, came in carrying a young boy. He greeted them. "My son vomits and has diarrhea. He can't sleep and he's got a fever." In the powerful grasp of his father, the boy's emaciated legs and arms dangled in the air. His eyes, blazing with fever, stared aimlessly into space.

"For how long?" Abdoulaye asked.

"Less than a week," the young father answered. "He's lost weight and is too weak to walk. I don't want him to die."

"Only for a week?" Abdoulaye asked, examining the sorry state of the boy.

"Maybe longer. I've been away. Maybe longer."

"Sickness is gripping this poor boy's stomach," Abdoulaye said to me. "Does he complain of pain in his stomach?"

"Yes," the father said, his face setting into a frown. "He grips his stomach and bends over. Then he gets diarrhea and when that's finished, he throws up."

"Don't worry," Abdoulaye said. "Your son's condition is common. We'll give him medicine that will kill the sickness and make him better."

"God is great," the father chanted. "God is great."

Abdoulaye tore up several pieces of cloth. When traveling on healing missions, he always brought several large strips of white or black cloth. When giving out medicine, he'd tear the cloth into smaller strips, pour herbal medicines onto them, roll them up, and tie them into a knot—a medicine bundle. He gave three such bundles to the man, who held them in his massive open palm.

Abdoulaye pointed to the first bundle. "This black bundle is for your son's vomiting. Take three pinches of it and put it in water or milk that has boiled. Give this to him first thing in the morning, at midday after lunch, and after dinner. In one day or two, the vomiting should stop and he'll start to eat again." He pointed to the two black bundles. "These," he told the father, "will kill the sickness in his stomach and intestines. Put three pinches of it in boiled water. It's better if you put it in milk that has boiled. You can even use the powdered milk that Ibrahim sells in his little shop. Give him this medicine in the morning for three days."

"And that will make him better?" the father asked.

"It should," Abdoulaye said. "If it doesn't, bring him to Tillaberi and let the clinic people look at him."

"I don't like the clinic," the father said. "I don't trust the clinic."

"You know, sometimes the clinic can be good," Abdoulaye said. "Sometimes our medicines can't kill some of the sicknesses that the children have." He took a deep breath. "In your son's case you probably won't have to go there."

"May God will it!"

Abdoulaye shifted his position on the mat. "Does your son drink water that comes from the pond?"

"Yes, we fetch some of our water from the pond. Some comes from the village well."

"His sickness comes from the pond water," Abdoulaye stated. "Make sure he drinks well water."

"Thank you," the man said. Taking his medicines and his son, he slipped through the hut's opening and returned to his home.

They again heard three claps that announced the arrival of another client. An old boney woman with loose skin that hung limply from her arms led a young boy, perhaps seven years old, into the hut. She wore a course indigo wrap-around made of homespun cloth. Her exposed gray hair was plaited. "My grandson has a fever." The boy wore a pair of dirty underwear. His stomach was distended and his legs and arms shook. Abdoulaye touched the boy's forehead.

"He's got a high fever," he told Omar. Abdoulaye turned to the woman. "Has he been able to sleep?"

"No," said the old woman. "He tosses and turns."

"Has he eaten?"

"No appetite."

"Has he thrown up?"

"Yes," she answered, "thick and yellow."

"My mother," Abdoulaye said to the woman, using a term that signified respect for an elderly woman, "your grandson has malaria. I'll give you some medicine. He should get better in a few days." He rummaged through his sack and produced several pieces of reddish tree bark. "Pound this bark into a powder. Heat up some water and after it has boiled put three pinches of the powder into a cup. Do this in the morning, midday and before he goes to sleep."

The woman nodded. "Can I give you something for your trouble?"

"If the child gets better," Abdoulaye said, "you can give me some eggs, a bowl of milk or some millet."

The woman led her grandson out of the hut.

"It's not too bad today," Abdoulaye explained. "Sometimes people have sicknesses that I can't treat. I tell them to go to the clinic in Tillaberi. They say they'll go, but they don't. They're afraid of dying at the clinic."

"Why is that, younger brother?"

"Because they wait too long to go. When they finally go, it's too late and they die." Abdoulaye stood up. "Today was a good day—not too many sick people."

Another series of three claps announced the arrival of yet another client. A thick-bodied man entered the hut. He wore threadbare black cotton trousers. His muscles, shaped from years of hard work in the fields, bulged under a frayed indigo tunic fashioned from homespun cloth. His large round face sat atop a neck that looked like a thick tree trunk. Despite these menacing features, a soft expression had set into his face. He sat down in front of them. "My greetings to you both."

"We ask after your well-being and the well-being of your family," Abdoulaye stated.

"We're fine," the man responded formulaically.

"You don't look like you need our attention," Omar interjected.

"I'm in good health, Praise to Allah." He frowned and looked down at the sand. "It's my wife who is not well."

"Can you tell us what's wrong?" Abdoulaye asked, sensing the sensitive nature of the exchange.

"Her bleeding has not stopped in months. She's very weak and very discouraged. We have two young children, and she doesn't have the strength to look after them. Our youngest is not yet weaned, but my wife's milk has dried up. I've got to buy powdered milk for my infant son."

Abdoulaye looked at the man who farmed three fields and who was known as a good provider for his family. "Do you have a horse or donkey?"

"I've got both," the man said.

"We're about to return to Tillaberi," Abdoulaye said. "Get your wife ready to travel. You'll come with us. We'll take her to the clinic. The nurses there know about women's illnesses. She'll be in good hands. You can stay with us until she is ready to come home."

The man extended his hand to us. "Thank you, brothers. Thank you. I'll go and get ready."

"We'll leave when you get back."

The man left the hut. Abdoulaye and Omar gathered their things.

"A man can never examine a young woman," Abdoulaye stated. "That makes my job difficult."

"What about older women?"

"Same thing, if the problem is a women's illness. All you can do is suggest a female healer, someone like our mother, may she rest in peace, or the female nurses at the clinic. Sometimes they wait until the women have lost so much blood that they never get better."

"It's a touchy business."

"That's the truth," Abdoulaye said, sighing, "but there are many rewards. When you heal someone, it's a wonderful thing."

CHAPTER 15

When Abdoulaye and Omar returned to Tillaberi that afternoon, they showed their farmer friend to his guest quarters. Then they bathed. In the late afternoon, Abdoulaye and Omar lounged on long leather pillows that they had placed under a thatched canopy, the shady space where musicians positioned themselves during spirit possession ceremonies. As they chewed on kola nut, their father's co-wife, Maymouna, approached.

"Hello, my sons," she said. "How goes the afternoon?"

"It goes well, my mother," Omar replied. "We're just back from work in the bush. We went to Gusuberi to care for the people."

"Gusuberi," she repeated, unimpressed by their healing efforts. "I've got important news for you." Maymouna informed them that Moussa and Seydou, their younger brothers, had returned from an extensive and successful musical tour of the villages in the region. Their musical virtuosity had apparently attracted large audiences. "And," she added, "the spirits were quite pleased with the music. People gave them generous gifts. They brought back ten sacks of millet, sorghum and rice, several goats, one sheep, and much cash."

"We're pleased to have our brothers at home," Abdoulaye said. "Are they in good health and good spirits?"

"They are," Maymouna replied. "They want to hold a spirit possession ceremony here. You see, they want everything to be in harmony when Issaka Dia makes his last journey."

"What does Issaka Dia say to this idea?" Omar asked.

"He agrees."

"When do they want to do the ceremony?" Abdoulaye asked

"In two days, my sons," she recited, "on Thursday, the day of the spirits."

"We'll look forward to it, my mother," Omar said to his father's second wife. "When was the last time you saw a spirit possession ceremony, Omar?" she asked.

"A long time ago, my mother."

"Well, I suppose Abdoulaye can explain things to you," she said, hunching her bony shoulders. She turned around and walked back to her mudbrick hut.

Omar turned to Abdoulaye. "She's always been like that, hasn't she?"

Abdoulaye smiled. "Always, older brother. She's a hot ember."

"Well put, Abdoulaye."

"It's best not to touch a hot ember, don't you agree?"

"Completely, younger brother. Completely."

During the next two days, Omar didn't encounter his younger brothers, Moussa and Seydou, who preferred to remain in Tillaberi proper rather than sleep in the distant family compound. In their absence, Omar's rather peaceful routine continued. In the mornings, he talked with Abdoulaye until lunchtime when they shared a bowl of millet porridge. In the afternoons, Omar might take a siesta or talk with Issaka Dia, who continued his short course on family history, medicinal plants, and the treacheries of the "path of power." In the late afternoon, Abdoulaye and Omar walked into the bush. After sharing a dinner with Abdoulaye and his young sons, Omar received a few night visitors. Later still, Issaka Dia might teach Omar additional incantations.

On the eve of the spirit possession ceremony, Omar sat next to his dying father who by then was too weak to sit up by himself.

"Father," he asked, "is it good to have a spirit possession ceremony now?"

"It's always good to give thanks to the spirits, my son. They know my body is weak. They'll soon search for a new body."

"I thought sorcerers like you had no spirits," Omar stated.

"No, no, my son. I have four and when I die they'll be looking for new bodies. Maybe they'll choose you."

"I hope not," Omar admitted.

Issaka Dia laughed a bit and then coughed. "The spirits are a burden. No one wants them in their life. And yet, once they choose us, we're obligated to them. Once we have them, they give us power."

"Power," Omar asserted, "has a front side and a back side."

Issaka Dia smiled. "You understand. You'll make a good sohanci."

After leaving Issaka Dia, that evening, Omar slipped into Fati's hut. They lost themselves in their growing passion.

CHAPTER 16

That Thursday morning passed like most days in Issaka Dia's compound. Just as the sun peeked over the rim of the eastern sky, Abdoulaye and Omar built a small fire. They then filled a large teapot with water and put it atop the fire. After the water hissed, boiled vigorously, and then bubbled out from the teapot's lid, they poured it over mounds of Nescafé, powdered milk, and sugar that they had shaped in the bottom of their plastic mugs. Coffee mugs in hand, they repaired to long red leather pillows that had been placed on two straw mats situated at the end of Abdoulaye's house. Reclining on their pillows, they looked out toward the bush and sipped their coffee, saying little to one another. In short order, Abdoulaye's daughter, thin as a blade of desert grass and perhaps ten years old, brought them a pot of rice and sauce—the previous evening's dinner that had been reheated. Another young girl, shorter and thinner than Abdoulaye's daughter, walked toward them, a tin platter balanced upon her head.

"Hayni masa ne ah," she cried.

Omar turned to his brother. "Care for some fried millet cakes, Abdoulaye?"

"My favorite food for breakfast."

Omar bought eight cakes and they feasted on this delicious fare.

In the afternoon streams of spirit possession, spectators flowed into the family compound. Unlike the family members who, following the traditions of Omar's sohanci ancestors, wore black every day, the spectators transformed the rather drab space into a sea of bright colors—red and green print shawls adorned with Technicolor peacocks, bright baby blue head scarves, tops with blue, black, and white backgrounds bursting with yellow, orange, purple, and black geometric motifs. Wearing a purple *fez*, a man arrived sporting a long shirt and matching trousers fashioned from damask cloth dyed gold. Dressed in soiled shorts, three sizes too big, and torn dirty white tee shirts, a group of young boys entered the compound balancing small roughly hewn wooden tables on their heads. From these tables, they would sell chewing gum, hard candy, kola nuts, and individual cigarettes.

As the crowd thickened, Seydou and Moussa, both sporting large gold-plated aviator sunglasses, sauntered into the compound. The spectators showered them with praise. Knowing how to work a crowd, they mingled with their fans, slowly making their way to the hangar—the spirit canopy—under which they would play spirit music.

A large woman dressed in a matching black wrap-around skirt and top made of homespun cloth put her hand on Seydou's arm. Looking into his round high cheek-boned face, the woman complemented Omar's younger brother.

"Your violin music, Seydou, is sent from heaven," she announced. "It's a blessing that brings us good fortune."

Revealing a mouth of missing teeth, Seydou smiled, but said nothing. He was dressed for playing the music of the spirits—a sleeveless black shirt and a pair of black balloon trousers. Seydou, who carried his one-string violin in a black sack slug over his shoulder, made his way to a small stool set behind a row of three gourds—the spirit possession percussion instruments. These had been set over resonating holes that had been dug in the sand. As Moussa and two other drummers, whom Omar did not know, situated themselves behind their drums, Seydou, the violin master, carefully removed from his sack, his one-stringed instrument, the godji. He also removed a bow the string of which was made from horsetail. The musicians loosened up. Drummers hit their gourds with bamboo drumsticks, which, shaped like a human hand with a palm, a wrist and a set of fingers, created a series of clacks and snare rolls. Meanwhile, Seydou tuned his instrument by tightening the horsehair attached to the fret. He connected the single string to a bridge that stretched over a chamber—a small gourd, covered with lizard skin pulled taut over its surface.

From just inside the spirit hut, Omar watched the crowd expand. Men, women, and children bought goods from the "table chiefs," who, stationed on the periphery of the compound, always profited from the festive atmosphere of a spirit possession ceremony. Dancers urged the musicians to play. And so they did. Beyond the rhythmic clacks and rolls of the drums, Omar heard the "cries" of Seydou's violin. Even if Omar's younger brother was full of himself, his music was nothing short of sweet. The woman had been right. He had a gift and his music had blessed the village.

When Omar saw a group of old women saunter on the dance ground, a sandy expanse in front of the spirit canopy, he left the spirit house and found a place behind the musicians. He wanted a good view of the dancers. At first, they danced slowly in a counterclockwise circle. Holding black cotton scarves between their hands, they glided along the sand. Moussa began to chant a spirit song, and the women nodded their aged heads. One dancer spat out some chewing tobacco that had been wedged under her lip. The pace quickened and the women stopped gliding and stood in a row. They faced the musicians. Pointing his drumstick toward the women, Moussa sang praises to the spirits. The pace quickened and one of the dancers, a tall fat woman, stepped toward the musicians, stomping her feet flat on the sand and swaying her wrinkled arms. The loose flesh of her face flapped to the rhythm, her smile evoking the pleasures of dance. The other dancers followed suit. Sweat beaded on their noses and dropped onto the sand. Men and women shot onto the dance grounds to place money on the dancers' foreheads. What a gift it was to see these women! What a pleasure it was to see the audience appreciate so deeply their rhythmic grace!

And then Abdoulaye, resplendent in flowing black robes and a black turban, emerged from his house and walked toward the dance grounds. Tall, thick, and imposing, people made way for him. Seeing him, the musicians picked the tempo, and Abdoulaye nodded as he walked in front of them. He nodded again and the musicians played music associated with the spirits of the earth, also known as the black spirits. No more dancing for the pleasure of it. No more dashes of gratitude. What had been something akin to a party had been transformed into a serious ceremony.

A group of men and women who had been sitting passively to one side of the dance grounds pushed themselves up and circled counterclockwise to the slow melodious tempo. The audience pressed closer to the dance grounds. A tall thin man also dressed in black put himself in the middle of the circle of movement. Wagging his finger at the dancers, the praise singer chanted spirit poems. The tempo quickened and the dancers faced the musicians. One by one they glided forward, swaying their arms like flying birds, moving their heads from side to side as they rhythmically stomped their feet on sand. An obese woman whose flesh jiggled as she moved to the beat, danced up to the drummers and stopped. The musicians played a different tune, and she began to dance with greater intensity, arms flailing, feet kicking up sand, head moving back and forth. Tearing off her top, the woman groaned. She then bent over and dropped down on her hands and knees, her heavy breasts hanging toward the ground. Taking handfuls of sand, she showered it over her head and torso and then rubbed the sand into her body. Sand on glistening skin gave her black flesh a reddish hue. A woman rushed to the dancer and slipped a black and white striped tunic over her head. The medium, no longer a woman, sang in a primordial language only a few people, including Abdoulaye and the praise singer, understood. The black spirits soon took other mediums, dousing themselves with sand as they sang spirit songs. One woman, taken by the spirit known as the snake, slithered on the sand, flicking her tongue like a reptile.

The snake reared his head like a cobra and spoke to the praise singer. "There is change in the wind," the spirit proclaimed. "Your great sohanci will soon die and you must prepare for what follows. If you give us a black goat today, you'll have good times in Tillaberi. You'll have food and water and health. If we do not taste goat blood, our anger will be felt." The snake dug its head into the soft ground and emerged with a face covered with dirt. "Do you understand?"

"We do," said the praise singer, who turned to find Abdoulaye behind him. After explaining the request to Abdoulaye, Omar's younger brother waved his hand. Moments later, a boy, perhaps ten years old, pulled a very reluctant black goat onto the dance grounds. Someone gave Abdoulaye a large butcher knife. When the black goat had been secured, Abdoulaye slit its throat. Blood spurted out and soaked into the sand. The black spirits rushed to the dying animal to drink the gushing blood. Smearing their faces with it, they proclaimed their satisfaction with the sacrifice.

By now, the deepening light of late afternoon signaled the approach of nightfall. One by one, women took the spirits behind the spirit hut where they would separate spirit and body, returning the mediums to the everyday world. Little by little the spectators trickled away, slowly returning the compound to its normal state.

Still under the spirit canopy, Moussa and Seydou carefully stored their instruments. As they conversed with their mother, Omar approached them.

"Your music was sweet today, my brothers," he said.

"You can't hear this kind of music in Paris, can you?" Moussa asked.

"I'm afraid not."

"I bet you can't see the spirits in Paris either, can you?" Seydou stated.

"I've never seen them there," Omar admitted.

"How can you understand the spirits, Omar?" Maymouna asked, a sneer etched on her face, "You're an infidel who is lost to us."

CHAPTER 17

Around sunset, Omar placed a palm frond mat at the back of the spirit house and sat down to look at the darkening sky. Fluffy soft pink clouds swirled like so many feathers across the western horizon, but shafts of dark orange and red light cut through the swirl, bringing a touch of celestial violence to the peaceful end of daylight. Although Omar tried to ignore Maymouna's biting comments, they stayed with him. Who was he kidding? He had been away for so many years and had adopted the French way of life. Could he take on the sorcerer's burden in a matter of weeks? Did he not deserve the resentment of his mother's co-wife and his younger brothers? And how could Abdoulaye not harbor the same resentment? For many years, Abdoulaye had tended to the family, sitting at Issaka Dia's feet, watching him, learning from him. Abdoulaye had the cool temperament that a sorcerer needed. How could Abdoulaye be so kind to his interloping older brother? And what of Fati, Omar's new lover? The more time Omar spent at "home," the less he understood it.

Lost in his thoughts, a faint breeze of presence swept over him. When he sat down next to Omar, Abdoulaye's majestic black robes swooshed. He touched Omar's shoulder, which magically released from his body the pressing weight of malaise. That moment sealed a deep bond between Omar and Abdoulaye.

"What's wrong Omar? You look sad," Abdoulaye said.

"I'm sad today. I feel like I don't belong here."

Abdoulaye spat some tobacco on the ground. "How can you not belong?"

Omar hunched my shoulders. "There are many here who wish me ill."

"And many who want you to stay, including our father. Issaka Dia knows your heart, Omar. So do I. Our father's second wife and our younger brothers will never know you." Abdoulaye cleared his throat. "At first I wasn't sure about you, Omar. Now I know that you'll be able to take up the sorcerer's burden."

Feeling the weight of the sorcerer's burden that had once again been placed on his shoulders, Omar nodded—with resignation.

Abdoulaye appreciated Omar's gesture. "The sohanci's path is a difficult one. I can answer some of your questions, but in end you'll have to find your own way. This work is no game and is nothing to be happy about. You may not believe me, Omar, but I don't envy you."

They sat there in silence for some time as deep red and purple bands, losing their luster at the end of daylight, flowed into the inky blackness of night.

––––––

One day later, after darkness settled in, Abdoulaye lit a small kerosene lantern and placed it next to Omar on a mat that had been unrolled next to his house. Just then, Abdoulaye's daughter brought them dinner—a big calabash of millet paste smothered in okra sauce. They said their blessings and ate the food in silence. Slowly and methodically they consumed the food—just being with one another.

Midway through the meal, they heard the clapping of hands. A young boy, perhaps 12 years old and dressed in a tattered sleeveless tee shirt and a faded pair of black drawstring trousers, came forward. He greeted them respectfully.

"To what do we owe this visit, Mounkaila?" Abdoulaye asked.

"My fathers," the boy said, "I have to tell you what I saw this afternoon in the bush."

"What did you see, young man?" Omar asked.

"Your brothers, Seydou and Moussa."

"Where exactly were they and what were they doing?" Abdoulaye asked.

"They were at a fork in the road," the boy reported. "Moussa held a black chicken by the neck and Seydou twisted its neck until it died."

"At the fork in the road?" Abdoulaye asked

"Yes."

"Thank you, Mounkaila," Abdoulaye said. He gave the boy a few coins and dismissed him. After the boy had left, Abdoulaye spoke softly. "That's death magic and I fear they've sent it to you, perhaps to both of us."

"What do we do?" Omar asked Abdoulaye.

"I'm not sure. We need to talk with Father. He'll tell us what needs to be done."

"Maybe we should go and see father in the black of night."

"We'll do that, Omar. I'll put some charcoal in the brazier and prepare us some tea. It's going to be a long night and we'll need to be very alert."

Abdoulaye turned toward his house. "Hey, Sidi, hey," he called out to one of his sons, "bring us some charcoal and the brazier." Within a few moments, a completely naked boy, perhaps eight years old, appeared with a bucket of charcoal and brazier fashioned from metal wire.

"Sidi," Abdoulaye said next. "We'll need the box of tea, the teapot and three glasses, the small ones made of glass."

"Yes, Father," the boy said as he disappeared into the darkness.

Abdoulaye lit the charcoal, which burned brightly. Sidi quickly fetched the necessary elements for brewing tea.

When the coals glowed red, Abdoulaye filled the teapot with water and placed the small enamel pot on the small hill of glowing embers. They waited silently as the water began to boil. Abdoulaye emptied three measures—a measure being one small glass of tea—into the boiling water. He then added ten cubes of sugar for the first batch.

"We'll go to see Father after our third glass?" Omar asked.

"By that time it will be the black of night."

They both stoked the embers and enjoyed the tea. Abdoulaye talked about how much had changed in Niger—and how much had not. Omar talked to him about his life in France.

"Your life in France sounds good, Omar. It sounds like you have a wonderful wife and good kids."

"They are wonderful. It's good to be their father."

"I wish you could bring them here, but it's too dangerous, isn't it?"

"They've wanted to come for a long time—especially Chantal. I made excuses, but never told them how they tried to kill me."

"Probably a good way to deal with it, Omar."

"Maybe. But I'm tired of it all—the drama, the danger. Will it ever stop?"

"You should still bring them, Omar. They're family. Things will soon change here. I can sense it."

Omar shook his head. "I don't know what to do."

Abdoulaye finished his third glass of tea. "I can't tell you what to do, but I can recite my favorite proverb."

"Which is?"

"An old man's talk may appear to be tied in knots, but in the end it straightens itself."

Omar smiled. "That's a good one."

In the black of night, Abdoulaye and Omar made their way to the entrance of Issaka Dia's hut. They clapped three times to signal their presence.

"Who comes to disturb a sick old man in the black of night?" Issaka Dia asked.

"It's Omar, your oldest son and Abdoulaye, my true brother."

"God be praised," Issaka Dia said in his raspy voice. "Come in, my sons. Come in."

They bent down and slipped into the hut. In the darkness, Abdoulaye found a lantern and lit it. Resting in the shadows, Issaka Dia lay on his side propped up on his elbow.

A silence settled in between them, creating a distinct heaviness in the hut. "What evil brings you to me in the black of night?" Issaka Dia, prescient as always, asked.

"Death magic has been sent to us, Father," Omar said.

"Who sent this death magic?" he asked.

"Our younger brothers, Seydou and Moussa," Abdoulaye stated.

Issaka Dia coughed hard and struggled to lean over the edge of the bed and spit. "Nothing has changed in this family," he said harshly. "This is a bad business, especially when brothers want to kill their kinsmen. A very bad business." Issaka Dia shifted his position, pushing his torso higher against his bed pillows. "We've often had this bad business between brothers. Your brothers are jealous and have filth in their hearts. They must be taught a lesson." He sighed. "We've got to put an end to this strife."

In great detail, Issaka Dia explained how Abdoulaye and Omar could repel the death magic and return it back to those—Moussa and Seyni—who had sent it. "You must do it," Issaka Dia stated, "so they will never try anything like this again, so that they will respect and fear both of you."

The old man told them where to find a cloth bag that contained a bundle of tree roots that had been whittled into stakes. They quickly found the wooden stakes and showed them to their father. "This very night and before dawn," Issaka Dia instructed, "find one of our red chickens and slit its throat. Let the blood flow over the stakes. While the blood is flowing say this: 'Whatever is in my heart is in your heart; whatever is in my mind is in your mind; whatever I want, you want.' Then visualize their faces and think this: 'I want you to suffer for what you did. Then after you have suffered, I want you to fear and respect me forever more'." The old man coughed again. He then told them to bury the stakes at the entrance to the compound, at the entrances of all the compound houses. He also told them to bury the stakes under the spirit canopy and at the north, south, east, and west points of the compound. "My sons," he said in a barely audible voice, "you've got work to do. Let an old man rest. Very soon, you'll see what happens."

Before dawn, all of the stakes had been buried in the appropriate places. At first light, Omar went to Fati's hut to explain what had happened. He laid down to rest. Before he fell asleep, he asked her to wake him before midmorning.

For three days, nothing happened. Thankfully, no one died in the compound. What's more, Omar had not received any news of Moussa and Seydou. The absence of results brought back much of Omar's initial skepticism about the efficacy of magic. Could a set of words and the sacrifice of a particular animal create or counteract death? The waiting game made life in the compound intolerable. When Omar saw his mother's co-wife, he shuddered. Here was a woman, whom he disliked intently, who most likely wanted him dead. She was probably wondering why Omar was still alive? Omar had never been a patient person. When faced with a task, he could not rest easily until he had successfully completed it. That's probably why he had done so well at the local school and the high school. For every course, he made an effort to complete all of his assignments on time. That's how he had made his way through the university and how he had methodically conducted the research for his books. That's why his lectures were usually well received. In the academic world, completing a task provided not only a sense of pride but also a feeling of control. In the magical universe, though, control seemed only a fleeting possibility, if a possibility at all.

Toward the end of the afternoon of the third day, Bari, a childhood friend of Abdoulaye, came to visit the compound. He was tall and lanky with an angular face. His eyes were as small and sharp as black pinheads. He wore a loose-fitting white shirt over a pair of brown trousers.

He joined Abdoulaye and Omar under the spirit canopy. After his long journey from town, Omar offered him water and dates. Bari took a deep swig of water from the plastic cup Omar had filled for him.

"I have news of Moussa and Seydou," he said.

That caught their attention. Abdoulaye pushed himself to a seated position on his pillow. Omar sat up straight on his stool. "Tell us," Omar commanded with no small degree of impatience.

"They arrested Moussa today. They say he stole from a shopkeeper in the market. Earlier today he was taken to a jail in Niamey. He'll be tried there. People say they'll send him to prison for three to five years."

"And Seydou?" Abdoulaye asked.

"During the night his foot swelled. It's so swollen, he can hardly walk."

Abdoulaye and Omar looked at one another. Omar noticed a very slight smile on Abdoulaye's face. Omar tried to remain solemn. "We hope that Moussa will not suffer too much in jail," Omar said, "and we wish Seydou a speedy recovery."

"May God will it!" said Bari.

"May God will it," Abdoulaye chimed in.

Omar stood up and shook Bari's hand. "Thank you for coming, Bari. We're very grateful."

"We, too, are grateful for your work in the village. You have our thanks and our good wishes for your work."

At dinner, Abdoulaye and Omar talked of the weather, the health difficulties of the poor people in the bush, and the progress Abdoulaye's son had made in school. It would have been unthinkable for them to gloat over the "success" of "work." Sohancis, Issaka Dia had often said during their childhood, are modest about their abilities and never boast of successes. If sorcerers do boast about their magical capacities, they should be ignored. And if they step over the boundary of good taste, they must be taught a lesson. Even so, their silence on the matter betrayed a deep satisfaction, which, through idle conversation and subtle smiles, they shared.

After dinner, they visited Issaka Dia. He seemed to be growing weaker and weaker. He coughed incessantly and could hardly prop himself on one elbow. More often than not, he seemed to be unaware of his surroundings—as if he had already traveled part of the way to the next world. When they entered the spirit house, Issaka Dia lay on his back and talked to invisible presences. His breathing had become labored and wheezy. After a few moments, the presence of his older sons broke his connection to the invisible world.

He smiled at them. "Ah my sons, what brings you to me?"

Omar explained to Issaka Dia what had transpired. His face remained expressionless. "The work of the sohanci," he said, "is no game."

"That's the truth, Father," Omar said.

"You speak the truth, Father," Abdoulaye said.

A coughing spasm rocked Issaka Dia's body. With great difficulty, he leaned over the edge of the bed and spat on the floor. He hauled his body back over the bed and fell back. His chest heaved with the effort of breathing. "My time is near, my sons. Stay close to me. Make sure to visit several times a day. Before I leave this earth, I must tell you some things."

They nodded their agreement.

"Now, leave me to sleep, my sons," he said as he closed his eyes and drifted off.

After such an emotionally draining day, Omar looked forward to being with Fati. They now had a wonderful routine. He'd slip into her house in the "black of night" and they'd make love. Then they would talk—sometimes for hours. On this night, Omar surprised the young widow with what seemed insatiable desire. Spent, they lay naked on Fati's bed, looking up at the rafters—sticks sealed with daub attached to log joists.

Fati had known about the death magic and Omar's response. He filled in more details and told her of Moussa's arrest and Seydou's swollen foot.

"The sohanci's work," she said, almost formulaically, "is no game."

"No it's not," he affirmed.

"What do you really think about the sohanci's work?" she asked.

He explained to Fati his previous doubts about sorcery. "Now," he admitted, looking directly at Fati's beautiful black face, "I feel proud to be Issaka Dia's son." Omar sat up on bed. With his back to her, he confessed his newly discovered sense of power. "I feel like a warrior," he said, feeling a bit embarrassed. "I confronted enemies who wanted to kill me. I repelled them and emerged the victor. I'm ashamed to admit it, but I feel powerful right now."

Fati placed her hands over Omar's eyes. "I don't think your eye will flutter anymore, Omar, but be careful," she warned. "Don't let this feeling overtake your good sense. Don't let this success make you forget your obligations."

"What do you mean, Fati?"

"Don't you ever think about your wife and your children?"

The question hit Omar like a punch to the stomach. No matter how hard he tried, he hadn't been able to stop thinking about Chantal and the kids. In truth, he had no idea how to reconcile what had become a life in two worlds. Suddenly, Omar's body took on the weight of guilt. His head fell limply to his chest. He breathed deeply and tried to think of how to respond to Fati's question. "I think about them all the time," he admitted.

"Of course you do. They're family. They know the world of France, but when will they learn about life here?" she asked.

Not knowing how to respond, Omar said nothing.

Fati put her hand on Omar's back. "Let things play out here. When the time is right, you'll find your way, and that way will bring you great satisfaction. Of this, I am certain."

The next morning seated at the morning fire, Abdoulaye and Omar shared a breakfast of coffee and fried millet pancakes. One of Abdoulaye's sons announced that their younger brother, Seydou, had come to visit his mother. In short order, Seydou and Maymouna emerged from the latter's house. Seydou, whose swollen foot had been wrapped in white cloth, walked with a crutch. Maymouna walked slowly toward them, her face set in a frown.

"Good day to you, our father's wife," Omar said. "How was your sleep, younger brother?"

"We praise God and the wisdom of our sohanci ancestors," Maymouna responded.

"We give our thanks," Seydou said.

Abdoulaye turned toward his house. "Hey, hey boy. Bring us two stools."

Seconds thereafter, Seyni, Abdoulaye's oldest son, brought two stools. Maymouna and Seydou sat down, the latter extending his swollen foot away from the fire.

Abdoulaye offered them coffee and food.

"Thank you," Maymouna said. "We've already had breakfast."

Silence lowered a wall between them. Maymouna fidgeted on her stool. Seydou stared at the ground. Abdoulaye and Omar gazed at them. Omar decided the break the silence.

"What's wrong with your foot, younger brother?" he asked.

Before he could answer, Seydou's mother chimed in: "He was fine, but two nights ago, he went to sleep and he woke up with the swollen foot." She stared at Omar. "You know how it works, don't you?"

"How unfortunate for you, Seydou," Omar said. "Do you mind if Abdoulaye and I look at it?"

Without comment Seydou unwrapped the cloth bandage, revealing a grotesquely swollen foot and ankle, covered with lesions oozing pus—not a pretty sight.

"That looks pretty serious," Omar said. "What do you think, Abdoulaye?"

Abdoulaye examined it. "It's serious, but we might have something to treat it." He turned to Omar. "What do you think?"

"Yes," Omar said solemnly. He looked at Seydou and Maymouna. "There are powders that will dry up the pus and heal the lesions. We have another powder that will reduce the swelling. It might take several days, but the swelling should go down." Omar turned to Abdoulaye. "What do you think?"

"Let me go and get the medicines."

Seydou rewrapped the bandage.

In Abdoulaye's absence, Omar asked after Moussa—a rather nasty and manipulative inquiry, of which, in retrospect, he was not proud.

Maymouna's eyes got misty. A single tear dropped from her left eye. "Did you hear that they took him away yesterday?"

Omar falsely professed his ignorance.

"They said he's in a Niamey jail. There's going to be a trial. They said he could go to jail for 20 years," she said, clasping her hands.

"Wife of my father," Omar said looking at the spiteful woman, "we hope that all goes well with the trial. I know people in Niamey. We'll get him a lawyer. Perhaps they'll set him free. If not, then maybe he'll get a short sentence. We'll do everything we can. Blood, after all, is obligation."

"True," Maymouna admitted, "and we need to take care of one another. You have our thanks, gratitude, and respect, Omar Dia."

"There's no need to say more, wife of my father. We're family and we are in this life together."

"Well said," Seydou stated.

Just then Abdoulaye returned with two satchels of medicine. He asked Seydou to remove the bandage, revealing once again the swollen mass of his ankle and foot. Abdoulaye took a black powder and covered the pus-filled lesions. "Younger brother," he stated, "this powder will draw out the pus and dry the soars. Wash your foot at sunset and apply more powder. At dawn tomorrow, wash it and apply more powder. By tomorrow, the sores should begin to heal."

"What about the swelling?" the violinist asked.

Abdoulaye produced another satchel with green powder. "Take three pinches of this green powder and put it in your coffee or milk in the morning and after dinner. Continue the three pinches morning and night for one week. You should see the swelling begin to go down after a few days."

Seydou looked at both of us. "I give thanks to you both."

Abdoulaye echoed Omar's sentiments. "No need for thanks, younger brother. We are brothers. May God provide you a speedy recovery."

"Amin," said Maymouna.

"We give thanks to God," Seydou said, "and to the traditions of our family."

"Well said, younger brother," Omar said, smiling inwardly.

Mother and son got up slowly and made their way to Maymouna's house. Abdoulaye and Omar savored a brief moment of satisfaction.

"What would you say is the state of our family, now?" Omar asked Abdoulaye.

"There are always problems, but things are much better now."

"They are, Abdoulaye," he said patting him on the shoulder. "But we have many challenges ahead."

Abdoulaye nodded. "The sorcerer's path is filled with challenges."

CHAPTER 18

An uncommon peace settled over the once-turbulent compound. Following the death magic crisis, family tension dissipated slowly, but not completely into the dry desert air. By now, the weather had also cooled off a bit. The midafternoon sun still produced hot air, but cool night winds brought a dry chill to the compound—good sleeping weather. Abdoulaye and Omar removed the objects they had buried to protect them from death magic. Moussa received a reduced sentence for theft and would serve two years in a Niamey jail. Prior to his trial, Omar contacted a high school friend who had studied law in France. His friend agreed to take on Moussa's case *pro bono*. Although the prosecution had clearly established Moussa's guilt, Omar's friend had managed to shave years off the sentence. Moussa sent word of his deep gratitude. For his part, Seydou took his medicines, and in short order, the skin lesions had healed and his foot had returned to its normal state. Several nights a week, the once spiteful Maymouna sent food over to Abdoulaye and Omar. It was no secret that Jitu, Abdoulaye's loyal wife, was a very good cook, but Maymouna's cooking knew no bounds. Omar and Abdoulaye savored her sumptuous sauces, all of which had been flavored with butter oil.

By the time the new moon had shone itself, Omar had gained a few pounds, mostly in a slightly expanded belly. Abdoulaye's weight gain surpassed that of Omar. The abundance of good food seemed to have extended considerably his already ample midsection. For poor millet farmers living in a place like Tillaberi, corpulence had always been a sign of prosperity, well-being, and good health.

On a more somber note, the new moon also signaled Issaka Dia's impending death, which, according to him, would take place seven days after the beginning of the new month. Although Omar had little contact with his father over the years, he had continually felt his presence in this world. No matter the circumstance, no matter how much time and space had separated them, he could depend on Issaka Dia to point him in the right direction, or, if necessary, to set the broken bones of his existence. The prospect of Issaka Dia's death made Omar tremble. How would the world ever be the same? Now more than ever, Omar needed his father's advice. How could he reconcile his life in two worlds? Thinking these thoughts reminded Omar of one of his father's favorite proverbs: "One foot cannot walk two paths." How many feet would Omar need to walk the various paths that wound their way through two worlds? He had no idea of where to go, let alone how to conduct himself on the journey. What's more, he knew that Issaka Dia would not resolve his son's dilemmas. Like any wise sohanci, he would say that Omar had to struggle. He would say that with the grace of the ancestors, Omar would find his way in the world.

To push these gloomy thoughts into the background of his consciousness, he and Abdoulaye resumed their afternoon forays into the bush. They walked along sinuous trails, observing the texture of the land, the curve of wadis that carved their way through the deep brown of clay and rock. The light of late afternoon shimmered on the high cirrus clouds so typical of the cool dry season in Tillaberi. For some reason, this desiccated landscape, which reminded Omar of a surrealist dreamscape painting, brought him peace.

Three days after the new moon, Abdoulaye and Omar decided to ride their horses to *The Place Where Stories Are Told*. They headed out into the bush and gradually made their way up toward the two-peaked butte that overlooked the Niger River valley. Afternoon light had deepened the blue of a cloudless sky. A cool wind blew in from the east. They tethered their horses and sat on the smooth boulder that gave them a glorious late afternoon view of the Niger. Taking in the scene, they sat in silence for a long time. In search of carrion, a vulture circled high in the sky.

Breaking the silence, Omar injudiciously mentioned to Abdoulaye the impending death of their father.

"Omar, even if it is on our minds, we should not talk of these things," Abdoulaye cautioned. "Our father still lives."

Omar nodded.

"It's going to be difficult for you and for me," Abdoulaye observed.

They lapsed into silence, sharing their despair, their fears, as well as their uncertainty about the future.

"Yes," Omar said after minutes of quiet contemplation. "I need to work things out...after."

"Your path will open, Omar. Be patient. You'll find your way."

Now a mass of molten red, the sun shimmered low in the western sky, casting a pink glow on the clouds that had formed on the eastern horizon. They mounted their horses and, once they had descended the butte, came upon flat trails. Sensing food and the comfort of home, their horses galloped all the way back to the compound.

Nothing feels better than a cool rinse after the sweaty heat of horseback riding on a dusty afternoon in Niger. Dressed only in a pitifully thin white cotton towel and a pair of tire-tread flip-flops, Omar carried a bucket of cold water, a plastic mug, and a bar of Palmolive soap to the washing enclosure. A three-foot millet stalk fence protected him from the curious gazes of family members, but he didn't care. He needed to rid himself of grime and sweat. Omar sat down on the stool and poured a cup of deliciously cool water over his head, which immediately brought him a small measure of relief. Outside the enclosure, he heard three claps. Then he heard the thin voice of a young boy.

"Father, they say that in the black of night you must go to the old man's hut."

"Thank you, my son."

Omar told no one of his assignation with Issaka Dia, who clearly wanted no one else to know. The boy might inform Abdoulaye. But his younger brother was astute enough to maintain his distance. Later, he shared a meal—millet and peanut sauce—with Abdoulaye. Sitting on leather pillows arrayed on a straw mat, they talked about the possibility of a meningitis epidemic and what they could do to help prevent the spread of the dreaded disease.

"Just getting people to cover their noses when they sneeze and their mouths when they cough would help," Abdoulaye suggested. "We could take a tour of the bush and give people advice."

"Sounds like a good idea," Omar affirmed. "And if a child gets sick, what can we do?"

"Our medicines don't work so well with the stiff neck sickness," Abdoulaye admitted. "We'd have to take them to the clinic to get a shot and give everyone else some pills to take."

"Let's hope the stiff neck sickness isn't too bad this year."

"It's always sad to see a child die."

They talked about food shortages in the region and how malnutrition had made people less resistant to infection and disease. Time flew by and Abdoulaye soon stood up to go to bed. "May we both pass the night in peace, Omar."

"May it come to pass," Omar said.

They both knew, though, that Omar anticipated an eventful evening.

Omar moved on to Fati's house. Usually he revealed to her his deepest concerns, but that night, he kept his thoughts and feelings close to himself. Sitting on the edge of her bed, she tried to ignite a conversation between them, but Omar remained uncommunicative. His head hung over his chest. As always, Fati demonstrated an inconceivable prescience.

"You're meeting the old man tonight, aren't you?"

"Yes," he said, with the timbre of surprise in his voice.

"He doesn't have much time left, does he?"

"Just a matter of days."

Fati hunched her shoulders. "Sometimes when old people are close to death, they get a burst of energy. They want to take care of business."

"I think you're right, Fati."

"Lay down on the bed and rest. When the black of night arrives, I'll make sure you're awake."

During a fitful sleep of several hours, Omar dreamed that he was walking on a desolate path that cut through an arid and empty landscape dotted with a few isolated trees and bushes without foliage. The sky was white with spots of red that looked like blood. A single bird, black as a moonless sky, flew high above. The scene frightened Omar. He wanted to turn back, but when he looked back, a violent fire blocked his way. Fearing for his life, he trudged on with no small amount of resignation. In short order, he came to a point at which the path split. A tree had sprouted at this fork in the road. A small black bird perched on one of its branches.

"Stop," said the little bird. "Stop, traveler."

Not knowing which direction to take, Omar stopped. His discomfort slipped him into a deep silence that he didn't want to break.

"Which way do you want to go, my friend?" the little bird asked.

Omar looked at two paths that led to uncertainty. "I don't know."

"You have to decide," the bird insisted. "It's very important."

At that moment, Omar woke up in a cold sweat. Completely disoriented, he cried out in French. "What's going on? Where am I?"

Fati put her warm hand on his forehead. "You're here with me, Omar. Go to your father, now. It's the black of night."

Omar made his way to Issaka Dia's spirit hut and clapped three times to signal his presence.

"Come in, my son," Issaka Dia said in a surprisingly strong voice. "Come in."

Two lanterns had been lit and adjusted to provide brighter-than-usual light in the hut. Issaka Dia sat propped up on two pillows. He seemed stronger than he had during Omar's most recent visits. "How's your evening, Father?" Omar asked.

"Tonight," he said, "I feel good. My strength won't last. My time is near."

"It's an end," Omar said, following the Songhay adage, "that we all face."

"That's the truth, my son." He shifted his position on the bed. "We've much work to do tonight. Come closer."

As Omar edged closer to his father, Issaka Dia's smile deepened the creases in his face.

"My son," he began, "we have to give away my work things." He pointed to a large orange and red carrying bag crafted from what looked like remnants of a Turkish carpet. "Bring me that bag," he commanded, "and open it."

Inside Omar found dozens of cloth satchels. "Those are my medicines. After I die, you'll give them to Abdoulaye. Tell him to divide all the powders between the two of you. You may not know how to use some of them. But Abdoulaye can tell you their names and uses. Keep some of your medicine here and take some with you to France. You'll soon know where to find these plants."

"Thank you, Father."

"Don't thank me, Omar," Issaka Dia said. "I'm passing on to you a lifelong burden."

"Understood, Father."

He next pointed to a long iron lance that had been planted in the sand next to the hut's center pole. Scores of brass, silver, and copper rings had been pushed into a locked position along the lance's expanding diameter. Years of sacrificial blood dulled their features. A red leather tassel had been tied to the lance's thicker end. "Bring me the *lolo*," he said, referring to the sorcerer's lance.

Issaka Dia gripped the lance in both of his hands. "My son, you will take possession of this lance. It has been in our family for hundreds of years, so take good care of it. Make sure that it is fed the blood of a red chicken on the third Thursday of every month. You're now a warrior, my son, and the lance gives you power in the world of the spirits." He extended it to Omar. "Take it, my son, and feel its power."

When Omar took hold of the lance, his arms convulsed as if he had received an electric shock.

Issaka Dia chuckled. "You see, my son, the lance contains the force of the past, the power of the ancestors. Abdoulaye is on the path of plants. You, Omar, are on the path of power and you'll need the lance to make your way." He patted Omar's hand. "Put it back where it was. Soon this spirit house will be yours and yours alone. You must know where things are, where things belong."

"Yes, Father," Omar said, feeling overwhelmed by the momentousness of the occasion.

Issaka Dia grunted as he tried to sit up on the bed. Omar helped him to a more comfortable position. The once massive and powerful body of this great man had become just a little more than skin and bones. "Help me take off my shirt," he asked.

Dozens of leather pouches attached to woven cords crisscrossed his chest. A leather belt circled his waist. A large brass ring had been attached to a leather cord around his neck. These amulets encased magical substances that sorcerers needed to walk the path of power. "Take these my son and wear them always. They will protect you from the dangers of the bush, and make you a strong spiritual guardian."

"Do these need to be fed?"

"No, my son. But you'll need to eat magic cake three of four times a year to feed their power."

"I will do so, Father."

He took the large brass ring from his neck and told Omar to put it on. He then extended both of his hands toward Omar. "Take off my rings and bracelets" There were several rings on each of the fingers of his left hand as well as one silver bracelet. No rings or bracelets had been worn on his right hand. "Always wear the large brass ring around your neck but keep it hidden under your shirt," he instructed. "Wear the copper rings on the third finger of your left hand—that's the finger of power and copper is the sorcerer's special metal."

"Understood."

"Give your brother the other rings, but not until after the cleansing ceremony 40 days after my death."

He put his hand into the side pocket of his shirt and pulled out a ring Omar had heard about but had never seen. The ring, crafted from silver, featured a simple band onto which a small post had been soldered. Attached to the post was a horse and a rider—both with vulture's heads. "This ring has been passed down from our distant ancestors. The sohanci gives it to his successor—that's you, Omar." He paused a moment. "Never wear this ring. Show it to no one. Keep it in your pocket or in your special container, your *baata*, which, you'll need to feed once a week with perfume, aromatic roots, and chicken blood."

Omar took the ring and put it with the other objects in the side pocket of his tunic.

Issaka Dia sighed as if a great burden had been lifted from his shoulders. Exhaustion pulled at his face and dimmed his eyes. "Help me to lie down," he asked.

Gently, Omar helped his father to extend himself on the bed. Cough spasms racked his body.

"Omar," he said, weakly. "Our work is almost over. One day, you will give these things to your son." His eyes closed and he fell asleep.

CHAPTER 19

For the next few days, Issaka Dia received no visitors. But suddenly on a Sunday, his strength returned. He wanted to see people. At first, only a trickle of well-wishers flowed into the compound. By Tuesday, the trickle had become a flood, people standing in line to pay their respects. In the afternoons, the wait was more than two hours. The family gave the well-wishers plenty of water and millet gruel and insisted that the older people sit in the shade while they waited.

The size of the visiting multitudes surprised Omar. He knew that his father was a great man, but hadn't realized how many people he had protected, how many he had healed. They came and came, some from great distances. Having heard of Issaka Dia's sickness, one man, perhaps 80 years old, had taken a series of dusty and uncomfortable buses all the way from Bamako, Mali. Another old man, too poor to take a bush taxi, had walked 80 kilometers from Ayorou. A rotund woman, well into her 70s had come from Ouagadougou in Burkina Faso—more than 500 kilometers to the south and west.

"Are you not tired from your trip, my mother?" Omar asked her.

"I am very tired, my son, but what choice do I have? Your father brought us health and happiness. He's my guardian—a great sohanci." She shook her head. "Men like your father will never be seen again."

"That's the truth," Omar stated.

"Death awaits us all," she said. "When he's gone, a powerful force will be lost. What will become of us?"

"Things will never be the same," Omar admitted, "but there are still sorcerers. Things change, but the ground remains firm," he said, reciting one of his favorite Songhay proverbs.

The visits continued well into the night. If a visitor had come a long way to see Issaka Dia, the family insisted they share meals and sleep in the compound.

After dinner on a Wednesday evening, Abdoulaye and Omar sat on pillows and mats under the spirit canopy and brewed tea. In the distance, a donkey brayed. In the compound, they could hear the soft din of evening conversation. Closer still, they heard the crackle of embers in the brazier.

"Abdoulaye, so many people have come, and from so far away."

"You are tired, no?"

"Very" Omar admitted. "And yet, I haven't had to talk with everyone. How does Issaka Dia do it? He has received everybody. Maybe he gives them a blessing. Maybe he just has a pleasant conversation. They tell him how much they'll miss him, how grateful they remain. How does he go on in this state?"

"These are his people," Abdoulaye reflected. "He's protected them, given them advice. He's been their rock in the world. They give him strength—the strength of the sohanci, Omar."

Omar nodded, wondering how long the visits would continue, for according to his father's own prediction, his time was near—very near.

Abdoulaye poured the first glass of tea and handed it to Omar. In deep reflection, his brow furrowed. After a few more moments, he asked, "How long will you remain with us?"

Omar had been so pre-occupied with Issaka Dia's impending death and with the crowds of pilgrims, he had neglected to think about the future. From the very first day of his visit, despite an array of pre-occupations— his birthright, learning the family business, his relationship with Fati, and death magic—he couldn't avoid thinking about how his life had quickly changed and how that change would affect his family in France. In his life, he had always preferred to take the path of least resistance. In his youth, it was easier to leave Tillaberi and Niger than to confront the obligations of the sorcerer's burden. In Paris, it was easier to profess ignorance than wto help that destitute woman on the rue de Charonne. Now in Tillaberi, he had reached an impasse and would finally have to confront a destiny that would not only allow him to fulfill his obligations but also enable him to live well in two worlds. To paraphrase Darwin, his life had become a tangled bank. It wasn't going to be easy. And now, Abdoulaye, much to his mounting irritation, had once again brought up the troubling subject. "I don't know, Abdoulaye," Omar said sharply. "How can I know that?"

Abdoulaye gave Omar a knowing smile that increased Omar's irritation. "You can't know," he said, "but in time, your path will open and you'll find you way."

"Yes, yes." Abdoulaye always said the same irritating thing when it came to Omar's future. "I'll find my way," Omar repeated formulaically.

The clap of hands woke Omar from a fitful, dreamless sleep. It was the black of night, and Omar staggered to the entrance of Fati's hut. Standing in the darkness, he found the unlikely figure of Maymouna, mother of the disgraced Seydou and Moussa and surviving wife of Issaka Dia. Why would this spiteful woman who had probably plotted his death want to talk to him in the black of night?

"I've just left the old man," she said. "He says that you should come to him right away."

"And you?" Omar asked.

"I've made my peace with him. He wants to be with you—alone." She began to walk back to her house and stopped. "I must respect my husband's last wishes," she said as she disappeared into the darkness.

As Fati silently watched Omar dress, he wondered about the vicissitudes of human character. For years, he wondered how his father had tolerated Maymouna's spitefulness, her vindictive character, and her endless series of dangerous plots to advance the fortunes of her sons. Perhaps he was able to see into her being and sense a deeply buried decency, or some sense of responsibility. Perhaps he was able to perceive her sense of devotion to him. Both Maymouna and Omar knew that her announcement signaled the passage of power from one generation to another, from father to son. Although Omar had heard many stories about what transpires during a sohanci's last moments on earth, he had no idea what to expect.

Dressed, he quickly and quietly made his way to the spirit hut. Lantern light cast a dim glow onto his father, who lay on his back. Gasping for breath, his chest heaved. Omar found a cloth, dampened it with water, and pressed it to his father's sweaty forehead. He opened his eyes and smiled at his son. "Come close, my son," he rasped. "Your ear..."

Omar lowered his ear to his lips and Issaka Dia whispered to him his "gind'ize gina," the magic word beyond all words and incantations. From the time of Sonni Ali Ber, emperor of Songhay in the fifteenth century, the great sohancis used their last breath to transfer this powerful word to their successors. He smiled briefly. His chest heaved and shuddered.

Eyes wide and mouth open, he put his chin to his chest and vomited. As a thick gob of phlegm pooled on his chest, the great Issaka Dia died. The press of grief and obligation made Omar's head and shoulders heavy. In the gob of phlegm, Omar found three small chains, the fabled *sisiri*, the physical manifestation of sohanci power. Only a few sohanci possessed these chains, and in most of these rare cases, there was but one chain for each person. Issaka Dia had three, which marked him as an important and powerful practitioner. He stared at the chains, knowing it was his duty to swallow them and become Tillaberi's next sohanci. And yet, the chains repelled him. How could he swallow such things? Did he want to? Shouldn't he go and fetch his brother, Abdoulaye, and have him swallow the chains? Omar hovered over his dead father for what seemed an endless period of time. In a flash of images, his life zipped by—a childhood of denial, an adolescence of fun and avoidance, a young adulthood of serious purpose, and adulthood of satisfying recognition—colleagues, students, family, and good fortune. What a good life! At least that's what he had thought. Those images faded into the body of his father and the pool of phlegm on his chest. Seeing his sacrifice to him triggered a deep force in Omar's body. He stopped thinking about past, present, and future, about the rough rub of desire and obligation, about the nether land between Niger and France, between Tillaberi and Paris. Possessed by an unfathomable will to act, he cupped his father's chain-laced vomit in his open hands. As he brought it to his mouth, the gut-wrenching smell, like the rotting corpse of an animal, made him dry heave three times. That same will to act suppressed his nausea. He opened his mouth and quickly swallowed his birthright, his family's ongoing legacy to the world. Again, he suppressed the desire to vomit. Breathing deeply, he gradually got control of himself. Then he began to feel it—a tingling sensation throughout his body, like gentle electronic impulses. The warm tingling spread throughout his body and took hold of him. In other magical rites, like the one that gives divinatory sight, the ritual gives one the disposition to acquire a skill or power. It is a first step on a long path to awareness and mastery. These magical chains were altogether different. He felt their impact immediately. It was as if Issaka Dia's kind and wise soul had entered Omar's body. Although Omar sensed his own character, Issaka Dia's force had somehow merged with his own being, which gave him immeasurable strength. For the first time in his life, Omar felt comfortable in his skin.

Omar stood up straight and walked away from his father's body. He knew that they would always remain connected. He knew that Issaka Dia would often visit his dreams and offer him comfort and advice. When Omar emerged from the spirit hut, the cocks crowed and a ribbon of red light rimmed the eastern horizon. He clapped outside of Abdoulaye's house, Abdoulaye soon appeared, dressed only in his balloon drawstring trousers. Seeing Omar, he knew immediately the news he had brought him.

"When, older brother?"

"In the black of night," Omar stated.

"Then, our father's work is done," Abdoulaye said.

"It is, younger brother."

Abdoulaye looked at Omar without expression. He understood what had transpired.

"We need to bury Father in the spirit hut," Omar said. "We should waste no time. You and I should do it, Abdoulaye."

"Yes. He'll be with us always."

CHAPTER 20

When death occurs among Omar's people, they say that it covers the family with filth—the filth of death. Mourners must live with this filth for 40 days, after which a cleansing ceremony is performed. During the ceremony, the deceased's objects are purified, and then distributed to rightful heirs. During this period of time, mourners wear white clothing, a defense against the filth. They refrain from any kind of work—other than receiving visitors. Neighbors prepare food and clean the compound.

The présence of filth is a challenge to every mourner, for it weakens a person, making her or his body vulnerable to physical disease or, worse yet, a sorcerous attack.

The night after Abdoulaye and Omar buried Issaka Dia, they reinstalled the stakes that repel death magic—to protect the family compound. Omar also began to sleep in the spirit hut—right next to his father's gravesite, which was marked only by several large smooth rocks found in the shallows of the Niger.

Death's filth made Omar sluggish. Grief consumed his being. He relived the regrets of his youthful mistakes. His insistence on living in France meant that he had lost many years of contact with Issaka Dia. He had learned a great deal in a relatively short period of time, but lamented his stubborn refusal to visit his father more regularly. He could have learned so much more. He could have built a deeper bond with his father. They could have had so many conversations in the black of night. In truth, Omar had been afraid to visit—fearful for his life. When he swallowed the *sisiri* chains, literally fusing his father's being with his own, he vowed to never turn his back on his relatives in Tillaberi.

Despite his new state of being, Omar had not figured out a way to accommodate his French family. How could he ever return to France, to Chantal and the kids, to the classroom at the Sorbonne? His life in France now seemed remote and inconsequential.

Life in the compound resumed a comfortable routine, except for the swell of visitors. People came from far and wide to pay their respects. One gentleman, named Diallo, came all the way from Dakar. Thirty years earlier, he had come to Issaka Dia to seek relief from persistent headaches and incessant nightmares. After listening to the man's complaints of a horrific woman who haunted his dreams, Issaka Dia treated him for spirit spouse sickness. He put him on a regimen of plants. He then burned resins in a brazier and had the man place a cloth over his head to inhale the aromatic smoke. He told the man to accept the spirit in his dreams, a beautiful but overbearing woman. He told the man, who had always been a prosperous merchant, to travel to Cote d'Ivoire and describe his dream woman to a sculptor who, for a modest fee, would carve an image of her.

The man followed Issaka Dia's instructions. When he returned home, statuette in hand, he put the spirit spouse at the center of his house. He made offerings to her every Thursday and Sunday. Once a week the man slept with his wooden spirit spouse. The man followed these prescriptions religiously and soon began to enjoy a happy and prosperous life. He never forgot Issaka Dia. For almost 30 years, he sent Issaka Dia small sums of money during the hard times of the year—especially just before the millet harvest when food was scarce and funds were tight. When he heard of Issaka Dia's death, he came to pay his respects.

"Your father," he told Abdoulaye and Omar, "was a great man. These days it's hard to find a man like him in Africa."

Omar nodded.

"That's the truth," Abdoulaye said.

As the hot season approached, the days became almost unbearable. On some days, the dust of the Harmattan, the desert wind, saturated the air like a fine mist, which sometimes made it a bit difficult to breathe. By late afternoon, though, cool winds would often cleanse the air of dust and drop the temperature.

The well-wishers continued to visit the compound. Omar and Abdoulaye were happy to feed and house people who had traveled from far away to pay their respects to Issaka Dia. They were also happy to feed local friends of the family. There were, indeed, local men and women, not well known to them, who came to the compound night after night to fill their empty bellies. It was their obligation to feed them as well. In other circumstances, these obligations might have placed a burden upon the family. But the relatively small cost of meeting this social burden hardly made a dent in Omar's salary.

After relatively quiet meals, a fire would be built, hot coals would be placed in a brazier, and tea would be brewed—the perfect setting for the telling of tales. Indeed, their guests regaled them with glorious stories of Issaka Dia's exploits. One family friend, Moustapha, an 80-year-old man from Tillakayna, a small village just to the north of Tillaberi, recounted Issaka Dia's practice of love magic.

Love Magic

My friends, listen to my story, for it is a great one. It was during the time of the great drought. You remember it, do you not? The rains had stopped, and there was little food in Niger. After people ran out of millet to eat, they would gather grass and tree barks and pound them into a flour, which they would put in boiling water and stir into a terrible paste. God provided me with some food during that hard time, but I was very, very sad. You see, my beautiful young wife had run away. At the time I was maybe 50 years old and I had paid a steep brideprice of a young girl of 18. She was tall and slender with smooth black skin that glistened in the sunlight. I got along well with her father, who was a friend of mine and I looked forward to many fine years with her. I had already fathered 8 children, but four of them had died in early childhood. I wanted more children and so I married Fatima. In truth, my friends, Fatima did not want such an old man for a husband. Although I was 50 years old, I enjoyed robust health. Work in the fields day and night hardened the muscles of my body. I liked to travel to markets and buy things for my wives and children. In truth, Fatima saw me differently. She even told me that she liked another man who was close to her age. She never smiled and even though we lived in the same compound and I provided her food, clothing, jewelry and perfume, she did not let me near her.

One day, I woke up to discover that Fatima had run away. She had taken her clothes, some of her finer rings and bracelets, leaving behind her dishes, pots, pans, blankets and so on. Aside from being heartsick, I worried about how she would survive the famine. Could her lover provide for her? Would she have enough food? What would she do for shelter? Although I was angry with her, she was still my wife and I did not want harm to visit her.

In my despair, my friends, I made my way to this very compound and met with Issaka Dia. He listened to my story and told me that he would try to do some work that would lure Fatima back to me—her husband. "And if she comes back," he said, "she'll be happy in your house. She'll never leave you again." Issaka Dia said that the key was to get her to come back. And so Issaka Dia, the great sohanci, began his work. He prepared a gourd and filled it with water and perfume and plants that had been ground into powder. He recited some incantations over it and then spit into the gourd. "Take this gourd and go to our washing hut. Take off your clothes and wash with it." I washed with the solution and returned to the spirit hut. Issaka Dia gave me resins to burn in a brazier. "Burn some of these every night until her return. It may take some time for her to come back—if she comes back." I wanted to pay Issaka Dia for his services, but he refused. "Pay me if your wife returns. If she does not come home, I do not deserve payment." Time passed and nothing happened. Frustrated, I once again came to see Issaka Dia. I told him of my despair. He said to continue burning the resins. After three months, my wife returned home. And when she came home, and God is my witness, she was no longer disdainful. She expressed her gratitude for my kindness and concern. My Fatima is still with us, the mother of two daughters and two sons. Every time I see her, I give my thanks to God and to the great sohanci, Issaka Dia, whose power saved my family. God be praised.

On another night, an old man from Burkina Faso told his story. He was a Gurmantche man who had trekked to Tillaberi from Fada N'Gourma, a village in the vast West Africa grasslands, perhaps 300 kilometers from Tillaberi. The distance from Fada to Tillaberi was not that great in kilometers. In terms of culture, though, Fada was in another universe. At Fada's center stood a Catholic Church. Indeed, Fada was well known for the quality of its *dolo*, or millet beer. How did Michel, the man's name, come in contact with Issaka Dia? As it turned out, Issaka Dia circumcised Michel when the latter was a small boy.

Circumcision

I met Issaka Dia one time—the day of my circumcision more than 70 years ago. At that time, Issaka Dia, I was told, traveled much of West Africa performing circumcisions. Later, I found out that Issaka Dia was called a guunu, the sohanci who cuts young 10 year-old boys—and sometimes not so young boys who have become teenagers. In time, I found out that the guunu has a special genealogy: his father must be a sohanci and trace his descent to Sonni Ali Ber; his mother must be a witch. This combination gives him the special force needed at the dangerous time of circumcision, when a boy's fate is sealed. As you know, my friends, if a man is not properly circumcised, his life will be miserable and he will not be able to have children. The fate of our village depended upon having

*a proper ceremony. For this we turned to the sohancis of Niger, the most power-
ful and famous sorcerers. Seventy years ago, only a few sohancis traveled in our
country and the name of Issaka Dia was well known.*

*Months after the elders of village sent a messenger to Niger, we received word
that Issaka Dia would soon visit our village to perform circumcisions. Late one
afternoon during the cool dry season, he arrived on a majestic white stallion.
Dressed in flowing black robes and a black turban, his presence made us both
fear and respect him. He met with the elders and ordered that the circumcisions
should begin just after dawn.*

*Accompanied by their fathers and uncles, more than 300 nervous boys from
all the surrounding settlements assembled outside the village under a large
shady tree. Issaka Dia told us to remove our clothes and approach him one by
one. He stood by a wooden platform, the chopping table, and asked us to lay
our penises flat on its surface. First he recited a short incantation that brought
harmony to our surroundings and then asked the spirits to protect us on our
paths. Then in a swift motion, he stretched our foreskins onto the wood and
removed them. Then, chewing on seeds, he spit lightly on the wound. The spit
made the pain go away. Then, he gave our fathers a green salve that would heal
the wound. "Take them to a cool hut," he said to everyone, "feed them well and
have them rest. After three days, they will be ready for their new lives."*

*Issaka Dia worked very hard that day. By sunset he was tired. The elders
thanked him for his work. Then, they slaughtered a cow and roasted the meat.
The elders feasted well into the night. The next morning, Issaka Dia left before
dawn to visit another set of villages.*

The stories continued well into each and every night—more tales of love
magic and circumcision. They heard how Issaka Dia had buried objects in
the soil that transformed a man's barren fields into fertile farmland. One
man, an elderly neighbor, told the story of Issaka Dia's ability to fly like
a vulture. As a child, Omar had heard that the great sohancis could fly to
distant places to scout a battlefield or perform healing rites. Until that
night, Omar had never linked this capacity to Issaka Dia.

Night Flight

*It has long been known, my friends, that the sohanci is special. They say that
the sohanci has no fear—not even of God! They say that the sohanci defies death
itself. They say that the sohanci can transform himself into his familiar—the
vulture, a creature that knows no fear, a bird that soars high in the sky and
catches the wind to travel great distances very quickly. Twenty-five years ago, I
thought little of these tales. How could anyone defy death? How could a man,
I asked myself, transform himself into a vulture and fly great distances? I kept*

these doubts to myself during a visit to the spirit house. One evening in the black of night I sought the advice of Issaka Dia. You see, I had received word that my younger brother was terribly ill in Abidjan in the Cote d'Ivoire and I didn't know what to do. Issaka Dia asked me to describe what I knew of my brother's symptoms and to tell me exactly where he lived in Abidjan. Because I had visited my brother several months earlier, I could describe his exact location in Treichville. "Good," Issaka Dia said. "I'll see what I can do for him. Come back tomorrow early in the morning." I returned home and slept soundly.

The next morning, I returned to the spirit hut to consult with Issaka Dia. His eyes were puffy and he yawned. I had never seen him in such a state. "Sohanci Issaka Dia, you look tired today."

"I am, my friend," Issaka Dia stated. "The sohanci works at night, you know, and some nights, like last night, we get very little sleep."

"What kept you up last night?" I asked.

"I did work for your brother," he stated. "I went to Abidjan and visited his room. It's small and whitewashed. The windows are also small and the fan doesn't work well."

"That," I said with disbelief, "describes perfectly my brother's room."

"I found him on his cot, tossing and turning with fever. I touched his hot forehead, released some perfume into the room, and left him powders to mix in his morning coffee. By the time I left, he felt much better."

How could Issaka Dia make up a story that contained so much accurate detail? Perhaps he read my thoughts. "I'm glad to know that my brother is better," I said with much doubt.

"Your brother," Issaka Dia said, "asked me to give this to you." He fished a silver ring out of his side pocket.

It was my brother's silver ring, my friends. He had always worn it on the third finger of his left hand. There was no way that Issaka Dia could have given me that ring if he had not gone to Abidjan and returned—all in one night!

"Issaka Dia was one of the great ones," one of the elders said, the glow of firelight on his face.

"They don't make men like him anymore," stated the man who had regaled us the story of Issaka Dia's flight to Abidjan.

Listening to the stories on those nights made Omar proud to be the son of such a great man, a man who never let pride undermine his capacity to act with quiet effectiveness and, yes, a degree of genuine modesty. In this way, the legend of Issaka Dia was reinforced. At that moment, Omar wondered what his gift to the world would be.

CHAPTER 21

The days of mourning slogged on. The endless stream of visitors continued, and as the 40-day period of mourning neared its end, the visitors talked about the ceremony that would cleanse everyone of death's filth.

"When will you hold it?" they asked.

"Will you march out to the bush?" they wondered.

"Who will receive his spirits?"

When Omar was growing up, he remembered the days when his father's spirits—the powerful and mercurial Dongo, deity of thunder, and Hausakoy, deity of iron—took over his large, imposing body, making the sight of him, eyes bulging and forehead vein throbbing, an indelible memory. Issaka Dia had taught Omar and his other sons that being a spirit medium was both a blessing and a burden. It was a blessing because the spirit could bring peace and harmony to the world. It was a burden because the same spirit could also bring much pain and suffering to its medium and her or his community. Issaka Dia also told his children that a spirit stayed with its medium until the latter's death. After 40 days of mourning, the dead person's spirit would take new mediums, usually members of the late medium's family.

"Things are being arranged," Abdoulaye would tell them wearily. "We'll soon send out word about the ceremony."

The heat had begun its relentless siege. Every day, the sun blistered the countryside, which forced Omar and Abdoulaye to go about their business at a snail's pace. In the afternoons, it was far too hot to remain in the mudbrick or straw huts. The best strategy was to sit under the spirit canopy, drink as much cool to lukewarm water as possible, and engage in listless conversation that eventually drifted into fitful dozing. Although Abdoulaye had little trouble sleeping in the heat for an hour or so, Omar avoided such rest. Every time he took a siesta, he'd wake with a stabbing headache that would last well into the late afternoon.

On one such intolerably hot day when the heat burned his skin and made his head throb, a young boy arrived at the compound. Save for Omar, the other adults had dozed off. The boy walked up to Omar.

"I've got a letter from the post office. It's for Omar Dia."

"That's me," Omar said, stretching out his hand to take the letter.

"They say the letter is all the way from France," the boy said.

Omar smiled. "And you have walked all the way from Tillaberi in the hot sun. Sit, my son. I'll get you some cool water." Omar dipped a ladle into a clay vat, which kept water surprisingly cool, poured it into a plastic mug, and gave it to the thirsty boy.

"Thank you, sir."

He sat down and took deep drinks of the water.

"Would you like some more?"

"Please, sir. And then I have got to get back to the post office."

As Omar expected, the letter was from Chantal. Omar hadn't been a very good correspondent. So much had happened since his arrival in Tillaberi, he hadn't figured out what to write to her. What would she think about the familial battles, the rapid apprenticeship in sorcery, or his initiation as Issaka Dia's successor? Chantal's previous letters had been filled with news of Paris and the kids. They were breezy and rather short. The envelope he now held in his hands seemed more substantial, which made him hesitant to open it. Would the words of this letter help him to meet his destiny? Did they promise, struggle, pain, and malaise?

With trembling hands, Omar tore open the envelope and started to read.

72 Rue de Charonne
75011 Paris
FRANCE

March 06, 2001

Dear Omar,

I hope this letter finds you in good health and good spirits. Quite frankly, we are all disappointed that you have written to us only once since you left. We realize that you find yourself in a difficult and emotionally devastating situation, but WE are your family. I AM your wife, and Adam and Lilly ARE your children. Your letter told us very little about what is happening to you. You simply say you are fine and that everyone is doing okay. You haven't even mentioned your poor father. How sick is he? Do you think if he received proper medical attention, we could prolong his life? If you had let me come with you, even for a little while, I might have been able to help. But you refused.

The more I think about it, the angrier I get. You have closed off your world from the children and from me. Why haven't you ever let us travel with you to Niger? What are you hiding from us? Are you ashamed of your origins? If so, there is no reason to be. But we know nothing of your African relatives, of your previous life there. Why have you always run away from yourself? Once again, you seem to be running away, this time from your wife and children in France. We are worried about you. I miss your voice, your conversation, and your love. Your children miss their father. Every day, Adam and Lilly ask, "When is Papa coming home from Niger? Why hasn't he written? Why hasn't he phoned us?" Adam says, "Daddy has forgotten us, Maman." Lilly says, "Daddy doesn't love us anymore." Then she bursts into tears.

What am I supposed to tell our children? What should I expect from you, Omar? Perhaps you've found a woman there who is more in tune with your needs? I don't know what you've found there, but I don't like it. What can be so important that you neglect your wife and children?

From the beginning of our marriage, I've loved you. I've opened myself to you, and you have been a wonderful husband. You loved and cared for me and for the children. And yet, in your absence I've learned that something was missing. The Omar I fell in love with was somehow incomplete. You had professional success, a lovely family, a nice place to live, but despite all of that, there was an empty space—a spark was missing, something primordial had been left in the homeland, in Tillaberi. I don't know if you have found that something or if that something means that you will abandon us to our life in Paris. What would you do in my place? Would you file for divorce? Would you say, "Well, marriage and family was nice, now it's time to move on"? During the cold rainy nights when I shudder with loneliness, I ask those very questions, Omar. What will you do? Do you still love us or has your love shifted to someone else? Will you forever remain in Tillaberi or will you return to us?

How will you define yourself? In the future, how will you be yourself? Let us know. Let us know very soon. The silent waiting has been interminable. We can't wait much longer. We all love you very much and await your word.

Love,
Chantal, Adam, and Lilly

Reading Chantal's letter slipped Omar into a funk. Holding onto the thin sheaths of paper, he hunched over on his stool and stared at the dull brown of sand at his feet. In a daze, he gradually lifted his head toward the eastern horizon. In late afternoon, the sky had lost the white glow of midday heat and took on a powder-blue hue. Omar didn't remember how long he sat in that stupor, but eventually the sound of Abdoulaye's voice brought him back to the heat, dust, and life in Tillaberi.

"Omar, what is it? What's wrong? You look like you've seen a demon."

He waved the letter in the air. "From Chantal, younger brother."

"Bad news? How are the children?"

"They're in good health. So is Chantal."

"Then what's the matter?"

"You already know. Haven't you been talking to me about my obligations as a husband and father?"

Abdoulaye remained silent.

"Have I listened?"

More silence.

"Well, Chantal may want to leave me. She wants to know if I've met someone. She wonders what's so important here that I pay no attention my wife and children. How can I explain? How could she understand that 'blood is obligation,' let alone my feelings for Fati?"

"You'll have to try, Omar. Maybe she understands more than you think. Hasn't she always wanted to come here and meet us?"

"Yes, and I've always said no. I didn't want her to see how we lived. I worried about the children. They could get seriously ill—dysentery, jaundice, and malaria."

"But you never gave her a chance."

"True enough," Omar said, hunching his shoulders. "What about Fati?"

"That, Omar, is another matter. Western women don't want a family with two wives."

"In Paris I used to joke about polygamy. I used to tell people what an old man once told me while I was at the lycée in Niamey. He said that he was weary of a life with four wives. 'The Europeans are smart,' he said, 'for having one wife at a time. That works. Two wives means a continuous argument in the household. Three wives is continuous warfare. And with four wives, my dear friend, only death will bring you peace.' Chantal would never be part of a polygamous household. I wouldn't want it either. I just don't know what to do. I can't sort out my feelings."

Abdoulaye smiled at Omar. "I'll give you the sorcerer's response, Omar. Nobody can tell you what to do. You'll have to find your own way."

Omar nodded. That damned sorcerer's response to an imposing problem—"a path will open, a solution will present itself, be patient." Omar stood up and stretched his arms in the air. "Maybe my thoughts will clear up on a walk in the bush," he said.

"Would you like me to come along?" Abdoulaye asked.

"Not this time, Abdoulaye. I need to walk alone today."

"Are you going to *The Place Where Stories Are Told*?"

"Not today. I'm going toward Tillaberi Mountain."

"Go with God's grace," Abdoulaye said.

Omar left the compound in the late afternoon, time when the light turned golden, when the shadows stretched, and when the rhythmic clanging of bells signaled that the Fulan shepherds had begun to guide their herds of cows, sheep, and goats toward town. Because the wind had blown away a haze of fine dust, the light's resolution was particularly sharp that day. Omar walked toward the north. Slowly the path that cut between scraggly acacias and tamarind trees sloped up. Sand soon gave way to hard red clay interspersed with partially buried rocks and boulders. Omar noticed a square of hard clay covered with blackened rocks. On closer inspection, he realized that he had stumbled upon a field of slag, the refuse of an ancient iron-smelting site. Omar picked up a small craggy piece of slag and put it in his pocket. Issaka Dia had long ago told him that slag had protective properties. Sorcerers liked to bury slag around a person's house. In this way, the slag would protect a household from enemies. Perhaps Omar would bury it in the family compound—perhaps not. Maybe he'd bury it in Paris—to protect his house there. He wondered if Songhay sorcery would work in Paris. Would it protect his family from evil-minded compatriots? Better yet, would it protect his family from evil-minded Parisians?

When Omar reached the base of Tillaberi Mountain, the trek got steeper and rockier. He didn't expect to have enough time to make it to the summit of the domed mountain but wanted to reach an outcropping where he could see the Niger River, Tillaberi, and Tillakaina. As he climbed higher, the terrain became more austere—rocks, boulders, brown clay, and robust scrub brush. After about 20 minutes of scampering among the rocks, making sure to avoid putting his foot into a hole that hid poisonous snakes, he came upon an outcropping that provided a majestic sight of Tillaberi, the Niger River basin, and below a commanding view of Tillakaina—the straw tops of its round mud houses silhouetted against a darkening sky. For some romantic reason, Omar thought a solitary jaunt to a majestic spot would fill his mind with creative and constructive ideas about how to move forward. Where should he live and with whom? How would he juxtapose the life of scholar who writes books with that of a sorcerer who makes amulets? Should he end his marriage to Chantal? And what about kids? And what about Fati—that face, that smile, her intoxicating presence?

Omar sat down on the outcropping and took in the view. A cool breeze swept up from the river, filling his lungs with fresh air. He felt no inspiration. His mind was empty of ideas—time to return to the family compound.

That evening, Abdoulaye and Omar sat on a palm frond mat and silently ate their dinner—the usual, millet covered with a peanut sauce. Omar sensed that Abdoulaye, good soul that he was, wanted to talk about the future. Recognizing the inner turmoil that had gripped Omar, Abdoulaye remained silent, which, that night, Omar deeply appreciated.

It was Abdoulaye who broke the silence. "Would you like some tea, Omar?"

Thinking that the caffeine jolt of strong green tea would impel him to some sort of resolution, Omar said yes.

In short order, a brazier glowing with charcoal appeared, and Abdoulaye silently went through the motions of preparing tea. Maybe he thought that the consumption of tea, which was known to stimulate long conversation, would trigger an exchange of much-needed talk. The tea, though, did nothing to empty Omar's mind of its confusing clutter. After silently sipping for several hours, Omar thanked Abdoulaye for his fraternal fidelity and slinked over to the spirit hut where he hoped for, but did not expect, a good night of sleep. Just as he lay down on what had been his father's bed, Omar heard three claps just outside the hut's opening.

"Who goes there so late at night?" he asked.

"It's Mariama," a thin high-pitched voice said. "Fati says you must come to her house tonight."

"Tonight?"

"Yes. She says you must come right now."

Omar usually invited himself to Fati's house. As the period of mourning stretched on, Omar spent most of his nights in the spirit hut. Omar had wanted to visit Fati, but grief and mourning had forced him to confront the social obligations to his family, his wife, his children, and his birthright, a set of reflections that made him wary of his passion for Fati. One part of Omar very much wanted to see her, listen to her soft voice, and make love to her. Another part of him wanted to avoid Fati—perhaps a way of getting used to living his life without her.

Omar slowly put on his trousers and tunic and slipped into the night. A cool breeze blew in from the west. As he made his way toward Fati's hut, a donkey brayed in the distance. The dim glow of a lantern illuminated the inside of Fati's hut. Omar clapped three times to announce his arrival.

"Come in, Omar," she said.

Dressed in her finest cloth, she sat at the edge of her bed, a portrait of Songhay beauty—glowing black skin smoothly stretched over a heart-shaped face blessed with high cheekbones and large clear black eyes. Seeing her made Omar's heart skip a beat. He stood motionless, afraid to approach.

"Omar," she said. "Come and sit by me."

He hesitated.

"Come and sit," she insisted.

When he sat down, he smelled her scent—the intoxicating Bint El Sudan, the perfume favored by Dongo, deity of thunder. His head began to spin. In such a state, words escaped the new sohanci of Tillaberi.

Fati broke the uncomfortable silence. "Omar," she began, "I asked you to come because I need to talk with you."

"About what?" he asked in a barely audible voice.

"About you and me," she said resolutely.

"What about me and you?" he asked in large measure to compel her to talk.

"Omar, the past months have been the best of my life. Life with your uncle was okay. He looked after me, but I felt little for him. He was a good man, may God rest his soul, but he was much older than me. We had little in common. He was very traditional, and I wanted something new. I can speak a bit of French, and I did go to school. I wanted a good Songhay man who was more educated than my husband. Following the family, I married him and shared his bed. I didn't know what to expect when he died. I certainly didn't expect to meet you. I had heard about you—the wayward son, the oldest son of Issaka Dia who had left Tillaberi, left Niger, a man who had run away.

"That's what they said about you. And then, when your father got sick, you surprised everyone by coming to be with him. They said that Omar is lost to us. They said that the French language had spoiled his brain. French food had ruined his belly. They said that his French woman and his French children would keep him in France, where he is a big man." She took a deep breath. "Then you came here full of nervous feelings. I could see it in your face, in the flutter of your eyes. You were saying to yourself: 'What am I doing here? I don't want to be here.'"

"That's what I was thinking."

"You were the man I was looking for. I knew that you wouldn't be here for a long time. I knew you were married and had children, but here, that doesn't matter. I hoped you'd notice me."

"I did from the very first time you brought us food."

Fati smiled. "I made sure that I was the one to bring the food. I wanted you to see me and notice me."

"That seemed to work."

"You are a good and powerful man, Omar. I'm so grateful that our paths have crossed. You have taught me about life. You might not realize it, but you have. You have shown me how to enjoy life. I can't imagine going back to the life I had been living." She repositioned herself on the bed's edge. "During the past few days, I've wondered what would happen to us. Today, I heard about your wife's letter and the effect it had on you."

She paused, waiting for Omar's response, but he remained silent.

"When I heard about that letter, I started thinking about your wife and your children. If we were all alike, there'd be no problem. I'd become your second wife, and we'd live together here in a household. Here, we do that all the time. But we're not all alike. Your wife and children live in Paris and speak French. I live in Niger and speak only a little French. Your family is used to the life in the city. I'm a country girl who has never traveled far from Tillaberi. Omar, what I'm saying is that after the mourning period is over, you've got to go back to your wife and children in Paris. Talk with her and talk with your children. Don't ignore your obligations here or there. Like your father, you must walk strongly on your path. Don't retreat into the past. Dig deep and find your courage. I know you'll find your way."

Fati's eyes misted, but she would not allow herself to cry. She sighed, dropped her head down, and stared at the sandy floor of her hut. Fati possessed a clarity and courage that Omar lacked. She understood him profoundly and knew that they had reached a point where their paths would diverge. Omar wanted to resist this fate. He didn't want to give up on Fati, but how could they go on? "What will you do, Fati?"

"When you leave here, I'll go to live with my brother and sister in Ouallam. When your uncle died, they wanted me to go there and live with them. It was my duty to remain here. I'm happy I did because I met you." She took Omar's hand. "You'll be fine. I'll be fine." She squeezed his hand.

"Will I ever see you in the future?"

"I'm not going anywhere, Omar. Only God knows what will happen. I do know that you are the sohanci of Tillaberi. When you come back to Niger, I'll see you."

"Even if I come back with my wife and children?"

"That makes no difference to me. Even if I'm married, I'll come."

At that moment, Omar wondered how we live with so many loves in our lives? He stood up, looked at Fati, and, in silence, made his way to the hut's entrance.

"Goodbye, Omar."

CHAPTER 23

The next morning, Omar sat down at a rickety table and wrote a letter to Chantal, Adam, and Lilly. Up to that point, Omar had been too self-consumed to find his new path in the world. It was Fati who had wherewithal to lead Omar to a crossroads. Standing there, he wanted to express himself in just the right way. He wanted the letter to be the first step on a long, new, and winding path of life. Omar had no idea where that path would lead to, but could anyone know the unexpected surprises that life could bring?

Dear Chantal, Adam, and Lilly

I hope this letter finds you in good spirits and good health. It has been far too long since my last letter, and I apologize to you. I have not been a good correspondent, a good husband, or a good father. Tucked away in our isolated family compound, I haven't heard your voices or news of your life in Paris. I wonder how things are at the hospital and how Adam and Lilly are progressing at school. How is Adam's swimming and Lilly's ballet?

I've been so immersed here in Tillaberi, I have neglected you—the most important people in my life. I now realize that even when I was in Paris, I neglected all of you. I promise that that will never happen again. I hope you can forgive my neglect, forgive me for preventing you access to a most important part of my life—a most important part of me. I now know that that was wrong. I am no longer worried about my African family's way of life, about their modest circumstances, about their great and deep traditions of healing the sick and making the world a more peaceful place. In his dying days, my father—and other members of the family—guided me to a much deeper comprehension of what is important in life.

Tomorrow we will celebrate my father's life and cleanse ourselves of the filth created by his death. Believe it or not, I am my father's successor. I am the sohanci, the spiritual guardian of Tillaberi. Issaka Dia bestowed upon me a great honor but also a great burden—the sorcerer's burden, which is, among other things, to share the pain and suffering of others, to live with their uncertainties as well as my own. After the cleansing ceremony, I will have to attend to many new responsibilities, but after about one week, I'll be ready to return to Paris. Once I've made reservations, I'll phone and let you know exactly the date and time of my arrival.

I want you to know that when school lets out in the summer, I want all of you to come to Niger. I want you to meet your family here. I want all of you to learn the Songhay language. Chantal, maybe you would be willing to help out in the Tillaberi clinic? Your skills would help many people here. I am going to buy horses for all of you. I want you to ride in the bush with me. There is so much I want to show you—important things. There are many stories I want to tell you about past.

I don't know if you can accept this, but I've looked into the future, a skill my father gave to me, and what I've seen is good—very good.

When I get home, there will be much to do and much to discuss. I can't wait to see you all again. I've been away for far too long. I'm coming back now and with God's grace will never be away again.

Love,
Omar

He re-read the letter and took a deep breath, hoping that Chantal would read it in the open spirit in which it was written. He then carefully folded the thin sheets and placed them inside an envelope. Normally, Omar would ask one of Abdoulaye's sons to take the letter to the post office. For this letter, though, he wanted to go to the post office himself to make sure it would be properly stamped and sent. He also wanted to phone Chantal to tell her that he would soon be coming home. Things might have been easier if he had been using his cell phone, but since coming to Tillaberi, the battery died, and it couldn't be recharged.

Omar called out to one of Abdoulaye's sons, "Hey, boy, put a saddle on Sorba. I'm going to ride him into town."

After putting on his black robes and wrapping a black turban around his head, Omar took the letter and mounted Sorba. The mid-morning sun felt hot against his robes, but a stiff breeze from the west—the cool direction—made the air bearable. Omar had always hated the isolation of the family compound—so far from Tillaberi proper. During his recent visit, though, Omar grew to enjoy the isolation—the forays into the bush, the long conversations with Abdoulaye, and the continuous stream of visitors. He no longer cared what others thought of him and the members of his family. He chuckled to himself: No one in Tillaberi wanted to live near a family of sorcerers. No one wanted to play with what they perceived to be fire. Truth be told, it was inconvenient to live so far way. It would take him 15 minutes or so to reach the outskirts of town and another 10 minutes to get to the post office. It didn't matter. Omar wanted to savor the journey. He had written a heartfelt letter—one of the first acts of his new life. Why not take the time to enjoy the ride to the post office?

The narrow sandy tracks that cut across a barren plain dotted with scrub brush gradually widened into the road that led to Tillaberi. A maze of intersecting pathways bordered by walled compounds of mostly rectangular mud-bricked and tin-roofed houses marked the outskirts of town. Holding the hands of their children, mothers, wrapped in indigo blue robes, guided their toddlers toward the bush—the toilet of convenience. As Omar rode deeper into the town, a tall man in blue robes looked at him and raised both of his arms skyward—a respectful greeting of hello. Omar greeted him.

"How goes the morning, Sohanci Omar?"

Omar smiled inwardly. No stranger had ever referred to him as "sohanci," his father's title. It was a mark of respect for his family—and for Omar.

"It goes well," he said. "It goes well."

Further along the trail, other men and women greeted him in the same manner—an affirmation of his new status. Despite the considerable burden of the new obligations, Omar liked the acknowledgements of the townspeople. Sitting atop his black stallion, dressed in the sohanci's black robes, Omar felt the power of his new position.

At the post office, he dismounted, and a young boy ran over to his horse. "I'll look after your horse, Sohanci Omar."

The post office was a dust-dulled white cement building with freshly painted green shutters. When one walked in, a counter stood opposite the door. A series of phone cabinets were situated to the left. An anemic fan spun just above the counter, where Ousseyni stood arranging a book of stamps. He looked up.

"Ah, Sohanci Omar," he said to him in Songhay, "what brings you all the way to the post office?"

Omar gave him the letter.

"Ah, I see. A letter to France." He weighed the letter. "That's going to be about $1.00 in postage, sir."

He gave the postmaster the money, who in turn put the stamp on the envelope. "Your wife should get it in three days' time."

His comment shocked Omar. Did everyone know everything about him in this small town? Had someone been reading his incoming mail? Controlling his emotions, Omar did not betray irritation. "That's good," he said. "I need to phone her in Paris."

The postmaster passed him a sheet of paper. Omar wrote down his Parisian telephone number and gave it to him.

"Go to Cabinet 1, Sohanci Omar, and when the phone rings, pick it up. Your wife should be on the line."

He sat down in Cabinet 1 and waited for the phone to ring. It wasn't likely that anyone would be home at 10:00 a.m. But he wanted to leave a message on the voice mail—that would be less awkward. The phone rang, and as expected, Omar got directed to the voice-mail message. At the beep, he began to speak.

"Chantal, I'll be coming home in about one week—after the end of my father's funeral ceremony. I've mailed a letter to you about what has happened here. You should get it in three days or so. I love you and the children very, very much and can't wait to see you all again. I'll phone in several days and let you know when my flight gets into Paris. I love you all."

Omar opened the door and walked toward the counter. "Thank you, Ousseyni. How much do I owe you for the phone call?"

"You were on for only 30 seconds. Let me look it up." The postmaster consulted a chart. "That's $2.50 for today."

"Thanks, Ousseyni," Omar said, fishing out the money from the deep front pocket in his tunic.

"Please give my greetings to your family and to your wife and children in Paris," the postmaster said.

"I will, indeed."

CHAPTER 24

By the time the 40 days of mourning had nearly come to an end, Omar once again experienced a full Nigerien hot season. Days had become unbearably hot, and by now it didn't cool off until the "black of night." On the day that the family would wash away the filth of Issaka Dia's death, the sun rose like a red fireball that cast searing heat over the morning landscape. There was nothing to do about this kind of heat except to maintain a slow pace and cool off periodically with water.

The rhythm of the family's preparations slowed down to accommodate the heat. Omar's relatives cleaned and pressed their best white clothes—skirts, tops, headscarves, tunics, capes, and robes. One of Abdoulaye's sons accounted for all of Issaka Dia's clothes, herbal medicines, and ritual objects. These would have to be purified with fresh milk, which that morning had been poured into gourds and stored in a relatively cool corner of Abdoulaye's house. Omar wondered what would transpire later in the afternoon. He knew that the filth of death needed to be washed away in the heat of mid-day but had no idea what would happen after the mourners returned to the family compound. How would they respond to Omar and Abdoulaye? Could they accept them as the new generation of healers in Tillaberi? Would they consult them in the future? Would they be willing to bear their souls to Omar or Abdoulaye? Would they be confident of Omar's or Abdoulaye's ability to keep Tillaberi safe from the destructive forces of the social and spirit worlds?

Time would tell. Omar had great confidence in his younger brother. Omar had lingering doubts about his own capacities. He could see himself as a kind of itinerant spiritual guardian. His compatriots would certainly test him. Issaka Dia had thought that this oldest son could take up the sorcerer's border, and Omar was beginning to think so as well.

By mid-afternoon, a motley crowd of mourners, perhaps 100 people, had gathered in the compound—old women, wrapped in homespun indigo cloth, who had assisted Issaka Dia during possession ceremonies and all of the spirit mediums whom Issaka Dia had initiated, including many local people. Idrissa Maiga, the Nigerien Minister of Agriculture, came to pay his respects. Family members and friends, some of whom had traveled from hundreds of miles away, waited for the ceremony to begin. The presence of Omar's older sister, Salamatou, lifted his spirits. She had been traveling across the country and hadn't had time to come and visit him in Tillaberi. He didn't expect to have much time to talk with her that day. Their talk would have to wait until his departure for France.

The sun blanched the sky. The absence of a breeze made it difficult to breathe. Like a patchy fog, a fine dust hovered over them. Abdoulaye and Omar sat on stools under the spirit canopy and received the well wishes of each and every mourner. A tall, thin man dressed in black and carrying a forked stick approached them. He was Yacouba Dendi, the sohanci of the neighboring town, Tillakaina. He would lead them through the ceremony.

"Death is a necessary step on life's path," he said, reciting the greeting one makes to those who mourn.

"It is necessary, indeed," Omar stated.

"All is ready, my brothers. We're ready to march into the bush."

Moments later, Wigindi Godji, master of the monochord violin, began to play his instrument. Its high-pitched cries pierced the hot, dry air. Omar and Abdoulaye stood up and placed themselves behind the violinist, who would lead them all to a crossroads in the bush. A two-by-two line formed behind them. They marched in sync with the slow, sad music. Following a narrow sandy path that led to the east, they marched into the bush. They trudged along passing jujube trees and a few tamarinds. They walked across a rocky clay plain from which only scrub brush grew. After ten minutes or so, they left the plain and entered a rolling sandy expanse. In the near distance, a shady tamarind tree grew at the point where the path forked into two other trails. This crossroads marked the intersection of two worlds—the world of social life and the world of the spirits. It was the place where they would wash away the filth of Issaka Dia's death.

Black-robed and black-turbaned Yacouba glided onto the crossroads. There, he planted his forked stick in what looked like a snake hole. As Wigindi Godji, who stood behind him, played his mournful instrument, Yacouba Dendi recited the genji how, the incantation that harmonizes the forces of the bush. He followed the incantation with praise-poems that celebrated the life of the benefactor, the great sorcerer king, Sonni Ali Ber, father of all the sohanci. He raised his arms as if he, like a giant black bird, was about to fly. Flapping his arms like the sorcerer's protector in the bush, the vulture, he urged the mourners to sit on the sand.

Yacouba Dendi held onto his forked stick and began to talk about his friend and mentor, Issaka Dia.

> We come today to think about our departed friend, father, teacher, and guardian, Issaka Dia. He was a man among men, but he had the blood of Sonni Ali Ber running in his veins. He was a good man who lent himself to the world, taking into his body your pain, my pain, and the pain of the world. From that pain, he became a wise man, who made life sweet for us—for all of us. Everyone here has been touched by Issaka Dia's grace.

A series of piercing wails caused Yacouba Dendi to stop but only for a short moment.

> There are people whom Issaka Dia healed of incurable illness. There are those here whom Issaka Dia healed of love sickness or of homesickness. There are people here whom Issaka Dia led to the path of fortune and notoriety. And there are many here, most of you, whom Issaka Dia initiated as spirit mediums. He took you from sickness to health, from a life in the fields and in households to one of burden and service. He made all of us strong. He kept us safe from the forces of the bush. We honor and praise him today. We remember and revere him. We will never forget the man or his great deeds. We will talk about him. He will be with us. The sohanci's body may pass away, but the sohanci never dies. Issaka Dia is with us today and forever more.

The chorus of wailing reached a crescendo. Yacouba Dendi let it continue as men and women expressed their grief at the passing of a great man, an important figure in the history of Omar's people.

Yacouba Dendi's brother, Zibo Dendi, brought a large calabash to the crossroads and filled it with water. Yacouba Dendi pulled from his deep breast pocket three black cloth pouches and took from them an assortment of powders—ground tree barks, roots, leaves, and stems. He poured these powders onto a piece of white cloth and mixed them together. Then in a counterclockwise fashion, beginning at the edge of the calabash, he spread the mixture in concentric circles, creating a swirl of powder on water. He then took a vial of *Bint El Sudan* perfume and sprinkled its contents into the mixture. He recited incantations, singing praises to the ancestors of sohancis—warriors all—and to the deities in the spirit world who had been the allies of past and present sohancis. He then recited a text that offered protection from enemies, both spirit and human. "We ask that the power of Issaka Dia be transferred to his successor, Omar Dia. We ask that the spirits give strength and forbearance to Omar so that he as well as his younger brother, Abdoulaye, walks the path of the sohanci, that they heal the sick, that they give sweetness to those whose lives have been embittered by evil, that they maintain the balance between the spirit and social worlds." He then spat three times into the gourd.

Zibo Dendi produced two smaller calabashes and placed them next to the large container. Taking a wooden laden, the older brother emptied the sacred contents of the large calabash into the two smaller vessels. "Sohanci Omar Dia and Abdoulaye Dia come and accept this humble offering from your father's dear friend."

They stood up and walked to Yacouba Dendi, his tall, thin body majestically framed by black robes. He gave each of them a calabash.

"You are now warriors—our warriors. Take this sacred water into the bush and wash the filth of your father's death from your bodies and souls. Go now. We will see you back at the family compound."

With a deep silence that befitted the profundity of the moment, Abdoulaye and Omar took their calabashes and walked into the bush. In the distance, they heard the din of the mourners returning to the compound. They walked into a thicket of brush, a cluster dense enough to afford a measure of privacy. Without speaking, they took off their clothes and faced one another, the sweat on their naked bodies glistening in the sun.

"Turn around, Abdoulaye. I'll pour my ablution over your head and you do the same for me."

Holding the calabash, Omar recited the genji how as he slowly poured the fragrant solution over his brother's head. Abdoulaye spread the holy water all over his body.

"It's your turn, older brother."

Soon enough Omar felt the cool, fragrant solution cascading down his body. He rubbed his skin with it and immediately felt an indescribable lightness—as if the burden of Issaka Dia's death had been lifted from his shoulders. He smiled at Abdoulaye.

"Do you feel it, Abdoulaye?" Omar asked, laughing.

"I do, Omar. I do feel it."

They laughed softly for a sweet moment and then put on their clothes. Not wanting that moment to slip away too soon, they looked at one another and smiled, creating an even deeper bond between them.

"Time to return, Abdoulaye?" Omar asked.

"Our time has come, Sohanci Omar."

Feeling relieved and yet burdened by his new set of obligations, Omar looked north toward the family compound. A blend of dust and light gave the air a filmy quality. They slowly trekked toward the compound, where Yacouba Dendi would complete the ceremony.

As they approached the compound, they heard the wail of Wigindi Godji's violin and the claque of sticks on gourd drums—spirit possession music. Outside the spirit hut, a white cloth had been spread over the sand. Zibo Dendi had arranged all of Issaka Dia's things (lances, spears, amulets, rings, bracelets, clothing, medicine pouches, and gourds) on the cloth. When Omar and Abdoulaye appeared, Yacouba Dendi motioned for them to approach.

"We must wash the filth of death from Issaka Dia's things," he stated.

Zibo Dendi gave his brother a gourd of fresh milk, over which the latter whispered an incantation. Yacouba Dendi then spat into it. He then took some milk into his mouth and began to spray it over Issaka Dia's things. Yacouba Dendi made sure that milk droplets hit each object at least three times. In this way, Issaka Dia's objects could be distributed to his heirs— mostly to Abdoulaye and Omar.

Meanwhile, the music inspired spirit mediums to dance on the sandy expanse in front of the spirit canopy. Wigindi Godji, one of the most famous violinists in all of Niger, played the music of the Tooru, the nobles of the Songhay spirit world. He shifted to the music of Dongo, one of the spirits that Issaka Dia had carried. Abdoulaye's breathing suddenly got heavy. Tears streamed from his eyes. His arms and legs shook uncontrollably. He groaned. Omar had never thought that Abdoulaye was a spirit medium, and yet it looked like a spirit was about to take him. Abdoulaye groaned again. Yacouba Dendi and Zibo Dendi rushed forward, their robes caught up in a sudden wind gust. A small group surrounded Abdoulaye, whose body throbbed with power.

"It's Dongo," Yacouba Dendi announced. He looked at Omar. "Dongo likes your family," he said. "He spent many years with your father. Now he has come to dwell in your younger brother's body. Praise to the spirits!!!" With one arm around "Dongo's" shoulder, Yacouba Dendi cried out, "Fetch his hatchet and bring his cape and hat."

From the white cloth on which Issaka Dia's things have been spread out and purified, a young boy brought a hatchet encased in red leather. A small bell had been attached to the hatchet head. Another boy brought Dongo's indigo cape and hat. Wielding his hatchet, Dongo groaned and bellowed and stomped around the dance grounds. He came up to Omar. "Sohanci Omar, you will sacrifice a black goat tomorrow at the crossroads where you washed away the dirt of death. Then you will sacrifice three black chickens and drip the blood at the entrance to your family compound. Do you understand?"

"I do," Omar said.

"This blood will keep your enemies away. This blood will bring peace and harmony to your compound." His eyes flashed fire. "Do you understand?"

"I do, King of the Sky. It will be done."

"It must be done."

Taking the spirit with a gentle grip, Yacouba Dendi led him away in order to shake Dongo from Abdoulaye's body.

By now the sun was setting, and darkness gradually descended upon the compound. The crowd of mourners gradually left to walk back to their homes in Tillaberi. It had been quite a day—a funeral, purification rituals, and finally Dongo's possession of Abdoulaye. Dongo, the most powerful of all Songhay spirits, would live with Abdoulaye for the rest of his days.

PART III

Niger/Paris 2001

CHAPTER 25

After months of familial turmoil in Niger, the prospect of Omar's reunion with Chantal and the kids should have been stressful. As Omar's Air France flight headed northward over a moonlit Sahara, he should have worried about what might happen. How had Chantal reacted to his letter? Did she still love him? And what about the kids? Had they changed? Would they forgive Omar for his long absence? How would he approach his work? Could he go on as before, the cosmopolitan postcolonial professor who got passionate about the works of French philosophers? Thinking of these important matters, though, did not tie his stomach in painful knots or cause his eyes to flutter. In his gut, Omar knew that solutions—good solutions—would present themselves. He knew that his path, as his ancestors liked to say, would open for him. He knew that Issaka Dia was and would always be with him. Even 35,000 feet above the Sahara, Omar could feel Issaka Dia's presence. When faced with a future dilemma, Omar knew that his father would slip into his dreams and offer sage advice. Such certitude brought peace of mind.

Prior to his departure, Omar had had so much to do. Abdoulaye and Omar had to distribute Issaka Dia's things. As the successor to his father, Omar received the sacred lance, the *lolo*, which had been in the family for hundreds of years. When he took possession of the lance, Omar walked to a fork in the road near the family compound, where he planted it in the earth and sacrificed a black chicken. He let the sacrificial blood run down the blood-caked shaft. The lance would remain in the spirit hut, planted in the sand next to its center post. Issaka Dia's ritual vessel, the *hampi*, a large

147

clay pot in which potions were mixed, would also remain in Tillaberi. In fact, all items—costumes and objects—connected to the spirits and their world would remain in the spirit hut.

Abdoulaye and Omar divided the items associated with sorcery and healing. Omar received some of his father's rings of power, three of which he put on the third finger of his left hand. He attached a large copper power ring, much too big and heavy to wear on his finger, to a leather necklace and wore it under his shirt. Omar's greatest prize, which he would never wear, was a large silver ring on which was mounted a horse and rider—representations of his ancestor Sonni Ali Ber and his flying horse. Omar would keep this ring—and several others not meant to be worn or displayed—in his sacrificial container where, every Sunday and Thursday, he'd make offerings to the family ancestors.

Abdoulaye received several power rings and the bulk of Issaka Dia's medicines. As a recently initiated medium of Dongo, deity of thunder, he took charge of Dongo's great indigo cape and cap as well as Dongo's hatchet. Several rings had been allotted to Omar's younger brothers Moussa and Seydou. Moussa would receive his inheritance when the authorities released him from jail, perhaps in the coming year—perhaps not.

Following Dongo's instructions at Issaka Dia's funeral, Abdoulaye and Omar bought a black goat and led it into the bush, this time to spot on rocky plain that sloped up to Tillaberi Mountain. There they found a smooth cone of granite in the sand, the smooth edges and crater of which made it look like a volcano.

"Is this the place?" Omar asked Abdoulaye.

"It is, older brother. It's Dongo's stone."

Abdoulaye talked to the goat, which struggled as he stretched its neck over Dongo's stone. The words had a soothing effect, and the goat relaxed. Abdoulaye unsheathed a large butcher knife and slit the goat's throat. The blood pooled in the stone's crater, a sign that Dongo had accepted the sacrifice. Two of Abdoulaye's sons, who had followed along, now came forward to carry the goat back to the compound. That night, they roasted the goat and invited well-wishers to a feast.

The next morning, Omar joined Abdoulaye at his fire. He had a teapot, a can of Nescafe, a bowl of fresh milk, and an assortment of millet pancakes. Omar sat down next to him.

"Omar," he said, "you leave in two days. What will we do? We need you here in Tillaberi. You are the sohanci."

"I can't stay here year round," Omar stated. "I've got my family, my job, and my students."

"Of course." Abdoulaye offered Omar a steaming coffee mug. "And here you have the family."

After thinking long and hard about his new set of obligations, it was time for Omar to make suggestions. "Here's what I think, Abdoulaye. No one person can fill the shoes of our father. We should share his burden. I'll officiate the major rituals—the protection of the village, the rain dance—and when I'm in residence, I'll see people, perform divination, and try to fix their problems. If you agree, you'll be the healer here. You know more about sickness than I do. If there is need for a possession ceremony, you can organize it and perform the rituals. If there's a big problem while I'm away, you can phone me, and I'll come immediately. That's how we can try to honor our father and meet our obligations." Omar paused a long moment. "What do you think?"

Abdoulaye's large, round face looked particularly massive that morning. He took a sip of his coffee and smiled at Omar. "That's what I've been thinking. Most older brothers in your situation would take total control. I'm honored that you want to share the obligations with me. I accept the responsibility. I have no resentment toward you. In truth, I wanted to succeed Issaka Dia. We all wanted to take on his burden. He wisely left it to you, and you have moved forward with good sense."

"I'm happy you feel that way, Abdoulaye."

Abdoulaye nodded. Their map had been drawn. They would try to follow it as best they could.

On the day of Omar's departure, he packed his things, making sure to take a number of black capes, shirts, trousers, and turban cloth—sohanci clothes—with him to Paris. For the first time in months, he slipped on his muted gray suit—traveling clothes that he'd wear for his return. Several days earlier, Omar had arranged for Garba Hima, the chauffeur, to take him to Niamey, where he hoped to visit his older sister before going to the airport to board the midnight flight to Paris.

Garba arrived just after the mid-afternoon prayer, the hottest time of day. By now, Omar's body had adjusted to the stifling heat of Niger's hot season. Dressed in a loose shirt and gray trousers, Garba walked into the compound and greeted everyone. When he got to Omar, he bowed a bit.

"Sohanci Omar, I pay my respects."

"Thank you, Garba."

The family surrounded Omar. His stepmother Maymouna recited the praise poetry of the family's ancestor, Sonni Ali Ber.

Si flies in the night.
Si flies when the rooster crows
Si Baru....

The recitation this time, though, seemed more heartfelt than the one Omar had received months earlier. Though he wanted to smile at such recognition from such a social critic, Omar quashed his desire to do so. Even Seydou, his disgraced younger brother, came by to pay his respects.

"Sohanci Omar, may you travel with God's protection. May the spirits bring you back to us quickly and safely," he said.

"Amin," Omar said with no small amount of satisfaction.

Abdoulaye's children stuffed Omar's bags in the trunk of Garba's car, and in no time at all, they were careening over the rutted tracks that would lead them to the paved road and eventually to Niamey, Niger's capital city.

When they finally reached the relatively smooth contours of the paved road, they came upon a police checkpoint, a common site in the Nigerien countryside. They slowed down and two policemen, carrying machine guns, approached the car. They came over to Omar's open window.

Extending their open hands through the window, one after the other, they greeted Omar. "We pay our respects, Sohanci Omar. Travel with God's grace."

"Amin," Omar said.

With that they signaled for Garba to proceed. They encountered four more police stops and received at each of them a flurry of respectful greetings.

When, at dusk, they finally rolled into the outskirts of Niamey, Garba admitted that he liked traveling with Omar. "They usually ask me for my papers, and most times, I have to pay a small bribe to get through the checkpoint. That didn't happen on our first trip—probably because they saw you as an official. This time they feared and respected you, Sohanci Omar, just as they feared and respected Issaka Dia."

They drove into Niamey without further conversation. Pedestrians, donkeys, camels, and cars clogged the road. A low cloud of dust hung above the city. "We should go to the research center, Garba." Omar had arranged to meet his sister there.

They drove past the Palais de Congres, which had majestic views of the Niger River, and turned up a road that climbed an embankment on which the museum and zoo were located. Skirting by the French Cultural Center, they came upon the clutter and confusion of Le Petit Marche, where vendors sold, among many things, fresh vegetables, meat, and fish. Clogged in traffic, they reached the research center for the oral tradition, a two-story structure in which offices and lecture halls had been built around a courtyard.

Garba parked his car. Omar walked to a gate that led to the main lecture center, a spacious rectangular room with a long conference table. Salamatou sat hunched over the table, reading a book.

"The scholar never rests," Omar said.

She looked up. "Omar, at last we have a little time."

"At last, older sister. At last."

"Why didn't you come to see me here in Niamey? You know the difficulties I have in Tillaberi."

"Once I got there, I couldn't leave."

Salamatou nodded her massive head, around which she had rolled a shimmering black headscarf. Although Salamatou was a very large woman, her face looked like a fine statue—smooth forehead, straight nose, large round eyes, thin lips, and a finely chiseled jaw and chin. "Understood. You're the oldest son, after all. The tension must have been sharp, no?"

"At first, things go hot up there."

"I bet they did, but I also heard that you rose to the challenge. Now you're the sohanci of Tillaberi. Your life will never be the same."

"As always, older sister, you understand perfectly," Omar stated. "Do you have some time for dinner before my flight?"

Salamatou stood up. "You'll eat at my house."

"Wonderful. We'll take my taxi there."

They walked into a poorly maintained courtyard—the ferns and banana trees needed more water, and trash had been left in one corner. In one pot, a red-flowering plant had wilted. Salamatou looked at Omar looking at the courtyard. "What can we do? It's a poor country."

"True."

"But we're wealthy in traditions. Our father was one of the great ones, wasn't he?"

"They don't make them like that anymore."

"That's the truth?" she said.

When Salamatou returned to Niger from Paris, she became one of the most distinguished oral historians in West Africa. For her research, she had tape-recorded, transcribed, and translated the most important epics in West Africa. Steeped in knowledge, she was a repository of traditional wisdom. When they talked, Salamatou would always tell Omar that he was lucky to have a wife like Chantal. Although she had never met Omar's children, she always remembered their birthdays, sent them expensive gifts, and would always talk to them when she phoned Omar in Paris. Salamatou never married and had no children, but she would give financial support to promising students who didn't have the wherewithal to attend the university.

They drove through the now darkened streets of Niamey. Along the sandy byways that paralleled the streets, dim neon lights outlined shop entrances. Lanterns illuminated rough-hewn tables filled with cigarette packages, kola nuts, and chewing gum. Children played amid piles of trash and puddles of discarded dishwater. On the street corners, teenage boys roasted mutton on grills—a metal barrel, top and bottom removed, covering a fire and topped with a mesh of metal lathing.

They finally came to Salamatou's house, which was hidden from the street by an eight-foot cement wall. Inside the walls, the compound grounds were barren, except for a few acacia trees here and there. Beyond a sand-stained white veranda, on which a table had been set for dinner, stood the house, a one-level villa with four rooms.

"I spend too much of my time at the research center, and with what they pay me, Omar, I can't really look after the house."

Omar shrugged. "I'm just happy to be here with you."

"I do have a very good cook, Omar. For that I'm grateful." She turned toward the house. "Ali," she said, "we're ready. Set one more plate for my brother's driver."

A tall gangly man, perhaps 25 years old and dressed in jeans and sleeveless white tee shirt, emerged from the house and set one more plate. Ali more than met the expectations that Salamatou set for him. He brought them a large platter of grilled vegetables—squash, peppers, some hot, some mild—which was complemented by another large platter of grilled chicken, sautéed onions, and fries.

"This is good, Ali. Can you bring us water, juice, and beer?" Salamatou asked.

Ali returned with Coca-Cola, a plastic container of juice, as well as a cooler filled with Flag beer, one of the Omar's favorites. "Enjoy the feast," Salamatou said as she poured herself some fruit juice and added some ice.

Omar had always admired Salamatou's intellect, especially her wealth of knowledge about African traditions. Like Omar, she had lived in two worlds. Omar's solution to such a life had been to maintain a great distance—a buffer really—between the old and new worlds. Paris had been a great place to do so. Losing himself in his work on African literature and ensconced in his busy Parisian life, Omar had thought little about the texture of life in Niger. In the end, his wholesale denial had afforded him a sweet life. Salamatou hadn't had that. She received her doctorate in ethno-linguistics. Her thesis explored traditional African philosophy, which meant that she had always thought about the central issues of life in Africa. Her work was much appreciated by scholars in Europe but not so much by her African colleagues who felt that her studies had no practical utility. As a consequence, she labored alone. The dissonance between the old and the new worlds racked Salamatou with much existential pain.

Soon after her triumphal return from Paris, a previous government, considering her strong-willed intellectualism as a political threat, assigned her to a post in Maine Soroa, a small outpost on the edge of Lake Chad, which was more than 1500 kilometers from the capital city. She was told to "inspect" primary schools, a subject she knew little about. Cut off from her own people, the Songhay, who lived in the western regions of the country and from the university libraries of the capital city, she found herself isolated from family and friends.

Eventually, a sympathetic colleague arranged for her to be hired by the Organization of African Unity (OAU), which had in Niamey its Center for Research on the Linguistics and the Oral Tradition. She began to teach and continued her research. Her work left little time for her personal life. In time, Salamatou became Center's director, but her strong opinions about politics made her tenure a short one. Dissatisfied with her administrative performance, a team of evaluators demoted her. She became a senior researcher, and out of loyalty and respect for her scholarship, the OAU paid her a modest salary.

Salamatou raised her glass. "I offer a toast to our family and a toast to you, Omar. You've made me very proud. Let's make sure we see one another more often."

Omar raised his bottle of beer, and they toasted.

Garba and Omar silently savored their food. Salamatou talked about griots and the repository of oral memory in West Africa. She went on and on about the great epics of the Masina in Mali and the Garuol in Western Niger. "None better," she said. "Just three months ago I found an old man who recited the entire epic of Mali Bero. That founder of the Zarma people was a wise man. There is much we could learn today from his words…so much."

Salamatou shifted her talk to the modern griots, African filmmakers. The filmmakers, Salamatou said, used a contemporary art form to perform the same tasks of the traditional West African bard. As she was going on and on about film and memory, Salamatou suddenly stopped talking, gripped the edge of the dinner table, and squinted at Omar. "I almost forgot, Omar, why do I bother to extol to you the virtues of traditional African beliefs? You are no longer an African scholar living in France. You are a sohanci, a master of the social and spirit worlds in Niger." Salamatou paused a moment. "How will you walk your path, younger brother? Hasn't your mind been poisoned by both worlds?"

Salamatou's questions hit home. Omar's mind had been poisoned by its exposure to two worlds. He had used denial to dull the toxicity. "In the past I suffered like you have, older sister," Omar stated. "But Issaka Dia always looked after me. He made sure that my pain would never imprison me. Issaka Dia healed me. I'm whole again, older sister. It doesn't matter anymore if I live in two worlds. Do you know the proverb: 'one foot cannot follow two paths'?"

"Indeed, I do. It is the theme of my life, brother."

"If your heart is whole, the paths converge and you walk forward. Issaka Dia taught me that."

"How can you heal the heart?" Salamatou asked, her face set in a deep frown.

"Through love. It takes time, but if you let me help you, we'll try to heal your heart. Issaka Dia taught me how to do it."

Salamatou stood up. Arms and legs shaking, she came over to Omar. He stood up, and they hugged.

"Thank you, brother. I do need your help. Don't forget about me."

"I won't, older sister. I'll be coming back. I'll leave some medicines here."

Omar turned to Garba. "Could you bring my small bag?"

Seconds later, the driver retrieved the bag. Omar pulled out a small black satchel and gave it to Salamatou. "Take three measures of this green powder and put it in a mug of warm milk. Drink one mug in the morning and one mug before you go to sleep. It's a good medicine for the heart, older sister."

"You're a true sohanci, Omar Dia, a true sohanci! Issaka Dia taught you well. You'll bear well the sorcerer's burden."

When Garba dropped Omar off at the airport, the baggage handlers treated him with great deference.

"Let me take your bag, Sohanci. We have such respect for you and your father. May he rest peacefully among the ancestors."

The Air France officials processed his tickets and boarding passes with unaccustomed efficiency and then bumped him up to the first class.

"We're happy to be of service, Sohanci Omar. Our condolences on the death of your father. He was a great man, and we pray that you carry on in his spirit."

Omar thanked them quietly and moved on to the police and customs officials, who greeted him warmly and respectfully and quickly stamped his passport.

In the waiting lounge, the passengers gathered. There was a group of Europeans returning home from a business trip. Omar noticed a cluster of Chinese diplomats or perhaps technical specialists headed back to China by way of Paris. There was also an assortment of Americans, wearing cotton shirts, jeans, and baseball caps. The Nigerien passengers huddled in one corner of the lounge, speaking French, Songhay, and Hausa. Gradually, they came over to Omar's spot and offered greetings.

"Sohanci Omar, we are honored to greet you."

"Sohanci Omar, we knew your father—our condolences. May God protect you."

One man, tall and thin and dressed in loose white shirt and gray dress trousers, came over. "Can I get you some water or a coca?"

Omar politely declined.

"We're happy you are with us tonight."

"Thank you," Omar said.

They boarded, and the flight took off, flying north over the Sahara. After a few hours of flight, Omar stared out the window and saw the flickering lights of the Mediterranean coast. Soon they would be over Europe and fly into another reality. Omar didn't know what to expect, but he knew that with the help of Issaka Dia, his path would open—and open widely.

CHAPTER 26

Just before sunrise, Omar's plane landed at Charles de Gaulle airport. It was a misty morning and the fog-shrouded airport buildings looked eerie. Omar walked into the terminal, got his passport stamped, retrieved his luggage, and put himself into the taxi line. The damp chill of Parisian air shot through his body. Although he had pulled out his warm jacket, he shivered as he waited for a ride home. He had told Chantal that he'd be home for breakfast—it was a Saturday and the kids would be there. Omar didn't want a "public" reunion at the airport. He had always loathed public reunions. If he had learned anything from Issaka Dia, it was that a person should approach pivotal moments with cool resolve. That's what he wanted to do. He wanted to let things unfold as naturally as possible.

His driver turned out to be Idrissa, an African immigrant from Ouagadougou, Burkina Faso.

Omar told him that he was from Niger and was returning to Paris.

"Where in Niger?" the driver asked.

"Tillaberi," he answered

"My uncle traveled there once," he said.

"What a small world," Omar said, very much amused. "I've just returned from my father's funeral. My name is Omar Dia."

"My condolences, Monsieur Dia."

The clogged highway led them slowly into the outskirts of Paris, marked by tall ugly buildings distinguished by garish neon signs spelling out corporate names: DARTY, SONY, and so on. Headed to his home in the 11th arrondissement, they entered Paris proper through Belleville. "I love the architecture of Paris," Omar said.

"Your family is here?"

"My wife and children are here." Omar answered. Before his trip to Niger, that response would have concluded his answer. "But most of my family still lives in Tillaberi."

"What do you do?"

"I'm a professor at the Sorbonne."

The man chuckled. "Your father did a good job for you?"

Omar smiled back. "He's still looking after me."

When they arrived at Omar's address, the driver got his client's bags out of the trunk. Omar gave him a big tip.

"Let me help you with your things. I'll put the flashers on."

"I'd be very grateful."

They lugged Omar's bags up to the apartment. Wanting some measure of privacy, Omar asked the driver to deposit the bags in front of the door.

"Perhaps I'll look you up sometime, Professor Dia. May God protect you."

"May God will it."

Not knowing what to expect, Omar knocked on the door. Dressed in her characteristic black slacks and white top, Chantal stood motionless in the doorway—so thin and stiff. Omar crossed the threshold. She immediately relaxed and threw her arms around him.

"I'm so glad you're back, Omar. I didn't know if you were coming back."

Looking into Chantal's moist eyes, Omar said, "I'm back, Chantal. I'm really back." The look of the apartment hadn't changed—the same arrangement of furniture and the same aromatic traces of French cooking—onions, garlic, *fines herbes*. "Where are the kids?"

"It's early. They're still in bed."

"I'll go and wake them."

Up to that moment, Omar had been a rather preoccupied father. In truth, he had been more concerned about the flow of his next lecture than with the direction of Lilly's and Adam's childhood. Omar had decided that that was going to change. He tiptoed into the bedroom the children shared—Lilly's things on the left, Adam's on the opposite side. Like a visiting African, Omar softly clapped his hands three times. The kids stirred from deep sleep, opening their eyes.

Lilly, seven years old with a café au lait skin and braided hair, rolled out of bed and jumped into Omar's arms.

"Papa," she said, "you're back."

"I am, Lilly."

"Good," she said, giving him a big hug.

The commotion woke Adam, who, at 10, was more reserved and per-haps a bit more resentful about Omar's absence. He came up to Omar tentatively. Like his sister, he had café au lait skin. Tall for his age and skinny, he hugged Omar, but not tightly.

"I'm so glad to see you, Adam."

"Don't ever go away for so long again, Papa. Never again."

"I may have to go away from time to time," Omar told him. "But from now on we will take long trips together—as a family."

"Good," he said. "Next time I want to go to Africa."

"You will, son. You will." Chantal stood in the hallway, tears stream-ing down her face. "Kids," he said, "I've brought you things from Niger. Want to see?"

He led his children into the living room, unzipped his smaller bag, and pulled out a small doll dressed in brightly patterned print cloth. "This doll is for you, Lilly."

Taking the doll into her arms, she beamed.

He then showed Adam a small leather satchel attached to a cord.

"What's that, Papa?"

"It's a wallet."

"Doesn't look like a wallet."

Omar demonstrated how to separate the two parts of the satchel, revealing a hidden compartment where a person could keep coins or paper money.

Adam took it and put it around his neck. "But it needs money, Papa."

They all burst out laughing. Omar gave Adam a few coins, which he put into his new wallet. He brought out a few other items he had bought for the kids—some silver earrings, shaped like the Southern Cross, for Lilly and a slingshot for Adam.

"We'll go to the park, and I'll show you how to use it, Adam. When we go to Niger, you'll take it with you and use it in the bush."

Omar pulled out a box and gave it to Chantal. She lifted out silver necklace shaped like a crescent, a rare form of the famous Croix d'Agadez that Tuareg smiths crafted. "Thank you, Omar," she said, putting it on. "It's beautiful."

She turned to the kids. "Your father is tired from his trip. Go and play in your room, and we'll all have breakfast soon."

The kids scampered away, leaving Omar and Chantal alone.

"Some coffee?" Chantal asked.

"I could use some strong coffee."

Chantal gave him a mug of steaming French roast and frowned a bit. "You hurt us, Omar. You didn't write. You didn't phone. It was as if you dropped off the edge of the world."

Omar took a sip of coffee. "I offer no excuses. Gifts and promises can't replace the pain. I'm sorry that I hurt you. But I'm back now..."

"You do seem a bit different."

"I am different. One day you'll understand my silence."

"I'm not sure I can fully forgive you, Omar."

"I hope you will."

"So tell me what happened?"

"My father died, and I became his successor, which means I've become the sohanci of Tillaberi, Niger."

"What does that mean?"

"It means that I'm a spiritual guardian for the people there and that I'm supposed to help people wherever I might be."

"But you're an atheist."

"I'm now someone who takes on other people's pain." He explained to Chantal how he was thrown into a maelstrom of family conflict—the spite of his father's second wife and the derision of his younger brothers. Omar told her of his bond with Abdoulaye and of their healing forays into the bush. He described the conversations he had had with Issaka Dia. "His very last act was to give me his sisiri, his power, which I took into my body, marking me as his successor." Omar recounted the 40 days of mourning, the stories of his father's exploits, and the cleansing ceremony.

Chantal didn't know what to say. A surge of curiosity broke her silence. "You carry metal chains in your stomach?"

"I do."

She shook her head. "That's impossible. They should poison you."

"My father had them, and he lived to be nearly 100."

"It can't be."

"It is. You and the kids will come to Niger and begin to see for yourself."

"You never wanted us to visit your family in Niger. Why now?"

"Two reasons. I want our children to know their Songhay relatives. I want them to be able to speak Songhay and know the land of their ancestors. I want you to know me fully. You can't do that unless you come with me to Niger, to Tillaberi."

"I've always wanted to go...but..."

"I want to go this summer when the kids are out of school."

"What do I do about my job?"

"You're a doctor. Take a leave. Your doctoring will be much appreciated in Tillaberi."

"You're serious, aren't you?"

"I am, Chantal. I have obligations, and I'll need to be in Tillaberi for periods of time, mostly, I hope, with you and the kids."

"But it's such a change."

"For the good, Chantal. My relatives want to welcome you as one of them. Things are good there now that Abdoulaye and I are the family elders. Everyone is eager to meet Lilly and Adam. There's so much I want to show and teach them in Niger."

"And what about your life here in Paris?"

"I'll take up my teaching. I'll continue to write. But it will be different. I'll become more involved in the African community. Now that I am my father's successor, I want to help my brothers and sisters here."

"What do you plan to do?" she asked.

"I'm not sure yet, but something." Omar realized that he had put way too much existential food on Chantal's plate, but he needed to finish. "I want to arrange for a Songhay-speaking nanny for the kids. I like that Maria speaks to them in Spanish, but I want them to learn my language. I also want to arrange a tutor for you, Chantal."

Chantal put down her coffee cup. "I liked our life before, Omar. Yes, you were sometimes preoccupied. Sometimes, when I talked, I felt you were humoring me, that what I had to say was unimportant to you. Sometimes, I felt like you needed to pay more attention to the kids. Sometimes, your discomfort with Africa and your family angered me. I wanted to know more of your African side." She held Omar's hand. "But I liked our life here in Paris. And now after a long absence in which you didn't write or phone, you return a new man who suddenly wants to change our way of life."

"Not exactly."

"Sounds like that to me. It would be nice for Lilly and Adam to learn Songhay and spend their summers in Tillaberi. Remember, they also have family in France. Remember that I have a profession and that, everyday, I help people. I like my work, and I won't be able to keep my very good job if I take off for three months every summer."

"You can't be sure about that, can you?"

"That's not the point. The point is that you need to think more sensitively about others—not just yourself."

"I thought that's what I was trying to do," Omar said, his frustration mounting. He held on to her hand. "All I ask is that you give it a try. If it works out, that will be wonderful. You can't know the pressure of the sorcerer's burden—500 years of healing."

"Omar," she said tersely, "I'm not so sure."

"Look, I understand how difficult all of this is, but these spiritual obligations are important to me. Try to accept them. I'm committed to you and the kids. I love you all so much and don't want to be apart from you. Please, give it a chance to work."

Chantal's body softened. She let out a deep breath of air. "I'm willing to try. For the sake of our love and for the sake of our family, I'll try."

CHAPTER 27

In the ensuing weeks, Omar's family slipped back into a routine. Chantal put in her time at the hospital, the kids continued with school, and Omar worked on a series of lectures that he would give at the Sorbonne before the end of the academic year. His colleagues had kindly granted him an emergency leave with pay to tend to Issaka Dia's illness, death, and funeral. Even though Omar had returned before the end of term, his colleagues didn't expect him to teach until the fall. In gratitude, Omar volunteered to give a series of lectures on the oral tradition. The lectures, he told his colleagues, would reflect some new thinking, inspired by his trip to Niger, about literature and the African experience.

On the weekends, the family took walks in the Parc Monceau or the Parc des Buttes de Chaumont. Their favorite biking spot was the Bois de Boulogne, which had a vast and intricate array of trails. Along the way, they'd stop for lunch, a soda, or an ice cream. Sometimes Omar went with Adam to the local swimming pool to watch him practice. The coach told Omar that with proper training Adam could become a highly competitive swimmer. Lilly liked to dance, and Omar would sometimes take her to ballet classes, where he was usually the only male present.

Omar hired a young Nigerien, Salmu, to work for them. She was a 22-year-old economics student from Karma, a town midway between Tillaberi and Niamey. In addition to French and Songhay, she spoke excellent English. She was tall, thin, pretty, and proper, always dressed in rather modest jeans and a loose blouse. The kids adored her, and she loved them. She worked during the evenings and on weekends and would accompany them on excursions into the city. Because she spoke to the kids in Songhay, they began to learn the language, which made Omar look forward to the day he might speak to them in his mother tongue. Omar also hired a tutor for Chantal. Although her erratic emergency room schedule didn't permit regular classes, Chantal had always been a disciplined and energetic person. When she made a commitment to try something, she would always see it through. She met with the tutor when she could and, like the children, began to speak a little bit of Songhay. Her efforts filled Omar with gratitude and love.

Even though work depleted her energy, Chantal maintained her good humor, and Omar did his best to make her life sweet. Salmu and Omar made sure the house was neat and clean, and they combined efforts to prepare sumptuous African meals—meat in bitter leaf sauce; rice, chicken, and okra sauce; chicken in sesame sauce; as well as Chantal's two favorites, chicken in squash sauce and couscous with lamb and vegetables savored with spicy harissa.

One evening, after a long messy day at the hospital—a serious car accident—Chantal came home exhausted. Once in the living room, she plopped down in the leather easy chair and kicked off her shoes. Omar immediately brought her a glass of white burgundy—a bottle from her favorite producer and a good year to boot.

She took a deep sip. "It's delicious, Omar. It's just the way I like it— slightly tart with a trace of melon." She took another sip and sniffed the air. "I smell a French meal tonight. Is it beef bourguignon?"

"It is, Madame Dia," Salmu answered. "I followed a recipe."

"Whose?"

"An American woman named Julia Child."

"Oh, that funny lady," Chantal said. "That's a good recipe."

"We'll serve a red burgundy wine with the main course," Omar interjected.

Chantal continued to sip her wine. "I'm beginning to like this new life."

As the weeks slipped by, Omar continued to develop his oral tradition lectures. Chantal worked at the hospital. The kids went to school, ate Salmu's delicious food, and bantered a bit in Songhay. Despite these activities, Omar was still trying to find his Parisian legs. He spent time in his study but also began to write at his café, Le Chope, which was just down the street from the apartment. In time a few students found him in the café, a discovery that led to informal discussions about African filmmakers like Ousmane Sembène. Omar also attended several lectures at the Sorbonne and at L'École des Hautes Études en Sciences Sociales. There he met several colleagues and debated the whys and wherefores of French philosophy. Omar very much enjoyed this intellectual routine, which he had missed in Tillaberi. Even so, he soon realized that the Parisian intellectual life could no longer sustain him.

Early one evening after a lecture on the impact of global technology on the West African griot, Omar exited the Metro at the Bastille to walk home. The sidewalks were filled with people sitting outside, enjoying a coffee, tea, or beer. As he walked down the rue de Rivoli passing a variety of antique and furniture shops, the crowds thinned a bit. When he reached rue de Charonne, he turned left and began the gradual assent to his building. There were diverse groups of people on the street: young French girls, their hair dyed purple, wearing short leather mini-skirts, nose rings adorning their nostrils; heavy-set young men atop their motorcycles talking trash to one another; groups of slender Chinese, both men and women, dressed in loose-fitting dark clothing, scurrying around the sidewalks, looking nervous and lost; portly Arab men gesturing wildly in front of a Turkish kebob house; and groups of African men and women, most of them tall and lean, walking swiftly up and down the sidewalk. Some of them stared at Omar. A few greeted him in Wolof, a language he didn't understand.

Suddenly, Omar felt a tug on his sleeve and recognized a greeting in Songhay. "Omar Dia, how goes the early evening?" said the voice of a woman.

He turned to find a large woman dressed in a wraparound skirt and matching top. A scarf covered her hair. She was the very same woman who had, months earlier, stopped him on the street to ask for help. He had failed her miserably. What had become of her? What had become of her daughter who was so very sick? Omar's old self would have found an excuse to run away, but now he felt differently. "It goes well, madam," Omar said.

"And your father?"

"Issaka Dia has passed away," he answered. "I've just come back from his funeral."

"Issaka Dia was a great man."

"That he was, madam." The woman looked troubled. "How goes it with your daughter?"

"It's the same with her, Omar Dia…" She paused a moment. Then her eyes widened. "Should I call you Sohanci Omar?"

"You can if you like."

"Are you your father's successor?"

"I am."

"What are you doing in France?" "I hope to walk my family's path in France as well as Niger."

She hunched over and began to cry. "God has brought you to me, Sohanci Omar. I'm afraid my daughter will die soon. She's been to every clinic and has seen many doctors. They give her medicine, but nothing seems to work. I took her to Senegalese marabouts."

"They are strong," Omar interjected.

"Not as strong as the Songhay sohanci." She took his arm. "Can you help us, Sohanci Omar?"

"I'll try. Your name?"

"Hadiza Fari. Come with me to see my daughter."

She led Omar into a courtyard that he had passed many times on his walks in the neighborhood. Omar followed Hadiza down a concrete slope to a large rectangular space that was filled with plastic and tin garbage cans. Children played amid soapy pools of discarded dishwater. Dressed in long shirts covering trousers or in the boubous, men clustered in small groups and talked. Women, some with babies tied to their backs, squatted around large basins as they washed clothes. One large woman sat on a stool as she cooked beignets. It smelled and looked like Africa.

Bordering the courtyard, there were six stories of what appeared to be small apartments, the doors of which stood back from a balcony. Sheets hanging from the balcony railing fluttered in the evening breeze.

"What is this place?" Omar asked Hadiza.

"It is owned by a West African brotherhood. Everyone here is from Senegal or Mali. We're the only ones from Niger."

"Are they Muslims?"

"Every one. We pay rent to an association, and they take care of the rest."

"It's like an African village," Omar said, "right in the middle of Paris."

"Yes," she agreed. "It's like a village. The gossip is terrible. You can't keep a secret."

"I know about that," Omar said.

They climbed up a trash-strewn stairwell to the fifth floor. Hadiza opened the door, revealing a small one-room apartment. Hadiza's daughter, Rabi, lay on a cot covered by a thin blanket. The cot had been placed against one of the whitewashed walls.

"Hello," she said in a barely audible voice.

One small window provided little light or fresh air. Hadiza cooked on a hot plate. A small table was used to eat or drink coffee. Hadiza's bed, another cot, stood opposite that of Rabi. It was covered with a particularly beautiful Songhay blanket—white, red, and black geometric patterns woven into a white background. "Is that a tera-tera blanket?" Omar asked.

"Yes. I'm from Tera."

"My ancestors originally came from that part of Niger."

"I know about your ancestors, Sohanci Omar."

There was no toilet, shower, or sink in the apartment. The walls were bare except for clothing hanging from nails that had been planted in the wall.

Observing Omar's observation, Hadiza frowned. "Our life is difficult here. I have to wash clothes and dishes in the courtyard, and we've got to use the community showers and toilets. They're on every floor."

"You don't get a lot of fresh air in here," Omar observed.

Hadiza put a kettle on the hot plate. "Sit down. I'll make us some tea."

"That would be lovely," Omar said, looking in Rabi's direction. "Can I talk with your daughter?"

"Of course."

Omar took the chair and placed it next to Rabi's bed. He greeted her in Songhay and told her his name.

"I'll try to sit up," she said. She managed to pull herself up and sit on the edge of the cot. "I'm not well, Sohanci Omar."

She looked like a famine victim. Her cheeks had lost their elasticity, and her collarbone stuck out boldly from her neck and shoulders. Her arms looked like sticks, and her skin had lost its luster. "Can you eat?"

"I try, but it doesn't usually stay down. I drink tea, and Mother makes me millet porridge. I can sometimes eat that."

"What do the doctors say?"

"They don't know what's wrong with me. I'm 23 years old, and they've never seen anyone like me." She began to weep. "I'm so tired, Sohanci Omar. I've had so many tests, but now they've given up on me. Last month, I was in the hospital. They gave me treatments. They put a needle into my arm and dripped medicine into me. I stayed there for two weeks. After that, they said there was nothing more they could do. They sent me home—to die."

Omar took her hand. "Rabi, I'll do what I can for you. You and your mother must come to my house on Sunday, the day of the spirits. Do you understand?"

"Yes."

"I live right up the street. You come, and we'll see what can be done."

Omar turned around to Hadiza. "I live at 72, rue de Charonne. Come on Sunday around 4:00 p.m. Maybe we can see what's really going on." Omar stood up.

Hadiza extended her hands to him "Thank you, Sohanci Omar. Thank you."

Omar squeezed her hands. "See you on Sunday."

Omar returned home to discover that Salmu had made another sumptuous African meal—chicken in sesame sauce, his favorite. Lilly and Adam both greeted him in Songhay, which gave him great pleasure. Soon Chantal would be home from the hospital, and they could look forward to a quiet evening. Before dinner, he went to his study to consider what could be done. In the universe of the sohanci, there are no accidents or coincidences. Stumbling upon Hadiza had been a sign, marking a fork on the path. She led him in a direction, which he had followed. Omar knew what had to be done. He would convert his study into a consultation room and have it ready by Sunday, the time of his first appointment. By then, everything would be in its rightful place.

CHAPTER 28

When Chantal got home that evening, the family sat down to dinner. So far the new arrangements had worked well. Salmu did the shopping, cooking, and much of the childcare, which meant that Chantal could focus on her work and relax when she got home. She liked the fact that Salmu had been teaching the children Songhay. Her own lessons had been infrequent, but stimulating. She had never been particularly good at learning languages, but for some reason she seemed to pick up Songhay. She had already mastered the complex set of greetings and could make rudimentary requests—for some food items and other matters.

They were also spending a lot of time together as a family, which pleased Chantal and Omar. Omar thought that Chantal now considered him an attentive husband and father, which translated into wonderful sex. Even so, he wasn't sure how she would respond to having a "spirit hut" in their Parisian apartment. Learning some Songhay was one thing, but having a continuous stream of West Africans showing up for consultations with Sohanci Omar was quite another. Omar wanted to see people on Thursdays and Sundays—Songhay spirit days. For Thursday consultations, Chantal would be at work. Sunday might be a problem, though. For the French, including, of course, Chantal, Sundays were sacrosanct—a time for people to enjoy their families in the privacy of their home.

After they began to eat the delicious chicken in sesame sauce, Omar recounted his encounter with Hadiza. He told them of the deplorable conditions in the "African village" down the street. He described Rabi's serious health concerns.

"Has she seen a doctor?" Chantal asked.

"They can't figure out what's wrong with her. She's been through a battery of tests."

"I'd be happy to go over there and examine her," Chantal said.

Omar cleared his throat. "I invited them to come over Sunday afternoon—4:00 p.m."

"Isn't that family time, Omar?"

"It is. But you should see this poor girl. Besides, she may be suffering from something beyond the reach of modern medicine."

"What are you talking about, Omar?"

"I've seen cases like this in Niger," he stated in a calm and even voice. "My father taught me how to treat these kinds of sickness."

Chantal sipped her wine. "Do you want us to leave when they come?"

"No. I'd like you to meet them. It would be great if you could examine her before I consult with them."

"Are you becoming a doctor?"

"No, Chantal. In time, you'll understand."

"I'd be happy to examine the girl on Sunday." She took another sip of wine. "Any other announcements?"

"Yes. I'm going to make some changes to my study to make it look more like a space where Africans consult healers—just a few changes so I can do both academic and sohanci work there."

"Nothing scary, I hope."

"Nothing scary."

Omar set out to build a Parisian style spirit hut. At an Asian import store, he bought some woven thatch and some bamboo poles. Once properly supplied, Omar hired the neighborhood carpenter, Monsieur Dupont, whom he knew from time spent at the corner café. Monsieur Dupont came by on Saturday, his day off, to build the consultation hut. To avoid the commotion, Chantal, Salmu, and the kids went shopping on the rue de Rivoli.

"Why do you want to build a hut in your apartment?" Monsieur Dupont asked with genuine curiosity.

"It has to do with my family," Omar said.

"Well, the kids will enjoy playing in it."

"Exactly so. It will give them a taste of what it's like to live in Africa."

"Good idea."

Monsieur Dupont was a short, rotund man of 60 years or so with a head full of unkempt red hair and a bushy beard. He would set the spirit hut into the far corner of the room. He bent and attached the bamboo to the wall and to the floor, creating the skeleton of the hut. They then unrolled the thatch and attached it to the bamboo posts. It took him only two hours or so to build it. Omar put a palm frond mat down on the hut's floor space and placed two wooden stools opposite one another on either side of the mat. "This is terrific, Dupont."

"I think so, too, Dia."

Omar paid him and they left together. Dupont returned home. Omar went to the hardware store on the Boulevard Voltaire to find a shallow container into which he could pour sand. He quickly found a suitable candidate and bought a bag of beige-colored sand—to mimic the sand found in the Tillaberi spirit hut. Once he had poured sand into the container and spread it out, preparations would be nearly complete. Omar had brought a few of his "work" things from Niger—a black satchel of divinatory shells, one Dongo hatchet, and several small clay pots. He put them into the hut. To make things a tad more African, he hung two Nigerien blankets on the wall, making a collection of three in the study. It wasn't the real spirit hut, but it would do just fine for working in Paris.

Omar sat in the spirit hut for some time, perhaps more than an hour, soaking up its ambiance. Eventually, the door opened and he heard voices: the kids were laughing. Chantal told them to put down their bags.

"Where's Papa?" Lilly asked.

"In his office. Come and check it out," Omar said.

Moments later, Lilly came in and shrieked in delight. "Papa, is it a tent? Can I play in it?"

Adam ran in and clapped his hands. "Papa, it's very cool. We're the only kids in Paris who have a hut in their house."

"That's right, Adam."

"Can I invite my friends over to play in it?"

"Of course."

Adam jumped up and down and turned around in circles.

Chantal walked up to the doorway. "OH MY GOD."

"Do you like it, Mama?" Lilly asked.

"What is it?" Chantal asked.

"It's a Parisian version of the family's spirit hut. People will come here to consult with me and the hut will comfort them."

"Well, the kids will like it, but I don't understand why we have to have it here."

"This hut," Omar said, "is part of my heritage."

By the time Hadiza and Rabi knocked on the door, everything was ready for the consultation. Omar had gotten the name of Rabi's doctor who faxed Chantal copies of the young girl's medical history. After Chantal had examined Rabi, the girl and her mother would come back to the spirit hut for another set of consultations. As they walked into the salon, their eyes widened. Hadiza cleaned office buildings. Rabi did the same until she was no longer able to work. They had never been in the apartment of prosperous Parisians.

Hadiza bowed to Omar and to Chantal. In a rather broken French, she identified herself and complimented Chantal on the beauty of the surroundings. "You're kind to have us here, Doctor Dia."

"It's Doctor Martin," Chantal said. "We're happy to have you here. Salmu has prepared some tea."

Salmu entered with a tea service platter. Rabi hardly had the strength to sit down, but Omar helped her into a chair. Salmu and the women exchanged greetings in Songhay. To Omar's pleasant surprise, Chantal also greeted them in Songhay.

"Ah, Dr. Martin. You speak Songhay."

"Only a little. I'm trying to learn it."

"How wonderful."

Salmu poured the tea. Hadiza began to sing praise poems about Omar's family, the legacy of Issaka Dia, and how good it was that Sohanci Omar lived in Paris. Salmu translated for Chantal. Omar, of course, had told Chantal the story of his family and the inexplicable feats of Issaka Dia. At the time, she found the tales both fascinating and entertaining. Hadiza's telling, though, seemed to impress her.

Wanting to begin her examination, Chantal asked Hadiza and Omar to give them a bit of privacy. Salmu remained close at hand to translate. Chantal studied Rabi's thick medical file for several moments and looked at the young Nigerien girl.

"You've had a tough time of it," she said. "Staff infections, dysentery, and an ovarian cyst they removed one year ago."

Rabi stared at the floor. "As God is my witness," she said in almost a whisper, "I've had a hard time. I'm grateful to be alive."

Salmu translated.

Chantal continued to study the file. "You healed well. The staff infections cleared up, no more dysentery, and you fully recovered from the operation."

"But I'm so weak. I can hardly move. I'm very sick, Doctor."

Chantal read on. "Your blood test is completely normal. According to this test, you should be energetic—completely well."

"But I'm not, Doctor."

"That I can see, Rabi," Chantal said, tenderly taking Rabi's hand. "Can I take a look at you?"

Rabi looked nervously at her mother.

"It's okay daughter."

"Give us some privacy. I'll use the couch to examine her."

Omar and Hadiza went to his study.

"Great God, Sohanci Omar!" You have a spirit hut. In Paris!!!!"

"I do, Hadiza. You and your daughter will be my first clients. I'll do my best to help you."

Minutes later Chantal helped Rabi walk to the study.

"Mama, a spirit hut."

"Hadiza and Rabi, please sit on the stools in the spirit hut. I'll be with you shortly."

Omar went to the closet and put on his black cape, covering his black tee shirt and black trousers. He put on a cap and wrapped a black turban around it. A wide-eyed Chantal watched him.

"I've never seen these clothes."

"I brought them back. Doctors have lab coats; sohanci have black capes."

"Even though I think all of this is a bit crazy, you look incredibly handsome in your lab coat."

Omar smiled. "I thought you'd think so." They looked at mother and daughter patiently waiting in the spirit hut. "What do you think, Chantal?"

"There is nothing wrong with her as far as I can see. There's no medical condition causing her weakness, but she's wasting away. If she doesn't start to eat more, the internal organs will begin to break down and she'll die. Would you like me to set up a psychiatric consult?"

"Thanks Chantal. Let me try a few things before that."

"Fair enough," she said as she left the study.

Picking up a third stool, Omar looked at mother and daughter who cast furtive glances at one another. He sat down next to them "Give me your hand, sister and daughter." Thus connected, Omar recited the genji how after which the tension seemed to drain from their faces. "Rabi, put your stool in front of the sand." Omar took out his black satchel of cowrie shells, the very ones Issaka Dia used to probe the past, understand the present and see into the future. He took one of the shells and gave it to

Rabi. "Speak to it from your heart. Tell it your desires, your dreams, your hopes, and then spit lightly into it."

Rabi gave the shells back to Omar and he tossed them in his hands as he recited a praise- poem to Nya Beri, a deity, who could probe the past, understand the present, and see into the future. Finished, he spat three times onto the shells and threw them on the sand, waiting for something, an insight, a pattern, a voice. Nothing. He threw them a second time, again without results. On the third throw, Omar understood the situation. He pointed to the configuration, indicating a young man who had a black heart. "Rabi, did you have a boyfriend here in Paris?"

"I did Sohanci Omar. I stopped liking him and told him I didn't want to see him anymore."

"And what happened?"

"He got very angry and said that a woman can't make those decisions."

"Was he from Africa?"

"From Mali."

"When did your problems begin?"

"They began right after our break-up. He kept coming to see me and I refused him. He telephoned, but I wouldn't talk to him. When he saw that I was sick, he stopped bothering me."

Omar pointed to the configuration. "It looks like he has sent you sickness, Rabi and the sickness is in your house. Here's what we need to do. First, I will give you a medicine that you will take morning and night in coffee, tea, or milk. You will take three measures of it and put it in your cup. Don't miss a single dose. Second, I will come to your house on Thursday to find to the sickness, if I can, and destroy it. In case the sickness is in the air, I will spray your house with words and milk to cleanse it of its filth. You must also give me one of your rings, Rabi. I'll put it in my special container. When it's ready, I'll ask you to wear it on the third finger of your left hand." Omar looked at them. "We'll see if this works for you."

Rabi cried. Hadiza touched Omar's hand. "We want to pay you for your time and service, Sohanci Omar."

"I want nothing. You are poor and I cannot take anything from someone who has so little money. If the treatments work, perhaps you could prepare us a Songhay dinner, bring it here, and eat with us."

"May God will it," Hadiza said.

"God is strong," said Rabi.

Omar gave them the medicine and helped Rabi to the hallway. They said their goodbyes to Chantal, the kids, and Salmu.

"Be well, Rabi," Chantal said.

CHAPTER 29

Omar began to thoroughly enjoy his new routine in Paris. He worked on his new lectures. His goal was to chart a new course for his thinking about African literature and representation—something that reflected his experience in Tillaberi. Family life had never been so rewarding. He attended Adam's swimming meets, cheering him on. Adam's stroke had become strong and firm. Sometimes he would win his heat. Lilly's performance as a ballerina-in-training had also become impressive. She was taller than her classmates, but that didn't seem to hinder her progress. Omar looked forward to Lilly's first public performance, which would occur before their departure for Niger.

Rabi, too, had made progress. She had already gained weight and in a few weeks time would be strong enough to return to work. After their initial consultation, Omar had gone to their apartment and discovered a loose floorboard under which he found a small hollowed out goat horn in which there was a gob of substances. "Here is the source of the sickness," Omar announced. "I've got to purify your space."

Carrying a bowl of fresh milk to each corner of the apartment, Omar recited the genji how and sprayed milk to the north, the south, the east, and west. He gave mother and daughter an amulet to keep in a container that they would put in the "center" of their dwelling. Finally, Omar gave Rabi the ring that had soaked in the forces of his ancestors.

Several weeks after the initial consultation, Hadiza and Rabi prepared a Songhay feast and brought it to Omar's apartment: boiled leaves wrapped around peanut butter, millet couscous soaked with sweet milk, baobab leaf sauce over pilaf with *kusu masa*, the slightly burnt crust of rice that comes from the bottom of the pot. They all sat down and feasted, bantering in Songhay and French.

Chantal couldn't get over Rabi's new state of health. "You look wonderful, Rabi." She kept touching her arm, pinching it playfully. "It's really you, right?"

"Oh yes, Doctor. I feel much better."

Hadiza chimed in: "You know what they say in Niger, Madame Doctor.... They say that the work of the sohanci is no game."

"I'm beginning to understand that," Chantal said.

"It's the truth," Hadiza intoned.

"Cimi no," Chantal said repeating Hadiza's proclamation. Everyone applauded.

"You'll do fine in Niger, Doctor Chantal," Hadiza said.

Word soon spread among West Africans in and around Paris that a sohanci from Niger was seeing clients in his home. One might think that, that wouldn't stir widespread interest. After all, each ethnic group in West Africa has its own healing traditions. But for hundreds of years, the sohanci of Songhay had been known far and wide for their extraordinary capacities. In the past, they, like Issaka Dia, traveled great distances to heal the sick, to protect villages, to perform circumcisions, and to enhance the power of chiefs or kings. Word of Omar's presence in Paris quickly brought a steady stream of clients on Thursdays and Sundays. The number of people grew so large that Chantal asked that Omar no longer see people every Sunday. Omar agreed to see clients two Sundays a month.

The onslaught clients may have been tiring, but it also filled Omar with creative energy. Soon enough, the date of his first lecture arrived. Having been advertised one month in advance, Omar thought the lecture might draw a modest crowd. Omar had planned to deliver the lecture at the Sorbonne, but because the subject—the notion of representation and the power of stories—was one that interested a wide assortment of scholars, the talk was scheduled for 5:00 p.m. in a large auditorium at the École des Hautes Études en Sciences Sociales on the Boulevard Raspail. The title of the lecture was "Stories are Forever."

The day of the lecture, a Thursday, Omar saw clients in the morning and ate a light lunch at a bistro in the neighborhood. Late in the afternoon, he took the Metro to the lecture hall, wearing his lecture outfit, a muted gray suit, a white dress shirt, and black loafers—no tie. In the

Metro, he thought of his lecture the previous fall on the cosmopolitanism of la sape and he chuckled to himself. The time he spent with Issaka Dia had changed his thinking about so many subjects.

Omar exited the Metro at the Sevres de Babylon stop, taking in the majesty of the Hotel Letitia, headquarters for the German occupiers during World War II as well as a place where, just after the war, Jews congregated hoping to find—or find out—about lost relatives. That day, he wanted to enjoy a walk along the Boulevard Raspail, one of his favorite streets in Paris. Along the way, he stopped at a café, stood at the bar, and ordered an espresso. Sipping the espresso he felt anonymous, which was good. No one there knew his name. If they were seeing him for the first time, they might think he was a well-dressed African diplomat, or better yet, a soccer player. He enjoyed that brief moment of fantasy and walked on to the classroom building, turned left into a shady courtyard, and strolled to the stage door of the auditorium.

Jean-Pierre Caperan, who, like Omar wrote about comparative literature, opened the door. He was several inches taller than Omar, which made him very tall indeed, but his large, soft shape made his height less imposing. Unlike Omar, he wore rumpled suits and ties that did not match his outfit. His unruly blond hair was thick, long, and usually unwashed, though on that day, it looked like it had received a little bit of attention.

Omar peeked into the room—the din of a full house.

"A very good crowd, Omar. We've missed you in Paris."

"Thanks, Jean-Pierre. I'll do all I can to not disappoint them."

He took Omar's arm. "I'll introduce you. You speak for about 50 minutes and then save 30 minutes or so for discussion."

"That sounds good to me."

They headed out on the stage and people began to applaud. Omar wondered why they would applaud before he had uttered a single word. But they did. Omar was overwhelmed.

Jean-Pierre hunched his shoulders. "They like you already. Maybe this is a 'welcome home' salute."

Jean-Pierre raised his arms to quiet the crowd and soon enough the din died down. "Friends, it is my great pleasure to introduce Professor Omar Dia, a literary theorist whose ideas and works are renowned throughout the world. He is a leading authority on French philosophy, African literature, and African film. His recent work has focused on les sapeurs, the subject of his latest book, *Threading Identities: La Sape in Contemporary Discourse*, which, published only two years ago, has already been translated into five languages. That work is in its 5th printing. As many of you know, Professor Dia returned to Niger earlier in the year to be with his father, who recently died. Today, he wants to talk about the impact of that trip on his thinking about literature, about representation and about the texture of stories....Professor Dia."

Omar stood up to thunderous applause, which, again, he hadn't expected. He took in the crowd, recognizing a few faces here and there. Omar began with Songhay greetings, translated into French.

"My dear friends, I send you late afternoon greetings. I hope your day has gone well, without pain, without too much worry and that you find yourselves in harmony with your world. How goes it with you?"

The crowd caught on. "It goes well. It goes well."

Omar smiled at them. "It goes well with me as well. I want to tell you a story today and it won't take too long so there will be plenty of time for discussion."

> For more than 10 years, I have lived, thought and wrote about the philosophical dimensions of literary theory, applying the insights of French theorists to the study of expressive culture of West Africa. I thought that if I plumbed the nooks and crannies of theory I could valorize African expressive culture, lifting it to same level as European literary efforts. For the longest time, I looked upon that work with a sense of pride, not just for my own efforts but also for the artistry of my cosmopolitan African brothers and sisters.

Here Omar described how a small group of African intellectuals had brilliantly taken the European theories and applied them to African expressive culture, teasing out profound insights about African-being-in-world. Then he returned to the major theme of the lecture.

> Alas, my friends, I ventured onto a different path, as my ancestors used to say, and I now look at things a bit differently. You see, I recently went home to Niger for the first time in many years. Here in Paris, my work on African literature and film received a small degree of recognition. In Niger, no one knew or cared about my lectures, my articles in newspapers, or my books. There, people knew me as Issaka Dia's son, the one lost to us. In rural Niger, many people believe that if you learn a foreign language, you are irrevocably changed. If you speak a foreign language, your mind is no longer pure. You are no longer one of us. Still, because my father, Issaka Dia, was a great healer and, in his own way, a profound philosopher, people owed me respect. I was the son of a great practitioner who had the blood of sorcerers, the blood of the great Sonni Ali Ber, 15th century king of the Songhay Empire, running through his veins.

The lack of recognition angered me. But how could they know about me? Many of my neighbors and relatives were illiterate. And those who could read would rather lose themselves in silly gothic novels than in French philosophy. They would never understand me. They would never understand the philosophical significance of their expressivity.

Then I began to live with my family in our compound on the outskirts of Tillaberi, a rural town that hugs the eastern bank of The Niger River, some 120 kilometers to the north of Niamey, Niger's capital city. The pace of life slowed down. I once again saw hungry and sick children. I saw once again what a struggle it is for people to provide food for their families.

My father invited me to sit and listen to him. He recounted the great stories of our people, The Songhay, and he imparted to me much of the wisdom of our ancestors. Listening to my father convinced me that the path I had been following in France, in Paris, had led me astray. That path had led me to the considerable insights of theory, ideas so powerful that they blinded me to central issues of the human condition—love and loss, courage and cowardice, kindness and greed, desire and obligation. These are the things most human—the things that formed the centerpiece of my father's life, things that he acted on every day, things he tried to bring into a harmonious balance in his little corner of the world. After several conversations, my father seized upon my discomfort.

"You've strayed from our path, my son, but you'll find your way. Let my stories sink into your body for a few more days and then take one of our horses and go to The Place Where Stories Are Told. Sit there, think about what is important, and find your way in the world."

I took my father's advice. I listened to more of his stories about origins of the Songhay Empire, about the miraculous powers of my ancestor, Sonni Ali Ber and how that knowledge/power was passed down from generation to generation.

Then late one afternoon, I mounted one of our black Arabian stallions, Sorba, and rode east into the bush, following a trail that made its way to a smooth boulder situated between two towering buttes—The Place Where Stories Are Told. I sat down looked out over a vast Niger River basin bathed in golden light. I thought for a long moment of time and then came to a fundamental realization. Scholars in France and elsewhere in the modern world usually have a short-term focus. We are all passionate about the discourses of the moment, the theories everyone is talking about. You invited me here today because of that short-term focus. Like most of my colleagues I was one who tuned his intellectual antenna to the current frequencies, frequencies that affected how I asked questions, thought, and wrote. I had used literature to reveal, epistemes, genealogies, assemblages, frictions. Using these revelations, I designed texts that twisted and turned around the issues, but never really focused squarely on the issue itself. My works were read and appreciated by the intellectual community, which, in France, is quite extensive. For that I am grateful. And yet, I wonder about my work. Does it explore those issues most deeply human, the issues that formed the fabric of my father's life? I wondered if my work shed light on the important things. Sitting in The Place Where Stories Are Told, I knew that more often than not I had bypassed those most human of our concerns. I am reminded of Wittgenstein's wonderful aphorism: "we may think we know the thing, but we only know the lines that form its boundary."

Now don't get me wrong. I did not dismiss my previous work. I think it has made modest contributions to literary studies and to the human sciences, but, sitting there, I wondered what people would think of my work 25, 50 or 75 years from now? Would my texts pass the test of time? I knew that they wouldn't. They might have a certain currency today and maybe even 5 or 10 years from today. But would my books be read 50 years from now? I don't think so. They are too specialized and too abstract; they don't really connect a wide array of readers to issues that constitute the texture of the human condition. Does that mean we should stop writing theoretical treatises? No, they illuminate much in the world. And yet, they have a narrow appeal and a limited shelf life.

I then heard my father's soft voice in my ear. He said that the mark of a great master is the ability not only to act and produce something, a medicine, or a cure, but to pass that knowledge on to the next generation. How true! How can we produce knowledge that survives the test of time so that our successors use it in their own fashion? My father taught me so much about history, philosophy, medicine and the human psyche. In the future, I will use that knowledge not as he used it during his lifetime in Tillaberi, Niger, but in my own fashion both in France and Niger. In this way, the knowledge, the wisdom, if you will, moves from generation to generation.

And yet, how can we meet the considerable and important challenge that my father, an illiterate sage you have never heard of, put to us—to think about what's important. He would answer the question with deceptive simplicity: learn how to tell good stories. The stories, he would say, can take on any form, any genre. What's important about stories is that they force a connection between people that compels them to think a new thought or feel a new feeling— something that will move them into new spaces of imagination and creativity.

And so my friends, I will devote the rest of my life to trying, in my own small way, to make life a little bit better for my family, for the people I know and for the people who know me. I will tell and write stories—all kinds of stories—that I hope will expand the boundaries of consciousness and make life just a little bit sweeter.

The great American novelist, Tim O'Brien, knows about stories. In his wonderful novel about the war in Vietnam, The Things They Carried, *he wrote: "Stories are for joining the past to the future. Stories are for those late hours in the night when you can't remember how you got from where you were to where you are. Stories are for eternity, when memory is erased, when there is nothing to remember except the story."*

Omar bowed his head, signaling the end of the lecture. Applause echoed through the lecture hall. Some people stood up to applaud. During this ovation, he cast his eyes downward. When he raised his head, he saw Chantal standing by the exit at the back of the room. Like the others, she applauded vigorously. She had never liked listening to his lectures. Her presence brought Omar much surprise and happiness.

Jean-Pierre Caperan shook Omar's hand. "A beautiful talk Omar."

"Thank you, Jean-Pierre."

Jean-Pierre raised his arms to quiet the crowd. "I would like to thank Professor Dia for a truly inspiring lecture. He has given us much to think about. We have time for some questions. Please raise your hand and someone will bring you a microphone." There ensued a selection of the usual questions about French philosophy. Although Omar found these questions disappointing, given the subject of his lecture, it was to be expected in such a setting and he answered them with detailed responses. There were other questions about African social and cultural movements that he also discussed with the audience. Finally, a young man took the microphone.

"Professor Dia, I must say that I found your lecture refreshingly honest and inspiring. Given your position, it is easy for you to advocate such radical change. For those of us just starting out in literary studies, how can we follow your path? We are all part of institutions, which set the rules for each discipline. If we break those rules, how do we move forward? I wonder, sir, if your challenge is a bit unrealistic for most of us."

This was the kind of question Omar wanted to get. "I very much appreciate your question, for I, too, have been in your situation. I do not ask anyone to abandon the theoretical path that has marked literary studies as well as the human sciences for more than 30 years. My challenge is that you not let the 'mandarin discourse' obscure the most important aspects of the human condition. I ask that you reflect about how what you think and what you write will stand up to the passage of time. Theories, of course, are also stories, are they not? If you pay close attention to the story you are crafting, it may well be told, read, and debated for many years to come. Now that would be a real contribution to scholarship."

Other hands went into the air, but Jean-Pierre intervened. "Thank you all for coming. Please give thanks to our speaker, Professor Omar Dia."

There was a final burst of applause.

"That was a wonderful lecture and interchange, Omar. Shall we get a drink?" Jean-Pierre asked.

"Normally I'd love to. But my wife is here. She never comes to my lectures so I think we'll be headed to dinner somewhere near our home."

"Sometime soon then?"

"Come to my café, Boulevard Voltaire and rue de Charonne. I'm there every morning around 9:00 a.m."

"I'll do that."

Omar worked his way through a throng of well-wishers. When he finally reached Chantal, she threw her arms around him.

"Keep talking like that, Omar. Don't change. What you said today is very important. Your father was a wise man. Sorry I didn't get a chance to meet him."

"I'm sorry, too. But soon you'll see Tillaberi for yourself. You'll see the land from which his wisdom grew."

"I can't wait to go, Omar," she said smiling. "Where are you taking me to dinner?"

CHAPTER 30

Omar received much praise for his lecture. A radio personality invited him to be interviewed on Radio France Culture. Several print journalists interviewed him. Editors asked him to write essays for various newspapers. In the past, he would have been deliriously happy about these opportunities. In the spring of 2001, though, he had a new set of priorities. His caseload of African clients had increased, and he was busy organizing his course for the new academic year. What's more he was busy making preparations for the family trip to Niger.

In the days before the trip to Niger, there was much excitement at 72, rue de Charonne. Every weekend, they went biking in the Bois de Boulogne or went swimming at the local pool. Sometimes, they took day trips to Versailles and Chartes. Omar and Chantal dined at Bonfinger, Chantal's favorite bistro in Paris. Chantal also arranged to bring a shipment of medicines to the health clinic in Tillaberi. She also made sure that everyone got proper immunizations. The kids did not like their yellow fever, tetanus, and rabies vaccinations. Chantal also started the kids on an anti-malarial drug. Although Omar had told Chantal that they would find provisions in Niger, she sent him out for mosquito nets and powerful insect repellents, both for skin and clothing.

"But you won't need that stuff in Tillaberi in July and August."

She wouldn't listen, which meant that Omar went out and bought all sorts of supplies—sleeping bags, Petromax lanterns, water filters, water purification tablets, an elaborate first aid kit, and so on. Lilly and Adam pumped Omar for information about Niger, about how Songhay people lived, and especially about their relatives. Omar tried to answer their questions, telling them that they would soon know their aunts, uncles, and cousins—dozens of playmate cousins. Chantal was also excited. She had always had a fascination for Africa and had always wanted to meet Omar's family. In her spare moments, she studied Songhay, poring over the dictionary and a grammar book. Her progress was slow, but steady.

Soon enough the school year ended and they packed up their things, arranged to have Salmu stay in the apartment until their return at the end of the summer, and headed off to the airport. They processed their tickets, passed through immigration control and security, and walked to the gate. Most of the passengers seemed to be Africans, many, like the Dias, were going to Niger, but others were on their way to Ouagadougou. As soon as they were seated comfortably in the gate area, a few Nigeriens came over to pay their respects to Omar.

"We are honored to see you Sohanci Omar."

"May God protect you, Sohanci Omar."

"I give thanks," Omar said. "I give thanks to you."

"My husband gives thanks," Chantal said in Songhay.

"Hey, hey," said one woman in Songhay. "She speaks Songhay. How wonderful."

Chantal nodded and the woman held out her hand. "An honor to meet you. We hear you are a doctor."

"It's true," said Chantal, continuing on in Songhay.

"God be with you," the woman said.

"How do people know about you and me?"

"Word travels fast, Chantal," Omar stated. "When we land, people at the airport will know you and pay you their respects."

"It's like a non-electronic Internet."

"It's been that way for centuries."

"Amazing."

The five-hour flight was smooth. They landed a bit after 3:00 p.m. on a bright sunny day. According to the pilot, the temperature hovered around 104 degrees. Before Chantal, Lilly, and Adam stepped out of the plane and descended the steps onto terra firma, Omar warned them about the heat.

"It's going to grab you," he said, "It takes time to get used to it."

"Yeah, yeah, Papa," Adam said.

"No problem," said Lilly.

Chantal stepped into the Nigerien afternoon. "Good God, Omar. You weren't kidding. I'm sweating already."

When they entered the hot stuffy reception hall, a huge police officer, whose torso looked more like a thick baobab tree trunk than one that belonged to a human being, came over to them. "Welcome, Sohanci Omar. You all can come with me. There's no need to wait in line." The immigration and health officials welcomed them to Niger and immediately stamped their passports. They moved on to the baggage room, where after a short wait, they retrieved their bags and presented them to the customs officer.

"I don't need to look at your bags, Sohanci Omar. It is an honor to shake your hand."

Beyond the baggage room, Garba Hima, Omar's loyal driver, waved to them. Omar instructed a baggage handler to take their things to the car. After paying the handlers a small fee, they all piled into Garba Hima's car and began their trek to Tillaberi. Chantal, who had taken the front seat, greeted Garba in Songhay. From the back, the kids followed suit.

"Ah, how wonderful you're learning Songhay. You'll be speaking it well in no time at all," Garba said in French.

"We hope so," said Chantal, who wiped her sweaty brow. "Garba," she asked, "do you have air-conditioning?"

"It's not working, Doctor. Like the language, you'll get used to the heat in no time."

"I'm not so sure," Chantal said.

"It cools down after sunset," Garba reassured her. He turned to Omar. "Are you stopping to see your sister?" he asked.

"Not today, Garba. She's promised to come visit us in Tillaberi."

"May it come to pass," Garba said.

Chantal and the kids had never seen anything like the streets of Niamey, which were clogged with donkeys, camels, and pedestrians carrying baskets of mangoes and bananas on their heads. Cars passed them kicking up clouds of dust that partially obscured people bantering on the sandy strips that bordered the road.

"What's that?" Lilly asked, pointing to a man standing behind a grill.

"That's a man cooking meat," Omar said. He tapped Garba on the shoulder. "Let's buy some grilled meat."

They pulled over and all of them approached a man who had some filet in a porcelain basin. "We'd like some meat," Omar announced.

"Good." The man carved the meat and put many chunks of it onto a piece of paper. "This is the best meat you'll ever taste," he said.

"God be with you, friend," Chantal said.

"Ah Madam, you speak Songhay?"

"Only a little."

"Wonderful."

The kids thanked the butcher—also in Songhay.

"God be praised," he said.

As they munched on grilled meat, which, in Omar's view, was among the best you could get anywhere in the world, they left behind the dust and congestion of Niamey and drove into the quiet emptiness of the bush. The millet had yet to appear in fields dotted with thatched granaries that looked like beehives. Here and there, they saw a group of mudbrick houses that marked a family compound. Larger clusters of houses indicated small villages. In time, the car chugged up an escarpment from which Chantal, Lilly, and Adam had their first vision of the Niger River Basin.

"It is breathtaking, Omar. You never told me how beautiful your homeland is. I could look at it for hours."

The kids seemed more interested in children, some their age, walking along the side of the road.

"Where are their parents?" Adam asked.

"They're probably at home," Omar said. "Here kids begin to do errands for their parents at a young age. When I was your age, Adam, I herded the family's flock of sheep and goats."

"I know, Papa. You've told me that before."

"When I wasn't in school, I'd walk for hours with the goats and sheep. And God helped me if I lost one of them."

"We've heard that one, Papa," Lilly chimed in.

Every 20 minutes or so, they had to stop for police roadblocks. Each time, the young police officers peered into the car and, upon seeing Omar, gave them respectful greetings and then wished them a safe journey to Tillaberi.

"Everybody likes you Papa," Lilly said. "Why's that?"

"It's because your father is an important man," Chantal stated.

"It's true, Lilly," Garba Hima intoned. "Your father, Sohanci Omar, is a very important man. People respect him and his family."

"Even me?" she asked.

"Even you," Garba Hima affirmed.

In the late afternoon, they came upon the dusty byways of Tillaberi, all lined with tall mudbrick walls behind which were mudbrick houses. As in Niamey, the streets teamed with activity, though on a scale less congested than in the capital city. A man dressed in a long black robes and an indigo turban crossed the road forcing Garba Hima to slam the brakes.

"Are we finally there?" Adam asked.

"No," Omar said. "We have a long ways to go."

"Who was that man?" Lilly asked.

"I don't know his name, Lilly," Omar answered, "but he is a Tuareg. They're nomads from the Sahara."

"Cool," said Adam.

"How much longer?" Chantal asked.

"Maybe 10 minutes," Omar said. "We've got to go into the bush."

"This looks like the bush to me," Chantal said.

They turned off the main road and followed sandy tracks to the outskirts of town. Soon enough they were in the bush.

"There's nothing here," Adam said.

"We're going the live out here?" Lilly wondered.

"Where are you taking us, Omar?" Chantal asked.

"To the family compound. It's just a little farther along this track."

The car chugged up a slight incline. Gradually, the three-foot-high millet-stalk fence that circled the compound came into view. Beyond the fence, they could see seven mudbrick houses and the tall thatched dome of the spirit hut. Having heard the approach of the taxi, the family streamed out of the entrance and clapped their hands in welcome. Omar's stepmother, Maymouna, began to recite the praise poetry of Sonni Ali Ber. Abdoulaye, dressed in a flowing black cape, came to the front of the throng, his large fleshy face creased with a smile.

"Kubeyni," he said. "Welcome family. Welcome."

They got out of the car and the family rushed to them, shaking their hands.

Lilly, Adam, and Chantal remembered their Songhay greetings, which were met with howls of approval.

Abdoulaye approached Omar. "Welcome, Omar. We've missed you. There's much to do while you are here."

"I know. We'll meet our burdens, Abdoulaye."

"We're so happy that your wife and children have finally come here. We'll enjoy your visit."

"Did you arrange a ride for Chantal in two days?"

"I did. A Land Rover from the clinic will come to get her."

"Good."

Seydou, Omar's younger brother, who looked rather gaunt, introduced himself to Chantal and the kids. Turning to Omar, he said: "Sohanci, we praise God that you and wife and children are here. May your time here pass in harmony."

"Thank you, younger brother."

"It's good that your wife and kids speak a little Songhay," he said. "By the time they leave, they will be speaking it well."

"Let it be so, younger brother."

Omar looked for Fati, wondering if she might be there. She wasn't.

Their luggage and supplies were brought into the compound. They would stay in the three-room mudbrick house next to the spirit house—the Sohanci's house. Inside, they found four new beds, a double bed in Omar and Chantal's room, and two twins in the kids' room. Abdoulaye had put a table with hard-backed chairs in the sitting room. Two canvas directors' chairs had been positioned next to the door. Two lanterns had been lit, spreading a flickering glow throughout the rooms. It looked like the inside of the house had been freshly whitewashed. Recognizing the care his brother had taken to assure their comfort, Omar thanked him. Abdoulaye stood smiling in the doorway.

"You're welcome, Omar. You should rest now. I've slaughtered a sheep and prepared a fire. It's roasting. We'll eat in little while. See you then."

Chantal, perhaps out of a sense of cultural anxiety, busied herself with unpacking their gear and provisions. Two of Abdoulaye's children, Seyni and Belma, appeared at the door.

"Uncle, can Adam and Lilly come outside?" Belma asked. "We want to teach them a game."

"Kids," Omar said in Songhay, "do you want to go outside with your cousins."

They nodded and disappeared into the dusk, leaving Chantal and Omar a rare moment of privacy.

"This is not going to be easy, Omar," Chantal observed. "The conditions are just terrible—a dirt floor, no running water, no toilet, no shower or hot water." She continued to toil with the baggage. "It's just not sanitary here. We'll need to boil and filter the water."

"Actually I had a small bore well installed in the compound. The water is some of the best you can drink—not a problem."

"I'm very concerned about the children. I don't want them to get sick."

"If we're careful, they'll be fine. What about you?"

"I'll try my best, but I don't know if I'm up to it."

Omar took her hand. "I'm so happy that you're willing to try. Give it a chance and if you begin to like it here, we'll stay the entire time. If things get really difficult, you and the kids can return to France any time you want."

"Won't that shame you? You finally bring your family here to Tillaberi and they hate it so much, that they leave after one week."

"All I ask is that you try. Let Niger work its magic. If that doesn't work, go back to France. You're here. You're trying and that makes me happy, Chantal. Give it a chance to work."

Lilly came running into the house. "Mama, Papa, they're roasting a sheep. They said for you to come outside and eat."

Omar and Chantal joined Abdoulaye and the others who stood around a table on which the sheep, now wonderfully roasted, lay. Porcelain plates were passed out. Holding his plate in front of his body, Abdoulaye spoke: "This is a blessed event. For the first time, our older brother, Sohanci Omar Dia, has brought his family to the land of his ancestors. We rejoice. We ask for the blessings of God and our ancestors. May we be protected and may this meat we are about to eat give us strength and provide us well being the in days ahead." With that, Abdoulaye used his finger and thumb to pull a sliver of meat off the sheep. "It's good," he announced. "Time to eat."

Following the others, Omar, Chantal, Adam, and Lilly approached the table and, like Abdoulaye, used their fingers and thumbs to pull meat off the bones and put it on their plates. Once they had a good pile of roasted sheep on their plates, they walked to the cooking house, a small mudbrick room, where food was prepared. There they received helpings of rice and squash sauce to complement the meat. Having traveled so far, they ate with abandon.

Maymouna came up to Chantal and the kids who looked as if they had finished eating.

"What? You can't be finished already. You haven't eaten anything," she said in Songhay. Ni ma ngaa kungu," she said. "Eat until you are full."

"My grandmother," Adam said in Songhay. "We are full. We give thanks."

"Praise be to God," was Maymouna's response. "This one speaks our language."

"Only a little," Adam said.

"Only a little," Lilly repeated.

By the time the meal ended, Omar, Chantal, Adam, and Lilly could hardly move. Exhausted from a long day of traveling and eating, they said their goodnights. As they walked to their new summerhouse, Lilly looked up. "I've never seen so many stars. Look at them, Mama."

Adam also looked up at the star-filled sky. "Papa, what is that cloud that stretches across the center of the sky?"

"That's the Milky Way, Adam. You can't see it in Paris. But here, if you stare at the sky for maybe 30 minutes, there's a good chance you'll see shooting stars."

"That is so cool, Papa, really cool."

For two days, Chantal and the kids had adjustment difficulties. Lilly and Adam had diarrhea. While it's never fun to have "the runs," when you get them in a place where there are no toilets, "the runs" become "the race" to the bush for some measure of privacy behind a cover of scrub. They liked the food quite a bit, but got tired of a diet that never varied: coffee, milk, and millet cakes in the morning, millet porridge and rice and sauce at lunch, and millet paste with peanut sauce in the evening. That bush routine compelled a trip to town to find some roasted chicken, several varieties of fish in cans, and some cold Coca-Cola, with the option of beer for Chantal. Omar also knew a restaurant in Tillaberi where you could get a delicious steak and fries.

Adam and Lilly very much enjoyed playing with their cousins. Seydou took it upon himself to teach Omar's kids horseback riding, which despite their gastronomic and gastrointestinal difficulties, they enjoyed immensely. For her part, Chantal looked forward to delivering her medicines and her medical expertise to the Tillaberi clinic. It was with an air of great energy and anticipation that she got into the clinic's Land Rover and drove off to work.

She returned late in the afternoon, her face a patchwork of exhaustion. She had put in a very long day, indeed, with just a short break for a lunch of rice and sauce washed down with a tepid Coca-Cola. She trudged into the compound, her medical bag strapped over her shoulder, her blouse patched to her skin with sweat, her short hair dried out from the dust and dirt and sticking out in every direction. She came into Omar's house and threw her bag on our bed.

"Tough day?" Omar asked.

"Very tough day, but I'll go back tomorrow and the next day until we leave. I've never seen so much misery…and so much gratitude."

"Did you see many patients?"

"When word got out that a French doctor was in the house, a long line formed—so many sick people. I saw malnourished children with festering skin soars. We gave them this nutritious paste that they make here in Niger. It works wonders. So many children had ear infections and worms. We were able to give them medicine. There were several cases of malaria, and two cases of hepatitis B, one was late-staged and the girl had become jaundiced."

"That's difficult to see, no?"

"If only the sanitary conditions were better. If only the water were clean."

"There are many wells in town."

"People say they like the taste of river water. Many of the sick children came from the bush, where they get water from scummy ponds or from unsanitary wells."

"Did you see any cases of guinea worm?"

Chantal nodded. "Yes, there was a man dressed in an indigo veil and black robes. His leg was horribly swollen. The nurse was able to tease the worm from his leg and we were able to extract it. What a mess!"

"You must be tired."

"I am, Omar, but this kind of work is satisfying. Here, a little bit of medical intervention goes a long, long way. In Paris, there is the bliss of saving a life in the ER, but also the devastation of losing one. Here, a simple shot or a pill makes such a difference. I'm going to work hard here, Omar, and I'm going to somehow arrange for regular shipments of medicine so the clinic can be well supplied."

"How will you do that?" Omar asked.

"Maybe I'll ask for donations. I want to do all I can."

At that moment, Omar felt admiration for Chantal. She had left her comfortable and satisfying life in Paris for a much more physically challenging one in a remote area of a remote country where she knew little of the language and less of the culture. Despite these difficult conditions, she had made up her mind to adapt and make her experience a satisfying one. And she had extended all of this considerable effort to adjust to the fundamental change that had swept into and disrupted her life. Omar had worried that Chantal might refuse to take the kids to the Nigerien bush. If she did come, Omar wondered how she would react to the physical privations of the family compound. So far, her response had surprised him. She seemed to like his family and maybe she would be able to adapt to life in the bush. Not much time had passed and things could rapidly go downhill, but so far she was being a real trooper. Besides, her medical skills would go a long way toward helping many people—children, teenagers, adults, and old people. Despite these deep feelings of gratitude, Omar would sometimes wonder off to the edge of the compound and stare at the horizon.

Late one afternoon, before Chantal's return from the clinic, Abdoulaye came up to Omar and stood silently by his side.

"What's wrong, Omar?"

Omar said nothing.

"Your family is here. It's like a dream come true."

Omar remained silent.

"It's Fati, isn't it?"

Omar turned toward his brother and frowned.

"You're a strange man, Omar."

"She said she would come to see me."

"She's not in Tillaberi, Omar. I hear that she married a man in Ouallam. How can she come to see you?"

Omar nodded his head in resignation. "She said she would. I wanted to see her."

"You know what our father always said?" Abdoulaye asked.

"What?"

"A pure person does what he says."

"Our father said that often, didn't he?"

Just then, they heard the approach of Chantal's Land Rover.

"You have a rich life, older brother. Be grateful for it."

One week later, Abdoulaye organized a spirit possession for Dongo, deity of thunder and king of the sky. Even though it was early in July, only traces of rain had fallen. If the rains did not come soon, the millet crop would be completely compromised.

Another Tillaberi spirit priest had already organized a rain dance. The tooru spirits, nobles of the Songhay spirit world who control natural elements like wind, clouds, water, fire, lightening, and thunder, had taken the bodies of mediums. An assortment of chickens and a black goat had been sacrificed. Special powders had been put into the hampi, the sacrificial container, the contents of which had been spilled onto a sacred crossroads. Despite these efforts, the rains had not yet come.

Fearing the devastations of famine, a council of town elders asked Omar and Abdoulaye to intervene. The brothers made preparations to celebrate the mercurial life of Dongo, the deity who brought wind, dust, and eventually rain.

Omar looked forward to having Chantal, Adam, and Lilly witness their first possession ceremony. They all marched toward Tillaberi, where, just outside of town, a large audience of elders, officials, mediums, and interested by-standers had gathered on of a sandy field filled with the dried-out stumps of the previous year's millet plants. A square boulder of granite with a recessed pool on its surface rose in the center of the field. The audience surrounded the boulder—one of Dongo's stones and a point of sacrifice. The brother of Tillaberi's chief held onto a tethered black goat, Dongo's favorite animal. Next to the rock, Omar planted Issaka Dia's forked sick, which sanctified the ground, making it ready to welcome the spirits. Wigindi Godji sat down on a stool and began to play his one-stringed violin. His music "cried" out to the heavens, beckoning Dongo to take a body and speak to the people. Responding to the melodious violin music, the mediums began to move in a counterclockwise circle. A man, who inserted himself into the center of the circle of dancers, sang Dongo's praise songs. Abdoulaye joined the group and swayed to the music.

Omar rejoined Chantal, Adam, and Lilly and explained to them what was going on. He told them that the tempo of the music would soon quicken and reach a climax at which time one of the dancers would get possessed.

"Is it a hypnotic state?" Chantal asked.

"Not exactly. You'll soon see what it is," Omar stated, "and be able to draw your own conclusions."

The music captured the attention of Adam and Lilly, who could not take their eyes off of their uncle Abdoulaye.

"Why's he dancing?" Lilly asked.

"Because he's a medium. Sometimes spirits take his body."

"I don't believe it," said Adam.

"Just wait and you'll see for yourselves."

The tempo quickened and the dancers formed a line and moved closer to Wigindi Godji, flailing their arms, moving their heads from side to side. Then it was Abdoulaye's turn, an impressive figure dressed in black robes and a black turban. He held a strip of black cloth in front of him as he approached the musician, stomping his bare feet on the smooth sand. He then dropped the cloth and put his hands on each side of his head as if he were in pain. He howled like a dog. Large tears dropped from his eyes and mucous ran from his nose. He bellowed. Holding his hands to his hips, he took long exaggerated steps around the dance grounds. His eyes blazed brightly.

Adam and Lilly hid behind their mother, who had taken out her camera. In no time at all, Dongo, now in the body of Abdoulaye, stomped over to them.

"Sohanci," Dongo said to Omar in a gravelly voice, "tell this woman to stop or else."

Omar explained to Chantal that she shouldn't photograph a spirit in the body of a medium. "It's dangerous," he said. "If mediums see such a photo, they could get sick or even die."

Chantal put her camera in her bag. Dongo put his hand on her head. He then blew into the ears of Adam and Lilly. Finally, he walked away to talk with Yacouba Dendi, sohanci of the neighboring town, Tillakaina, who was helping with the ceremony.

"What's going on?" Chantal asked.

"He's giving a blessing to you and the children. It's a very good sign," Omar said.

Dongo was speaking to the crowd.

"I am very angry with you in Tillaberi," he said. "You are a village with two mouths and two hearts. There is so much betrayal here that I have withheld the rains. You have to work with one another with one mouth and one heart. There must be harmony between village and bush."

The audience pledged to work together with "one mouth and one heart."

Dongo continued, "You must make a sacrifice on my stone. You'll see how the blood flows and will know if the rains will come and the millet will grow. If the blood flows well and you are speaking to me with pure hearts, I'll drink it and bring the rains. If there are still two hearts and two mouths, I will not drink it and there will be famine and sickness in Tillaberi."

Yacouba Dendi motioned for Omar to approach Dongo's rock. He handed Omar a knife.

"Sohanci, you must cut the goat's throat and bring us harmony."

Omar chanted to harmonize the bush and spat lightly in the goat's ear, which seemed to calm the animal. Then he positioned its head over Dongo's stone and slit its throat. The blood spurted out of its neck, but the animal didn't thrash too much, which meant that the blood flowed smoothly, pooling into the recessed surface of the stone.

Yacouba Dendi removed the dead goat. Dongo kneeled in front of his stone and bent over the pool of blood. "This is good blood," he said, as he drank it in. He picked up his head and licked the blood off of his lips. "There will be rain in Tillaberi. There will be rain."

Yacouba Dendi led Dongo away so that the spirit might leave Abdoulaye's body. From a distance they saw Dongo lay down on the sand and then heard coughing, a signal that Abdoulaye was back in his body. They went to him.

"Thank you for your efforts, Abdoulaye," Omar said.

Chantal put her head on Abdoulaye's massive shoulder. "Are you okay?" she asked in Songhay.

Abdoulaye coughed. "I'll be fine, my in-law. Just fine."

"Are you sure?" asked Lilly.

Abdoulaye grunted as he stood up. "I'm sure, Lilly."

"Good," she said.

They walked back to the family compound, tired, but exhilarated by what they had witnessed.

"Will the rains come, Papa?" Adam asked.

"Time will tell," Omar said.

Two days went by without rain. Routine returned to the family compound. Clients came to see Omar every day. Abdoulaye rode his horse to visit people in the bush, treating them for their physical and emotional problems. Each morning, Seydou brought horses for Lilly and Adam and they rode off into the bush. In the afternoon, Adam and Lilly played with their cousins or walked into the town. A car came for Chantal in the morning and she went to work at the clinic.

At the end of the day, Omar, Chantal, Adam, and Lilly met in their house to talk about what had transpired. Lilly and Adam recounted many adventures. They had made steady progress as horseback riders. Chantal liked working at the clinic and felt that she was making a big difference in the lives of her patients. As for Omar, he felt the presence of Issaka Dia each and every day.

In the late afternoon of the third day after the spirit possession ceremony, Chantal wondered what had happened to the rain.

"Didn't Dongo say that there'd be rain?" she asked.

"We need rain, Papa," Lilly asserted.

"I wonder if it's coming," Adam stated.

"It's coming," Omar said with confidence.

Someone clapped outside the open door to the house. "It's me, Omar," Abdoulaye announced. "Come outside and look at the eastern sky. All of you."

They popped outside and saw a dark gray band on the eastern horizon. The wind had shifted from west to east and scent of rain was in the air.

"The rains, Abdoulaye?" Omar asked.

He peered at the expanding dark gray band. "Could be, but it could also be just wind and dust. We'll see. But for now, we need to get ready." He turned to Lilly and Adam. "Come with me and make sure the animals are tied tight." He turned to Omar. "You know what to do."

"What do you have to do?" Chantal asked.

"We need to make sure the windows are shut tight and remove loose objects from the ground and put them here in the house."

"But why?"

"Because there's going to be quite a storm—howling wind, dust, rain. Sometimes there's even a tornado."

As the band expanded even more, Omar and Chantal secured the household. Lilly and Adam returned. Omar gave them a strip of turban cloth. "Watch me," he said. "Tie it around your head and then put it across your nose like a mask. Keeps out the dust." Omar gave another strip of cloth to Chantal. "You do the same."

"But..."

"Do it, Chantal. You'll need it."

As the cooling wind stiffened, they went out into the compound to watch the storm come in. A tidal wave of brown dust had built up and loomed over them.

"I've never seen anything like it," Chantal said. "The wave must be 50 meters high."

"That's right," Omar said. "Let's go into the house, close the door, and ride it out. Let's hope that rain will follow the wind and dust."

They huddled in the main room of the house. The wind rattled the windows. The rumble of thunder could be heard in the distance.

"That's thunder?" Adam wondered.

"That, Adam," Omar said, "is the voice of Dongo. He's bringing us wind, dust, and maybe rain."

And then with a thump the wave of dust crashed down upon them, filtering out the sun and darkening the house. Adam turned on his flashlight, the light of which illuminated air filled with dust. The wind howled. Thunder rumbled.

"Is it going to rain?" Chantal wondered.

"I can smell it. Let's hope it comes," Omar said.

They then heard the slow splat and patter of raindrops on the roof and the sand. Then the sky seemed to open up. Windswept rain whipped across the compound. The temperature plummeted. The donkeys brayed.

The goats bleated. Muddy water began pouring through the roof, forming a puddle in the front room. "Adam," Omar said, "put that basin under the leak."

After about one hour, the rain slackened. Omar opened the door. The family compound had become a very large puddle. The air was remarkably free of dust. Omar took off his turban and breathed deeply. Chantal and kids did the same. The other children frolicked in the puddles. Lilly and Adam ran off to join their cousins.

Omar looked at Chantal. "Tomorrow we'll go and plant our fields. With luck, we'll have a good harvest this year."

"May it come to pass," Chantal said. "Dongo said that there would be rain and three days later there was rain," she stated smiling broadly. "This poor land is full of riches."

The morning after the first rain, they walked out to their fields, hoes in hand, to plant the millet crop. The family fields were on a sandy slope about three kilometers from the family compound. They had four fields, one each for Issaka Dia's sons. Omar hoed his field. Lilly and Adam threw in millet seeds into the shallow indentations and then covered the seeds with the displaced soil. Abdoulaye and Seydou did the same for their fields. It took them several hours to finish the job. Weary from the hard work, they retired to the shade of large tamarind tree to rest. About that time a line of children approached from the compound, clay jugs balanced on their heads. They had brought water and millet porridge for lunch. Surrounded by their children, Abdoulaye, Seydou, and Omar sat and sipped cool porridge. They had all worked to ensure that millet would fill the granaries and provide food for the long months of drought that lay ahead. After they had rested, the group moved on to Moussa's field. Because he was still in prison, they planted his crop—for his wife and children. With good fortune, he would soon be home to enjoy the fruits of their labor.

The rains began to fall regularly—a few more times in July and about every three days or so in August. The millet matured in the fields, and by the end of August, it was almost as tall as Adam who was big for a ten-year-old. When Chantal went to the clinic, Adam, Lilly, and Omar would sometimes ride their horses to inspect the fields. One time the whole family marched to the fields to rid them of weeds and to build a scarecrow to protect the emerging millet seeds from ravenous birds. By now, Lilly and Adam spoke Songhay easily—ah the wonder of children! They had become skilled riders. For her part, Chantal's Songhay had improved considerably.

With just a little assistance, she could take a medical history and ask people to describe their symptoms. She felt proud of herself. The physical resilience of the Songhay children impressed her deeply. Mothers would bring in a toddler who appeared to be at death's door. That child might be suffering from malnutrition, gastrointestinal disorders, skin lesions, ear infections, or malaria. But with a modicum of medical attention, most of these kids recovered—and quickly. Some days Chantal lost a child to a simple untreated infection. How could anyone accept the death of a child? These senseless deaths depressed Chantal, but then the next day she would able to save a child. In Niger, Chantal learned fully what it meant to be a physician. Healing people was important, of course, but she began to listen to the stories of her new patients, stories beyond her imagination. By listening to those often heart-rending stories, Chantal expanded the scope of her practice. In her own way, she had learned how to be a healer.

One evening after a strong thunderstorm, Chantal asked Omar and the kids to gather in the front room of their mudbrick house. "I am so impressed with my patients," she said. "Listen to this story":

One Strong Woman
Her name is Ramatou. She came in to see me with her 2 year-old, Fati. Ramatou looked like an old woman. She was frail. Her face was a patchwork of wrinkles. Her smile revealed missing teeth and several remaining teeth that looked like stumps. Her daughter was very underweight and her skin was lifeless. She seemed hungry and dehydrated.

"Is this your granddaughter?" I asked.
"No, no. Fati is my daughter, born two years ago."
"How old are you?"
"I don't know," Ramatou answered.
"How many children have you given birth to?"
"Around 20. Thirteen of them died."
"Do you get enough to eat?"
"We live on the other side of the river. Sometimes we get fish. We mostly eat rice and millet and not much of that."
"Why not?"
"My husband left two years ago when Fati was born. He said I was used up and no good anymore. He wanted a younger woman."
"What happened?"
"He left me with seven children and said I should fend for myself."
"He did that!"
"Yes. My family is far away and could not help me. So I had to earn money. Some women sell their bodies for money, but even if I wanted to do that, which I didn't, I was too old and frail to attract clients."

"What did you do?"

"I'm a good cook. My husband even said so. So I managed to get a loan from one of our village merchants. With that I began to cook fish, rice and sauce by the riverside. With cooking we could live in a small hut. I could feed my children. The older children did fine, but little Fati was always sick. Even before I weaned her she'd vomit and have diarrhea. Her skin would break out and she had no appetite. She didn't grow. There were no clinics in our village, so when I heard that a French Doctor was in Tillaberi; I took a dugout to see you. Can you help me?"

"Yes, Ramatou. I can help. Let me hold your daughter."

Little Fati looked at me with large sad eyes, but didn't cry. I arranged for her to eat the special paste for malnourished kids. We also arranged for Ramatou's other six children, who had been left for the day with her neighbor. We found rooms for her and her family at the clinic, where they would be well fed and well housed.

Ramatou began to cook for people at the clinic. In a few days, Fati showed remarkable improvement. Her eyes sparkled and she walked with a little bounce in her step. After two weeks at the clinic, we hired Ramatou as a cook and insisted that she and family live on the clinic grounds. Four of her kids have been enrolled in school.

Sometimes it takes so little to snatch glorious life from the grip of despair and death.

Chantal's story convinced Omar that spending time in Niger had compelled her to appreciate life more fully. How sad it would be to return to France where they would resume their conventional European lives—school for the kids, the ER for Chantal, and the university lecture hall for Omar. There was so much that Omar had grown to love in Niger: his brothers, cousins, nieces, and nephews, the pace of life, and, in all frankness, the sense of satisfaction derived from walking the path of Issaka Dia. Even so there was much Omar loved about France—the food, the exchange of ideas among colleagues and students, a multicultural social mix that led many people to accept difference.

Before their departure, Omar wanted to take his family to *The Place Where Stories Are Told*. He wanted to tell Lilly, Adam, and Chantal the story of his ancestors.

Two days before their return flight, they rode off toward *The Place Where Stories Are Told*. They left in the late afternoon, heading east and south away from the sun, but paralleling the great Niger River. Chantal, Lilly, and Adam enjoyed the ride. As they started to climb toward the twin buttes, the vegetation thinned out considerably—just scrub and an occasional scraggly plant.

"How can anything grow here, Papa?" Lilly wondered.

"It's amazing how living things can survive the most difficult conditions. Think of Ramatou, your mother's patient. With almost nothing, she cared for seven children for almost two years."

"The people here are strong, Papa," Adam stated.

"They are. They've lived here for centuries."

Chantal, Lilly, and Adam followed Omar onto the space between the two buttes. They dismounted. Omar showed them to the smooth boulder that overlooked the Niger River Basin.

"This is *The Place Where Stories Are Told*. My ancestors have been coming here for many generations to pass along the history of our family. It's finally time for you to learn of your present, past and future."

"This place is really cool," Adam said.

"I love it," Lilly said.

"It's magnificent, Omar."

"We'll come here every year to look, to sit, and to listen."

They sat down on the flat rock and gazed upon the haze that had rolled into the vast basin.

"Sit down and open your ears," Omar said. "Let my words enter your bodies so you, too, will know who you are."

They sat up straight and waited for Omar to begin just as his father had begun so many years before.

"There was once a great warrior. His name was Sonni Ali Ber, also known as Si, and he was a great emperor Songhay..."

Epilogue

They say that wisdom settles into certain places. Over the years, much wisdom has settled into the smooth flat rock that marks *The Place Where Stories Are Told*. Ever seeking that wisdom, Omar often went there to think about the past and present. Where else could he recount the story of his life?

Four years had passed since Omar first brought his family to *The Place Where Stories Are Told*. Time brought much change to Omar's family. Adam became a teenager and Lilly was about to become a young woman. They spent four summers in Tillaberi, which meant that the kids spoke fluent Songhay and knew well the African side of their family. They each had a horse that they groomed and fed. Adam and Lilly witnessed events that their French friends could never imagine. They learned who they were.

Time in Tillaberi changed the direction of Chantal's career. After the first trip to Niger, she began to study tropical medicine. Gradually, she became a specialist. Although working in the ER had brought her much satisfaction, she now saw mostly patients who had immigrated to France from tropical environments. Many French doctors, she came to realize, knew little of tropical diseases. Her growing expertise often helped to save lives. She was also committed to practicing medicine in Niger. Every summer she came to Tillaberi to tend to the sick. She always found time to listen to stories of her patients.

Abdoulaye became Tillaberi's itinerant herbalist. Several times a week he rode into the bush to treat the sick. He was also the priest of the

Tillaberi spirit possession troupe. Many of the spirit possession ceremonies he organized were held in the family compound. Seydou, whose violin playing had become sweeter, and Moussa, who gained his release from prison, assisted him with the ceremonies. Omar's younger brothers had also become devoted fathers and husbands. They traveled much less on the spirit possession music circuit. What's more, they moved back to the family compound. Everybody seemed to get along well.

Maymouna, who had mellowed with old age, lived long enough to welcome her son home from prison. Soon after Moussa's release, she developed what Chantal diagnosed as advanced ovarian cancer. Chantal was able to give her medicines to make her pain a bit more bearable. When she approached death's portal, everyone stood solemnly around her bed as she peacefully crossed into the next world.

Fati had married someone from a family of sorcerers in Ouallam and had given birth to a little boy—Ali. In time, she brought little Ali to Tillaberi to seek the family's blessings. Omar once thought that his passion for Fati would never subside. When he saw her again, his feelings for her were no longer strong. The threads that had connected them had frayed and unraveled, their passion having faded like a Songhay blanket left out in the sun. Traces of the pattern remained, but were now barely visible.

Omar continued the challenging task of leading a life in two worlds. Even though time had passed, he still found it difficult to bear the sorcerer's burden. No matter the strengths of his sohanci inheritance, it was not easy for him to feel completely at home. In France, Omar enjoyed teaching students at the Sorbonne. They especially liked his emphasis on storytelling and the great wisdom of African sages. That new focus resulted in a new biography of his father, Issaka Dia. Omar also collected and published the poetic stories recounted by famous Songhay bards. In his Paris neighborhood, he saw scores of people on Thursdays and every other Sunday. Their social resilience in a strange land never ceased to inspire Omar, which, in turn, compelled him to help them as much as he could.

When Omar spent time in Niger, which was as often as possible, sometimes alone, sometimes with Chantal, Adam, and Lilly, he tended to his obligations as Tillaberi's sohanci. In his spare time, he often rode to *The Place Where Stories Are Told*, and wondered about the future. Who would have thought that the rebellious "school boy" would have become his father's successor? Who would have thought that Abdoulaye and Omar would share the sorcerer's burden? Who would have thought that he would divide his time between Tillaberi and Paris, living life in two very different places?

Omar often brought his children to *The Place Where Stories Are Told*. In that glorious setting, he talked to them about the past and the present. His children listened intently. In the end, he understood that the most important charge of the sorcerer's burden was to pass on to the next generation what he had learned from the ancestors. Issaka Dia could have never imagined that his successor—Omar Dia—would meet the sorcerer's burden in such a "modern" way.

Omar didn't know what would become of his children. Despite that uncertainty, he was sure of one thing: that one day his children would bring their children to *The Place Where Stories Are Told*. He knew that they would ask their children to open their ears and hear the stories of the past that would mark a path to their future.

AUTHOR'S NOTE

A writer who is fortunate can sometimes stumble upon a life-changing literary passage. I luckily found such a passage in Tim O'Brien's incomparable novel *The Things They Carried*. Toward the beginning of the story, a gripping account of one company of American soldiers on patrol during the Vietnam War, the narrator contemplates the deep existential dilemmas of being young, at war and very far from home. "Stories," he says, "are for those late hours of the night when you can't remember how you got from where you were to where you are. Stories are for an eternity, when memory is erased, when there is nothing to remember except the story."[1]

That passage inspired me to devote my energies to crafting stories that connect writers to readers, a connection that might stimulate a new thought or even a new feeling. Reading Tim O'Brien compelled me to foreground narratives in my writing. No matter the genre I've employed (ethnography, memoir, scholarly essay, or fiction), the story has been front and center. As I wrote in my memoir *The Power of the Between: An Anthropological Odyssey*:

> Whatever form they take, stories are indeed for an eternity…they wind their way through our villages, and in their telling and re-telling, they link past, present and future. To tell a story is to take off on the wings of the wind,

---

[1] Tim O'Brien, 36.

a wind that takes us ever closer to the elusive end of wisdom. In the end it is the texture of the story that marks our contribution to the world, the contour of our stories that etches our traces in the world.[2]

Alas, there is no singular way of crafting a good story.

How does a writer decide how to tell her or his stories? My rule of thumb is to live with the subject material, letting it seep into my consciousness. In his *Notebooks*, the great artist Paul Klee wrote that to paint the forest he had to let the trees penetrate his being.

> In a forest I have felt many times over that it was not I who looked at the forest. Some days I felt that the trees were looking at me. I was there, listening...I think the painter must be penetrated by the universe and not penetrate it...I expect to be inwardly submerged, buried. Perhaps I paint to break out.[3]

I have a similar orientation to writing. When I've written about spirit possession, or the life of West African traders in New York City, I've tried to find a way to open my being to those realities. On that slow and deliberate path, a creative spark eventually revealed to me an opening—to the text. Thereafter, the books took shape on the page.[4] The same can be said of my works on globalization. My explorations of the global have been expressed in scholarly essays as well as two works of fiction, *Jaguar* (1999) and *Gallery Bundu* (2006). As for my approach to representing the mysteries of sorcery, I have heretofore used the memoir—not fiction.

Why would I choose fiction to write *The Sorcerer's Burden*, a story that describes the dynamic circumstances of sorcerous practice in a rapidly changing world? Like many sparks on the slow path of creativity, the idea for writing *The Sorcerer's Burden* came to me unexpectedly one day in 2006. I was thinking about a scholar I knew. He was a cosmopolitan African intellectual who had deep knowledge of literature and philosophy. At the time I didn't know much about his family, but I mused about the challenges he faced adjusting to a life in two worlds—the modern and the traditional. What if I transformed this celebrated scholar into the oldest son (and successor) of a great Songhay sorcerer—a great leap

---

[2] Paul Stoller (2008, 173).
[3] See Georges Charbonnier (1959) cited by M. Merleau-Ponty (1964, 31).
[4] See Paul Stoller (1989b, 1999, 2006). Chicago: The University of Chicago Press.

of imagination that created the character of Omar Dia? How would this cosmopolitan Parisian professor reconcile the challenges of his family life in Paris with longstanding obligations to his Songhay family in Niger? Would he be able to take up the sorcerer's burden? These questions, I thought, could be wonderfully incorporated into a novel.

From the beginning of the process, I knew that the narrative dimensions of fiction would enable me to apply my ethnographic knowledge of Songhay sorcery and rural Songhay family life to the emotional saga of Omar Dia's global family. I let this idea sink into my consciousness and lived with it for many years. The story matured slowly. I steadily developed a plot, constructed characters, and crafted dialogue. I took pains to depict where and how Songhay people lived in Paris and Niger. I attempted to describe Songhay rituals with ethnographic precision. Gradually, the novel took shape.

As is evident, *The Sorcerer's Burden* did not mystically materialize in my mind. It is the result of a 40-year association with the Songhay people of the Republic of Niger. *The Sorcerer's Burden* is also an attempt to use fiction to explore the social tensions created through the forces of global change. Can the religious traditions of a West African people survive the profound social and cultural change that global forces have unleashed? Can global families survive the cross-cultural conflicts that human difference generates? In the swirl of contemporary social life, can we learn to live well in the world? In *The Sorcerer's Burden*, thoughts about these questions emerge from the narrative.

Why write stories like *The Sorcerer's Burden*? Are they useful? What can they tell us about the imponderables of the human condition? In search of these imponderables, writers often wander the landscapes of the imagination. As the late Edmond Jabes once wrote:

I see myself again in the deserts of Egypt, looking for pebbles—yellow, sometimes brown, digging them out of the sand, taking them home for the sake of the human face that would suddenly emerge out of their nothingness—an eternal human face that time had modeled for centuries, not mere moments—their face alive against life.

Along amid sand, whose every grain bears witness to an exhausted wind, a desolate world, I was satisfied with appearance, whereas it is inside the stone that the heart of death is merrily at work, where, with a beat of heaven or hell, the closed universe of eternity is written.[5]

---

[5] Edmond Jabes (1984). Chicago: The University of Chicago.

Tim O'Brien had it right. "Stories are for an eternity, when memory is erased, when there is nothing to remember except the story."

That is a reason to tell and listen to stories. That is a reason to write and read stories. That is a reason for anthropologists to write fiction.

REFERENCES

Jabes, Edmond. 1984. *The book of margins*. Chicago: The University of Chicago Press.

Merleau-Ponty, Maurice. 1964. *L'Oeil et l'esprit*, 31. Paris: Gallimard.

Narayan, Kirin. 1999. Ethnography and fiction: Where is the border? *Anthropology and Humanism* 24(2): 134–147.

Stoller, Paul. 1989a. *Fusion of the worlds: Ethnography of possession among the Songhay of Niger*. Chicago: University of Chicago Press.

Stoller, Paul. 1989b. *The taste of ethnographic things: The senses in anthropology*. Philadelphia: University of Pennsylvania Press.

Stoller, Paul. 1994. Embodying colonial memories. *American Anthropologist* 96(3): 634–648.

Stoller, Paul. 1995. *Embodying colonial memories: Spirit possession, power, and the Hauka in West Africa*. New York: Routledge.

Stoller, Paul. 1997. *Sensuous scholarship*. Philadelphia: University of Pennsylvania Press.

Stoller, Paul. 1999. *Jaguar: A story of Africans in America*. Chicago: The University of Chicago Press.

Stoller, Paul. 2005. *Gallery Bundu: A story of an African past*. Chicago: The University of Chicago Press, 1999.

Stoller, Paul. 2008. *The power of the between: An anthropological Odyssey*. Chicago: The University of Chicago Press.

Stoller, Paul. 2014. *Yaya's story: The quest for wellbeing in the world*. Chicago: The University of Chicago Press.

Stoller, Paul, and Cheryl Olkes. 1987. *In sorcery's shadow: A memoir of apprenticeship among the Songhay of Niger*. Chicago: University of Chicago Press.

Printed in the United States
By Bookmasters